MESHKWADOON
Book 1

Alex Tilley

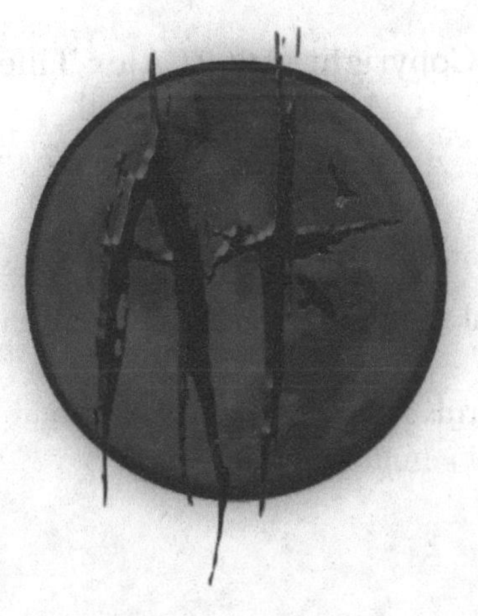

To Phil and Brandon.
Chantal and Natalie.
The Wickerman and weens.

Chapter 1

Hazelnut eyes, honey-blonde hair, thin wrists, and a mole like the tip of a pen on her left nostril. She couldn't escape the memory of a girl's face in a mirror with the heart of a flower. She turned her eyes to a sky of twilight. Stars peeked through like fireflies from behind clouds. The damp grass moistened her back as she listened to crickets' falsettos. Blowing reeds whispered suspiciously around her. The trees rustled misgivings and curses. She was a pale fungus in clinging black. She was a spiritless corpse. She felt nothing. She heard nothing. She was nothing. The dark night like pitch consumed her vision and she dozed without sleep into dreams. Flickering images, like passing lights in a subway tunnel, snaked through her mind.

She played quietly behind a purple velvet couch, bubbled by innocence. Large shapes of people were shifting blurs. It smelled like a roasting turkey and buttered rolls. There was a clatter of dishes being set, accompanied by the muffled sounds of family cordiality. A child's raspy whine grew distinct. Its screech grew from a chasm deep within her. The dream and its pieces drifted away like torn pages from a book.

It was snowing. She was nervously watching others take trips down a hill on curved wooden sleds. A man's large hand, with a flat black ring, held her by the shoulder. She felt warmth, despite the angered wind whipping the snow in swirls. She heard the revving of quads and drunken men's laughter. The screech became a humoured shrill.

She was on a worn, stone walkway, buildings like mountains loomed above her. People shuffled suffocatingly around her on all sides. A woman held her hand. Her mother held her hand. Her mother smiled. The shrill became a horrid laugh that began to blind her like a dark veil pulled over her face. She looked down to her legs surrounded by blackness and to her hand holding her mother's. The clouded darkness wrapped her limbs like choking vines. It consumed everything. It was everything. The shrill entered her like a knife.

She opened her eyes to trees leaning over her like curious physicians. Her chest struggled through quick, small breaths. Her eyes felt swallowed by swollen lids. She sat up from the grass and blinked at her empty hand. She tightened her grip and flexed away the remnants of her mother's touch.

The evening was quiet and peaceful. She found relief in the absence of the mirthless shrill that had penetrated her. She listened. The wind rustled the emo- tionless nature around her. Twisted trees like gnarled fingers of an ancient earth eyed her uncomfortably.

She stood slowly and brushed the front and back of her black dress. She looked around with no sense of expectation. The crickets were quietened by natured passions. The peeking stars were the only source of light. She wrapped her arms around herself and rubbed them up and down. Her neck hairs tingled.

Nothing stirred in her examination of the surroundings. Reeds continued to gossip in a small pool to her left. The dark water shone in spots where stars were bright enough to reflect off its surface. All else was filled with a depraved blackness.

She turned to the forest again and listened to its unaccommodating rustle. It groaned at her in aching sways. The need to hear its words crept inside her.

She took a few steps toward the trees then stopped. She looked at her naked feet and wondered at their nudity. Indentations from her heels were left in half-circles on each foot. She had no memory of what she was running from, or to, but she delved herself for the reality. She found only her echoing thoughts.

Despite her barefootedness, she abandoned her self-search and followed the call of the forest. Evergreens and other trees shuffled in around her. She ignored the pangs from the rocky earth and the reaching of low hanging limbs and scrambled through the twisted extremities that crowded her.

Her loneliness was a welcome consolation. She breathed in and out as she realized the sudden freedom of her lungs. She felt the lightness of her stomach. She smelt the summer air through the leaves. She felt the comforts of normal. She wasn't exposed like a slab of meat on display, raw and over spread like pages in an old children's library book. She could breathe freely. She wiped off warm dribbles from her forehead and pushed through the tangled brush. As she approached a declining edge of a tree topped ravine, she stopped to examine her path.

"Where the hell am I?" she whispered to herself.

She pulled a twist of her hair tightly. The path behind her was dense. A distinct trail was left by her clumsy walking. The darkness shaded all else. She hesitated in the silence and then kept going.

Water chittered in the dip of the ravine, and she hypnotically moved towards it. She felt some inkling of serenity in the feminine whispers of the soft rolling stream over smoothed rocks. Her anxiety hushed its unceasing demands.

She looked at her hands. She tried to wipe away a spot of dirt, but it didn't rub off. She spat on it and rubbed it, but the smudge was as deep as a stain. She looked back and forth between her crusted palms. Her breathing was laboured. She struggled through deep and shuttering gasps. Her eyes were locked on the stains. She heard the trickle of the water and looked up quickly. She ran toward the noisy stream. She tripped and fell to her knees. She got up wildly and stumbled through the slapping branches.

The trees thinned and she broke into a more committed stride until she reached the soft bank. She fell on all fours at its edge. She resisted the burning ache to cry.

She looked at her pitiful reflection in the pool of

deep ink. Her high cheekbones and slanted eyes looked childishly back at her. She stared without reservation into the abyss that watched her unblinkingly.

Her breath caught as her reflection broke from a diving frog. She looked immediately back into the water. A frightened girl with a ripple of scars returned her desperate stare. She thought suddenly of drowning in the black mirror. She imagined herself lowering without hesitation into the inky liquid. An unrelenting itch at her side broke her concentration. She tried to pull away, but the water's whisper pulled her back.

"I'm not crazy. Not like her. I'm not like her. I'll *never* be like her. I'm not crazy!" She screamed into the eyes of the wild woman who glared back at her. She gripped the grassy bank into fistfuls of dirt and whipped it into the water.

She sobbed. She was alone. She was always alone. The loneliness frightened her. She splashed her hands in the stream and washed them with an explosive vigour. She scraped at her skin with her chipped white fingernails. She scraped herself obsessively. She dug between her nails. She worked the thin crevices until they burned. She dipped her hands into the water and repeated the task over and over. She stopped when her palms were an emblazoned red in the lightless night.

She closed her eyes and listened to the unceasing chatter, a murky mockery to the sordid ferryman. Awareness of the darkness around her crept slowly into her mind. She quickly opened her eyes and the fear lifted with her lids, despite the remaining darkness. She cupped her hands and dipped them in the stream again to cleanse her face. She let the cold-water dribble slowly down her cheeks and off her chin. She shakily pushed herself up, like a fawn on spindly legs. She feared blinking and being caught again in the unknown black.

She breathed slowly. She shook her head in disgust at herself. She knew it was wrong, but she also knew that once the pecking mind takes over it is like a wildfire that consumes reason. It controlled her with its seeds of doubt that had blossomed and sprouted roots deep into her conscience. She fought herself for normal. She fought to be free of the burden of her nameless conditions. To be a woman who could reach out and embrace comfort without hesitation or fear…but it was a falling blade she couldn't catch. She rubbed her forehead with her palms and sighed. Her stubborn resolve to go onward into the forest diminished like a puffed-out candle flame. The wind was quiet. The small river softened.

She followed the water on its journey. She was embarrassed the idea of going back came to her, although unseen strangers' judgements weighed each step. Her bare feet squished in the mud. She had little confidence in her footing and found herself slipping and swearing at herself.

Her feet cramped. Her rashed skin burned. Her hair was a greasy mess along her forehead. She could feel the grime of each strand sticking to it. She had to go on in opposition to the drag of a semblance of her old life hanging off her, like an escaped caged animal only foreseeing its predestined prison.

She forced herself to stop as her lips tingled with the craving of a cigarette. She felt her fingers, imagining one rested between them.

"Ist good?" she heard whispered over the din of the nighttime forest.

"Bak ahway! Bak ahway! Ist Nanabozho's. Stop!" an answering squeal responded.

The whispers stunned her, as if lightning had struck the tree beside her. She felt no sense of self-preservation. She was paralyzed. She listened, like a child listening to a house's nightly creaks from under a blanket. She held her breath. The river calmed in the ensuing silence, as if it also strained to listen. Its mumbling became an indistinct background noise far away from the adrenaline that pumped like a drug through her blood. The trees danced softly in an intimate sway. Her feet sank slowly and silently, deeper, and deeper into the earth.

No voices followed. Her heart slowly returned to a stable rhythm. She exhaled after a period of utter silence. Her feet were almost entirely embraced in the cold, wet sludge. She considered if she had finally begun to lose herself to the degradation of her mind. Her eyes twinged. She understood the horror of her realization. She leaned against a tree and shivered.

Few moments passed before she began to smell some form of herbal aroma floating in the air. She heard a strange giggle. The giggle was met with a firm and deep bark of unfiltered enjoyment. The fumes thickened like clouds of a scented mist. A spiral of the aromatic smoke twisted away from behind a bush. She tried to edge toward it, but her feet were anchored by her torrent of self-depravations. The mud began to feel warm in its embrace. It accommodated her like a comforting friend.

Although she heard nothing else, the smoke rose in a continuous spiral from source to sky. She eventually convinced herself to pull away from the coddling riverbank and managed to trip silently to the edge of the bush. She brushed through it to peer into a patch of soft grass that lay in between four large trees standing like pillars of stone. Sitting comfortably in the middle, passing a roughly carved wooden pipe, were two small humanoid beings. They were like morbid rabbits. Their backs were toward her, but she could see the rough leafy skin that covered them. A strip of jagged spikes pointed out along their spines like thorns. There was a distinct glow of the cherried bowl of herbs that burned softly as it was passed between them. The shank of the pipe was as long as the beings' bodies, but she could see their bark-like hands hold and pass it with ease. They were otherwise motionless except when a momentary gust of wind shuffled the forest around them. The creatures harmoniously vibrated and shifted in the direction of the wind's path.

She watched them and breathed the aroma of their pipe deep into her lungs. It was strangely familiar. She edged closer. She was close enough where she could reach out and touch them. One slowly turned its head toward her. Its beady eyes caught her, and she froze.

It tilted its head. There was no mouth, no nose, no ears, just oblong eyes that were bloodshot and stony, like milky-red rocks protruding from an earthy garden gnome.

She tried to say something, but the words caught in her throat. She opened her mouth, but only a choking silence came out. Tears began to swell and form pools that blurred her vision. She wrapped her hands around her neck and begged silently for air. The being slowly stood up. Its body was still facing away from her before its beady-eyed head swiveled toward her. She pointed to violently to her strained throat. Her pointing quickly turned into manic clawing as she tried to rip open an airway. She could feel the blood trapped to bursting in her skull. She saw the creature watching her through her blurred and panicked stare before it straightened its head in a whiplash motion. She coughed and gasped hysterically, falling to her hands and knees, as air forced its way inside her.

"Ist sees," one of them squeaked.

Plumes of smoke excreted with each syllable from the one still facing the other direction. The small being facing her stared without motion. She reached deeply for each breath as she tried to keep her eyes on them. She felt the innocence of her naivete withdrawn from her as her vision caught its beady glare. Wariness weighed on her. She felt her body's exhaustion. Her throat burned and the tenderness of her neck felt like she was slashed with a rake. Her urge to cry maddened her.

"Please...please help me home?" she begged with a hoarse voice, barely able to hold each word that slipped out of her mouth.

The being facing away from her took a deep inhalation from the pipe. She wondered, as she massaged her tortured throat, from what orifice it inhaled into.

It soundlessly exhaled its consumed fumes. Smoke swirled above its head. A moment went by as the smoke dissipated.

"Yuh've seen. Yuh musstay," it stated with a slow, high squeal.

"I cannot stay...here? I don't even know where I am. I don't even know what I'm seeing. What the hell are you?" she replied stubbornly. A flare of prejudice clouded her fear.

"Musstay. Yuh musstay. Yuh musstay." Its own response was a heavier and more guttural squeal. The one staring at her nodded dreamily. Their voices carried as if part of the wind.

"You-you're not real. I-I-Stop, stay there!" she shouted as she gestured to the beings. The other turned slowly toward her. "Ju-just stay there."

She shot upward and stepped back. She coughed violently. Her chest pleaded for more air. Both beings tilted their heads and considered her. She was held by them and stared open mouthed. Their tiny heads straightened in unison. She felt them weighing her. They swept her slowly with their engorged pupils, testing her fortitude with their stony eyes.

"Yuh don know," the higher pitch being said.

"Ist don know," the other joined.

She found some semblance of breath in their considerations of her, quickly turned on the spot, and ran. With each pained step she felt the comfort, sanctity, and sanity of her thoughts slip away. She angrily brushed the tears from her eyes.

"Stay. Stay. Yuh musstay," the higher pitched being squeaked with the wind that rushed past her. She saw nothing behind her as she looked back. "Yuh musstay or yuh mussdie." She quickened her pace until she was into a blind sprint. "He comes. He comes." They chanted like a metronome in her head. "He comes. He comes. He comes. Yuh mussdie. He whill say yuh mussdie."

She kept running, but their voices echoed like a rolling drum. A maniacal and murderous laughter suddenly filled her, overcoming the beings' chant. It entered her like a predator's encouragement in her ear. She tripped and fell in a blur of darkness.

She pushed herself into a hasty sitting position and looked back quickly; she saw nothing. The forest around her was silent. The river continued its whisper in an eternal ode to the night. She despised her weak and clumsy nature. Her wariness planted her. Her loneliness was another dense weight on her shoulders. Her exhaustion beat at her. She delved herself for air. Each breath burned through her restrictive throat. Her body called to her to lie down and close her eyes, but she ignored it.

She tried to watch the trees for signs of movement, but the running water distracted her thoughts. She was left to her own crazed spins until her eyes caught a pale shape in the shadows. Her breath caught. A strange figure stepped eerily toward her. The darkness made it look like a silhouetted marionette. Its laughter ripped through her like the reverberation of gongs. She couldn't move. It came to her like a nightmare coming to light.

A red leather, fingerless gloved hand sprang forward and grabbed her roughly by the chin. Its fingers were pincers of ice. Tears partially blinded her. She could just see the figure's chalky white face pull toward her own. Its breath was like a Winter frost. Its grip tightened on her jaw. She couldn't pull away.

"You are mine, once again, ivory flower," it said with an accent. It cradled each syllable carefully, but its tone was deep like a whisper through a hollow tree trunk.

She struggled against its cold fingers, but its grip was immoveable. She shuddered. The blur from her tears made its starkly white face look like a smudged painting. She tried to push it away, but its shoulders resisted her like an iron door. She grabbed its wrist with her hands and tried to wrench its grip away from her. It laughed horrifically. She felt helpless. She *was* helpless.

"Just kill me," she cried. "Just-just kill me, please."

"Noooo," it laughed with a ripple of enjoyment,

mocking her. "Nooo, you must not die now. You cannot, though I would happily fulfill your desires. I would bathe in your tainted fluids. I would taste your ripened flesh. Alas, for you shall be harvested instead. Returned to the roots and worms who will feed on our seed to bring life anew. In honour of meshkwadoon… 'Tis a pity. Though, it shall not always be so, ivory flower."

She dug her fingernails into its arm. Its skin was deathly cold. She swallowed the tears that dripped into her squished lips, then shot her hand upward to slice its face. It shoved her backwards and she tripped. She scrambled to her feet. It touched its cheek and looked at its hand. It smiled, then it released its hideous shrill as it looked down on her. She twisted and stumbled. She pulled herself desperately up and ran. She followed the riverbank as it coached her with its quickened flow. Its whispers called to her excitedly. She looked back and saw nothing. She didn't look back again.

Chapter 2

Trees churned overhead like a twister of specters. Light fog misted the ground. Leaves, bushes, and fallen branches called out angrily from beneath her blind steps. Sweat matted her hair and her breathing was ragged. She listened for the red gloved apparition, but all she heard was the deep thumping of blood in her head.

Soon the trees began to thin on both sides. Branches hung lower and heavier, no longer reaching to the sky in exaltation. Thickets like gorgon hair grasped at her from out of the fog. She pulled herself relentlessly through the ankle gripping brush. She used thin trees for assistance until she was halted by a wall of evergreens that hung like a curtain of stone before her.

The barrier of deep green was a silent guardian that looked down on her. She hesitated before she rushed through its spiky arms. Needles caught her exposed skin like scraping Velcro as she spilled into a clearing.

She dropped her head and held her hips, as she tried to catch air from her burning lungs. Her feet were torn in a blistered agony. She lifted her gaze from the grass sticking between her aching toes and rubbed her sleepless eyes. She investigated the forest enclosed sanctuary. Wild grass showered in the morning rays. There were no sounds of birds, but the wind brought smells of pine in its delicate moaning. She was soothed by the soft green that cushioned her soles. She wondered regretfully of the heels she left behind, recognizing the pair by the indentation left like scars on her feet. She shook her head thinking of the black suede with the counterfeit red soles. She felt childish without them. She brushed her greasy, dangling hair behind her ears as she lifted her eyes to the sky.

Taking only the moment to correct herself and collect her breathing, she took the first pained limps forward. A light chirrup sprang out of the treetops, and it was returned in kind. As if awakened from a deep slumber, the morning stirred the world with an energy of life. Scilla's yawned to the sky, blue petals straining like stretched arms. Daffodils were exploding stars in the damp grass, a glistening field of crystals in the blossoming light.

She couldn't remember when she turned away from the river. She couldn't even recall when the darkness began to fade. All she could remember from the night was fear and the taste of iron in her parched mouth. Her memories were a darting shadow that she chased timelessly. She would have cried if she had the energy to. She hated herself for wanting to cry.

She could feel the dirt and sap plastered to her skin like splattered molasses. She angrily reminded herself to refrain from touching her face with her stained hands. She disgusted herself, a fungal taint in the scenic meadow. Her mind became obsessed with the bottle of sanitizer she knew was in her missing purse. She lost herself as she imagined rubbing it between her fingers. She closed her eyes in exploration of the relief.

Waking from an unexpected sleep, she lifted her chin slowly from her chest. She was unsure how she got to her knees. Each blink was flecked with spots like a dirty pub glass, as her eyes tried to adapt to the sun. She stood up and re-examined the clearing. It was an oval arena of soft hued flowers, orange and black butterflies, and low flying birds. The trees shaped it, like an impenetrable wall of emerald keeping an army of shadow at bay. The sky was a cloudless and soothing maternal blue, a swaddle that tucked in the fresh morning life.

She smoothed her black dress and began twisting her hair between two fingers. She twirled it neurotically. She closed her eyes softly. The strands of hair wrapped satisfyingly around her fingers. She tugged it with an unexplainable pleasure. She sighed after an aggressive pull and considered her path ahead. Societal expectations pulled her spirit to home, but the fear of unknown faces hung over her. She knew she could never really escape the mortal disorder that was the duty of life. An anxiety of missed work slowly crept inside her, but it was replaced quickly by the gap wedged between her past and her present. She felt like a hollowed-out shell, with the acceptance of her being carved roughly out of her. It was an unquenchable abyss inside her that swallowed her sense of love, her identity, her hope. She couldn't help but feed the rotting beast to keep it from devouring her. She could already feel the faceless eyes of everyone re-evaluating her upon her return, a meatless stack of bones splayed for judgement.

She grimaced tightly. Her swollen eyes burned like Hephaestion forges, each breath a bellow that stoked them. Any imaginations of the night slipped away from her, as she accepted each moment in the forest as an individual trial to maintain her sanity. She knew she had failed the tests miserably. She embraced the notion that what she ran from, the red gloved man, the beady-eyed beings, her life, were machinations of her decaying mind: a genetic suffrage.

She flexed and straightened her back muscles. She rolled her shoulders tightly and shook away her tensions with a deep sigh. With an inherent sense of impatience, she limped across the meadow. Each step was taken without care for the livery that decorated the grassy oval field, as her mind got caught in a web of insignificant flashes of thought.

Within a thoughtless blink, she found herself face to face with the opposing border of evergreens. Her arms tingled with the tattooed rash she carried from the other side. She scratched them compulsively in unison before she forced herself through. The needles barely seemed to touch her as she shouldered sideways into the swaying arms.

The forest on the other side was silent and dim. She stubbornly brushed through tall plants, long grass, and nature-shapened trees twisted by age and the crowding of branches. Nothing was familiar to her. She was lost. She was always lost.

She focused on the image of herself behind her desk, organizing files. Files of everything she was. Files of nothing. She felt the fear of her nothingness. It was the type of fear she would withhold from the eyes of the world. It was a shameful fear. She slouched from the sudden burden of her thoughts. She wondered if she had the determination to make it out. She wondered if she had the intent to.

While entangled by the deep roots of her mind, she missed her step as the ground below her dipped aggressively. She spilled clumsily forward onto a thin, hard trail. It was a dirt, rock, and root scaled snake that slithered between overhanging branches. It crested between two short dips at the base of the trees' edge. She sighed and rubbed her sore ankle.

She looked the trail up and down. Sunlight slipped through the gap in the greenery. It bathed the path in white light. As she attempted to stand, pain seared through her entire foot and lower leg. The stabbing left her clenching her teeth. Her eyes were simmering embers, but she continued her war against each tear.

Her body grew cold against the cool earth. Shivers quaked her. The sunlight and her fiery eyes did nothing to warm her. She braced her ankle in a fetal ball on the dirt. A light breeze excited over hanging leaves. They shook as they watched her hopeless display. She found no relief in her discovery. She clung to her ankle gravely, a child curled in despair. The ground began to vibrate. The vibrations grew stronger as the trail slowly awoke from its slumber. She tried to focus on the sensation, but the rumble faded through an unseen chrysalis. She blinked. She heard children's voices. She blinked. She saw only black. She heard nothing. There was nothing. She blinked.

Sweat danced down Arjun's forehead. It shimmered in the Summer's golden rays as it dripped off his face to make dark circles in the dirt. He dabbed his neck with the towel that hung around him, damp already from repetition.

His class shuffled along behind. They were a motley precession of prepubescent youth. He reduced his pace to examine his wild flock. He allowed the front of the line to wiggle past him. He was quietly amazed by the oddity of twelve-year olds: mismatched clothes, uncut mops of hair, and a blooming awareness of self. They were undulating beings caught in the current of culture and societal shifts. Rough carved figurines of innocence, they cracked like aged cement walls from a birthing ego that pushed heedlessly at the seams in an attempt to find any possible route to escape the confines of their awakening minds.

Talking and giggling faded in and out as the line

of children continued to pass him. He counted their numbers quietly and obsessively to himself as they did. Once the chubby little Mikayla shifted past, her bright eyes looking down to her pink and white sneakers, he snuck in behind. He couldn't see much beyond her through the twisting of the path. His lack of vision made his palms clammy with sweat, and he got anxious to recount them. He checked his phone to confirm the list. The continuous talking gave him little confidence that he lost no one.

"Mr. Kaul!" a child's voice screamed urgently from the front of the line.

He hastily pushed past Mikayla and wound through the rest of the children. Fear swept over him. The incident two years ago dripped like sludge into his gut. He knew he should've been watching them. He knew he should've got the educational assistant to join them. He started to run.

"Mr. Kaul! Mr. Kaul! Mr. Kaul!" other children began to echo. Their heads turned to him like a pack of spooked prairie dogs as he passed through them.

As he reached the front of the procession, he eyed the source of commotion cautiously. The kids were piled into a group blocking the path, but he edged above them and saw a woman in a black dress laying on her side. Her knees were pulled loosely toward her chest. Her bare feet were stained with dirt and dried blood. Her pale legs were uncovered, and they led like a serpentine curve to the exposed bottom portion of her buttocks. His eyes instinctively settled there for a moment before he abruptly brushed between the kids and went to his knees by the woman's face. The earth was rough and stray pebbles jabbed malignantly into his shins. He adjusted out of the pangs and motioned for the kids to wait.

"Stay there, guys. Kim-Kimberly, do a head-count, please," he delegated, attempting to pastor the panic.

The petite brown-haired girl awoke from her shivering petrification. She skittishly adjusted her black rimmed glasses, blinked quickly, and looked around her to the other stunned children as if expecting them to know how to respond. A moment later he could hear the girl's squeaky voice slowly begin counting as he returned his focus to the woman.

"Can you hear me? Are you alright?" he asked softly, leaning in toward the woman's expressionless face.

He saw her breasts gently motioning to and from her chest. She was alive. He breathed out deeply. Relief cleansed him.

"Caroline? Caroline, bring me the first aid pack from Yuuta," he stated, barely taking his eyes from the woman. The children stirred quietly trying to accommodate the two girls, as they simultaneously maneuvered to get their own individual looks at the scene.

He focused on the woman's face. She had fair skin framed by honey-blonde hair. Her dry lips were pink and slightly parted. Her high cheekbones were defined by the shape of her head. Her eyes seemed to shift excitedly under their lids, as if she was watching a gripping thriller in her dreams. She was like a plucked flower forsaken by its snatcher. He slowly brushed some of the spilled hair that cradled her jawline behind her ear.

"Mr. Kaul?" Yuuta inquired softly, kneeling beside him in imitation.

"Ah-yeah...umm, thank you."

He took the presented first aid pack from Yuuta. He opened it and sifted through the unorganized contents. He shifted Band-Aids and small instructional sheets to the side until he found the latex gloves he sought. He put them on his hands, removed the damp towel from his shoulders, dried the woman's forehead, and placed it to rest under her head. He was internally aware that he had never performed any form of first aid outside of the course he took every few years, but the kids eyed him expectantly. Sweat dribbled over one of his eyes, and he wiped it away quickly with the back of his forearm. He looked down at the woman and hesitated.

"Hey, you okay?" he asked again, as he snapped his fingers near her ear. He shook her shoulder lightly. She didn't blink. He sighed and reached into the pack. After another moment of annoyed searching, he pulled out a handful of disinfectant wipes. "Yuuta, grab some gauze for me, please." He passed the spilling pack to the boy, stood up, then kneeled back down by the woman's feet.

He struggled to pull his resisting gaze away from her exposed cheeks. White underwear peeked out at him. He had to drag his eyes like stone blocks down her legs. He hadn't felt the warmth of a woman since his wife left him. A twinge in his groin forced him to shake the thoughts out of his head, as the weight of shame burdened him in the spotlight of his kids' eyes.

After slowly opening a few disinfectant wipe packs, he massaged at the crusted dirt and dried blood on the woman's feet. He saw that her left ankle was swollen and red. He reduced the pressure of his wiping while he approached it. Neither she nor the kids budged. They watched him like swaying stalks of corn. She was a placid flower patch. He felt the sweat dripping down his back.

Once he was satisfied with his work, he looked to Yuuta who passed him a roll of gauze. While he wrapped the woman's feet and ankle, Yuuta gently pulled down the woman's dress to cover her exposure.

"Is she okay, Mr. Kaul?" Yuuta asked shyly.

"I'm not sure...I think she'll be fine," he said. Yuuta's concerned disposition didn't change. "I may need to carry her back to the bus. Grab Charlie for me?"

A short and skinny bespectacled boy emerged from the wide-eyed flock, responding to the summons before Yuuta could get off his knees. A wrinkled map was anxiously held in the boy's grip, as if he held it the entire trip fearing that at any moment, he would be called upon to fulfill his map reading duty.

"Alright Charlie, you're up." The boy stood beside him, and shakily passed the map over. "No, no. Sit beside me here and lay the map in front of you. Come on, bacha!" Charlie sat awkwardly but quickly beside him and sprawled out the map. The boy's eyes shifted between the map now and the motionless woman. Arjun examined the map. He mumbled thoughtlessly to himself. He traced his finger on a dark line and examined the shape of the trail. "Oh, shukr hai," he breathed in relief, "the parking lot is just a few hundred meters away. Everybody, listen up for a sec. Charlie will guide you for the remainder of the trail, stick behind him and when you reach the exit into the parking lot, Kim will do another headcount. You will need to wait for me there. Mrs. Freecomb should be there to meet you. Kim, there's twenty-nine, including myself. I swear on the ajna chakra…if any of you leave the trail for any reason…"

"Mr. Kaul…I-I don't know the way," Charlie stuttered. Fear dampened the boy's puny brown eyes.

"Charlie, just follow the trail. It's literally a straight line." Arjun expressed irritably. His eyes flicked from Charlies' face and back to the woman on the ground. She hadn't moved. "Go on, everyone… Yuuta, you're gonna help me." Arjun grabbed the boy by the shoulder and held him in place as the other kids shuffled past. They eyed the woman as if she was a coiled cobra. Once Mikayla, the last in line once again, was hidden by the sloped winding trail, he pulled off the latex gloves and stuffed them in his front pocket. He evaluated the woman, dropped his backpack to the ground, dipped down, and scooped her into his arms. Her skin was warm porcelain. "Grab my bag, please." He motioned to the lying green sac on the dirt with his foot. The boy picked it up swiftly as he collected the first aid kit.

Arjun carried the woman at a quick trot. Although she was petite, the density of her weight was a struggle for his aching biceps. He regretted his procrastination from physical activity, a blundering sweat soaked sloth, but he maintained his pace.

He broke the tree line to find the kids waiting expectantly. Dolores rushed over quickly. An unreasonable look of concern wrinkled her bug-like features.

"Oh dear, oh dear, Mr. Kaul…Mr. Kaul, is she okee?" the bus driver worriedly expressed, as she halted in front of him and Yuuta, her thick fingers spread over her gaping mouth.

"I'm not sure, Dolores. Please get the kids on the bus. We will need to take her to the nearest hospital," Arjun said.

"Yes-yes, of course, dear. It's about a fi-fifteen-minute drive to Huntsville Memorial… My granddaughter was delivered there in July. Such a sweet girl. She's walking now, did yee know?"

"Yes, Dolores, take us to Huntsville. I will let Cathy know why we'll be delayed," he said, ignoring her rambles.

"Dear-Mr. Kaul, yee don't think we should just call her an ambulance do yer?"

He hesitated. He looked at the woman's face cupped in his hand and his heavy breathing quickened.

An unknown force tried to convince him to hold her closer, tighter. He unwillingly restrained himself.

"Yuuta, Mrs. Freecomb is right. Grab me the fire blanket and pillow from the bus and we will lay the woman here until the paramedics arrive," he said to the boy standing quietly beside him.

Yuuta scrambled onto the bus and returned quickly with a gray blanket and a foam neck pillow. The boy laid them out on the grass. Mr. Kaul placed her softly on the blanket. He rested her head on the pillow and it sank into it like a marshmallow.

Yuuta touched her forehead with the back of his hand and watched her. The boy's eyes seemed to darken as he stared with an intense look of pained suffering. Yuuta looked up for a moment and Mr. Kaul saw that the boy's eyes had become like onyx stones. They were black as a pika's, like bored out caverns in a field of red lined snow. He didn't recall the true colour of Yuuta's eyes, but in that moment, they were gouged Oedipean sockets.

Yuuta twisted his gaze awkwardly back onto the woman's face. The boy was a ghost of his former self after the disappearance of his father and the death of his mother. A dilapidated up-and-comer. But as that boy looked upon the woman, Mr. Kaul saw an ember ignite in those pits of pitch.

"You can get on the bus now, Yuuta. Thanks, yaar," Arjun suggested. He tried not to distinctly wrinkle his brow.

"Yes-yes, sir. Yes, Mr. Kaul," the boy whispered.

He rose slowly but kept his eyes locked on the woman. Arjun watched Yuuta shiver and witnessed the colour in his eyes slowly fade to a soft green. "Yes, Mr. Kaul."

The boy worried his hands as he climbed the steps into the dated yellow vehicle. Dolores made a check mark on a clipboard she held. She had a cellphone hugged tightly between her shoulder and the side of her head. Maternal concern darkened her thick face.

Mr. Kaul's chest heaved Ribhusan anvils, as he suddenly realized the weight of his breathing. His eyes were pulled back to the woman. He licked his lips and forced himself to look to the forest's edge. A breeze shook the leaves of nearby trees and for a moment he believed he heard a satisfied whisper from within their depths, as they watched him unwaveringly.

The bus began to rumble as Dolores engaged the ignition. He could smell its diesel fumes permeate the air. The leaves had a sudden moment of violent stirring, but there was no wind. He eyed a disgruntled red maple, with roots that burrowed like python-sized worms into the earth. He could feel its anger. He shook his head and quickly looked back at the woman. Her breasts still shifted with each breath, no lighter nor deeper. He lifted his eyes to her closed ones and suddenly hers lifted open to reveal glistening hazelnuts desperate and hard as hungry soil. Her breath caught and she burst into wild tears. He pulled her into his arms as she sobbed hysterically, like a child devastated by its first confrontation with mortality.

After countless minutes, her cries became soft

whimpers, and he began smoothing her hair with his hand. Her whimpers slowly faded into sniffles, and he watched her use the back of her red arm to wipe away tear streaks.

They sat in silent contemplation of one another, until sirens called like heavenly trumpets in the distance. The sirens grew louder and louder like Christian angels diving to the earth. He stared down at her, realizing he may never see her again, and turned her face towards his own.

"What is your name?" he asked softly. Concern swelled his tongue.

She watched him, as if seeing another person for the first time. Her face was carved ivory, but it was cold, like a Shilo winter. It frightened him for a moment, until she licked her lips and sniffed one last time.

"Natasha…My name is Natasha," she whispered.

Chapter 3

The woman's face was like a pale light in Yuuta's mind, but the thought of Mr. Kaul's coal black stare disturbed the image. Every time Yuuta closed his eyes, he saw the unblinking black beetles staring back at him.

He sat quietly the entire bus ride, listening to, and envying, the whispering and laughing of the others. Charlie sat alone in front of him. Robert and Caroline talked suspiciously in the seat to his left. He watched them quietly without directly looking.

He stirred from side to side as the bus shook from the potholed highway. The windows rattled. He wished he had someone he could tell about the woman and Mr. Kaul's frightening face, but he also wished that he never had to talk to anyone. He immediately began to regret not bringing his book. He rested his forehead against the cool glass. It vibrated like a running dryer. He absently watched green highway signs shoot past, as he breathed his thoughts back inside. The woman's face casually slipped back into his mind, and he dreamed of her pink lips.

"What do you think happened?" he heard Charlie whisper excitedly.

Yuuta opened his eyes. He jumped when he saw

Charlie sitting beside him. The small boy was jittery and seemed uncomfortable.

"I'm not sure," Yuuta replied. "Her feet were-they looked…I don't know. I think she was running from something…or-or someone."

"You think she's one of those from downtown?" Charlie said absently, eyeing the seat ahead of them.

The seat was a thin, cracked, blackish leather. Carvings of previous riders made permanent marks in it. Yuuta watched Charlie trace an indented Nazi-symbol with his eyes.

"Probably," Yuuta replied, his mind grasped at the pink parted lips that threatened to slip away.

"Did you see Mr. Kaul's face?" Charlie asked. Yuuta hesitated. A foreign sense of annoyance disturbed him. "Did you see it? It was kind of creepy, but I had to stare too. She was better looking than Caroline on her best day. I hope she's okay-the woman, I hope the woman's okay."

Yuuta felt his fingers grip the seat below him, digging like picks into the veins of the leather. His blood bubbled like a cauldron of oil swaying with the vibrations of the bus.

"I-I don't know," he stuttered. "Do you-did you-did something about her…bother you?"

Charlie looked at him strangely. The boy adjusted his glasses.

"Yuuta…" Charlie was barely audible. He turned his face away; his cheeks were spotted with red splotches. "I saw her underwear." Yuuta's insides squirmed like writhing worms. He shifted awkwardly between his gripping hands. He began to sweat as an internal heat source was fanned by his heavy breaths. His heart pounded, a soundless and ancient forging being worked inside his ears. Charlie didn't seem to notice anything. "Did you see them Yuuta…You had to have seen them…Her butt too. I saw her butt cheeks. We were right there. He was touching her too. I wonder if he could smell her. I bet she smelt so nice. Robert says girls smell like flowers and fishes. I don't know what he's talking about though. Kim said that she must be a squaw hanging out like that. Do you know what a squaw is, Yuuta?" Charlie pressed his face closer to Yuuta's. "Robert said that she was just jealous because no guys will look at her. Either way, I'm just excited I got to see."

Yuuta's hands were vice grips that tightened on the seat. Shavings of leather clogged under his ungroomed fingernails as he dug them deeper. His heart pulsed violently. His groin began to swell, as he bathed in the flickering images of the woman's pale skin, her softly parted pink lips, and her lily-white underwear. Her unperfumed smell resonated in his nostrils.

"Please…don't," he groaned, whether to himself or to Charlie, he wasn't sure. "I don't feel well. I- Charlie…" Charlie gasped when their eyes met.

"Yuuta! Your eyes!" Charlie spluttered.

Robert and Caroline swiveled quickly in their direction; a pair of startled racoons caught rummaging through garbage. The bus glided along a rumble strip, and they all vibrated. Yuuta vomited violently.

"Mr. Kaul…I need Mr. Kaul. I need Mr. Kaul, please," he gasped, wiping away some of the mess from his mouth with his sweater's sleeve.

He struggled to see through watery eyes, but he caught shades of people poking out over the backs of seats and in the bus aisle. He could hear their accusing whispers. The screeching of a sound like a tea kettle escalated through his head. He was conscious of each breath, as he tried to fill the cavern deep within his stomach. The ringing got louder and louder, tearing through him like a storm. Laughter reverberated through his head.

He breathed in and out. In and out.

He opened his eyes. He was leaning into the cold glass window. He blinked quickly in an attempt to pinch out a small swell of tears. He faced the barrier of cracked black leather. He lifted his head up and looked hesitantly, and shamefully, to his left: no one was there, except for Robert and Caroline whispering to each other in the seat across the aisle. Charlie's bobbing head poked out from the bus seat in front of him. It was a dream, a nightmare.

He breathed deeply. He tried to forget the nausea that still tingled within him. He was thankful for the end of day quiet, the ringing a memory of another place and another time. He looked out the window and recognized the final stretch of highway. Although he couldn't say where exactly they were, he knew they were close by his recognition of the off-ramp they passed.

    He reached for the backpack and first aid kit at his feet and placed them beside him on the seat. The backpack was heavy with textbooks, but he didn't mind the extra weight. He thought of home and the burden of his school day being stationed beside his closet. He thought of his sobo, of the fish and bread and tea she would prepare for him while he watched his shows. He thought of his books. He looked down at the hands he twisted together silently.

    The quiet din of the bus gradually faded as others recognized the area near the school. A current of excitement conducted through them, as they saw local stores, parks, and homes. He was surprised in his eavesdropping that almost no discussion seemed to be on the woman, as conversations became personal or gibberish. They didn't feel her. They were incapable of recognizing the woman's plight or pain. Children. They were all children. He hated all of them.

    The bus slowly turned into the school's half-moon driveway. It trundled past an empty rusted bike rack. A yellowing soccer field crisped in the hot summer air at the centre of the half-moon. He always felt strange when he came to the school when no children or teachers were around, like a backyard trespasser. The vacancy weighed on him heavily.

    The school was a brown bricked twentieth century dungeon not unlike his sofu's descriptions of internment camps. A small garden bordered the worn walls that led to the main entrance, but the flowers drooped sadly. He could almost feel their hunger, as they huddled in the shade of the bleak high walls, starved by the local caretaker. The soil was dry and looked like it would crack and shatter before crumbling between grooming fingers. He felt pity for the fading foliage, but he didn't understand why he felt so. He continued to watch the flowers as the bus slowly came to a halt.

Preferring to be last off, he sat while the children who were already not standing out of excitement began to stand. Craning necks looked between windows and soft whispers became adolescent decibels. He sat quietly and watched them. His eyes caught the resigned sigh of Mrs. Freecomb. She looked tired. He eyed her sides, as they spilled over the edge of the seat. She was a big woman, with arms that drooped like the branchlets of the tree in his backyard. Her short gray hair projected her motherly nature. She always acted like she knew everything; that she knew what boys needed best. Sighing once more she stood to her feet dutifully.

"Alright children, off yous go. Yer mums and dads are waiting for yous. Everyone off! Come on now, I've got to get home to my Andrew," she shouted. A smile was drawn across her face. "Move along now, dears!"

As if rounding up a band of wild hogs, she waved her hands toward the front of the bus toward the opened exit door. Children shuffled along with her direction energetically like a hungry herd. Most of the chatter had subsided as the children quickly exited, but Yuuta remained in his chair. He watched until Charlie descended the stairs before he finally lifted off the seat with his bag on his back and the first aid kit gripped in his hand. He followed Mrs. Freecomb's sigh of relief out of the bus.

He held the handles tightly on the stairs as he descended them to the paved walkway. His classmates were already scattered, running or walking to their waiting parents. He walked his first aid kit to Mrs. Warren, who waited impatiently, talking into her earbud headset. She said nothing as she took it. He tightened his shoulder straps and quietly walked home alone.

The suburban streets were busy with traffic. Sirens sang in the distance. It was a common song that rang throughout the neighbourhood. Similarly de-signed bungalows lined the road, differentiated only by the gardens that decorated their exteriors. Maple trees were planted at the curbside of each home. Birds maneuvered determinedly.

The sun slowly dipped toward the horizon, shooting its final Apollyonic arrows onto the suburbia. The street was lit in an orange glow. He watched as his shadow stretched out before him and imagined himself at battle with the great black creature.

The evening cooled and the shadow fiend grew with the sinking sun. A river whispered softly under the bridge he quietly crossed. He stopped for a moment to consider the girlish whisper of the water, like a mumbling Naiad worshipping the shadow. He had crossed it everyday and couldn't remember the musical voice any other time. He looked over the edge and into the shallow water that frothed around big rocks and collapsed trees. A rusted barrel of trash stood near the bank.

He watched the bubbling river curiously. He tried to catch the words of her whispered song. She sounded joyful in her everlasting task. He watched and listened, hypnotized by her flowing music.

A sudden feeling of something watching him tingled up his shoulders and he looked along the sidewalk. A ragged man was standing a few paces away. The man stared at him. His disgruntled brown jacket covered much of his donation box outfit. A beard like twisted tree roots sprouted from his face. His hair was a wig of damp straw hanging to his neck. He stood haggardly, watching Yuuta. His eyes followed Yuuta's, as Yuuta looked from the top of the man's greasy top to his worn and muddied sneakers.

"I hear it too," the man said suddenly. His voice was a ragged exhalation of a history of smoking.

Yuuta watched the man with a curiosity that trumped his fear.

"What does it say? I mean...what does she say?" Yuuta asked. The man considered him without blinking but said nothing. "Well, I...I should get going. I really don't think I should keep my grandmother waiting. She can get pretty foul once excited." He said strategically. He backed away slowly. The man's arms hung loosely at his side, like an ape's. He had a mild forward leaning slouch. His eyes were like dark mud. He didn't respond, but he sighed. "Umm, okay, well…"

He began to gingerly walk around the man, but the man grabbed him by the shoulders. He tried to resist, but the man's strength pulled him in. The man's dark eyes burrowed into his own.

"They're everywhere. In everything," the man coughed. "Like mosquitos buzzing around your ears. Heimskr! You swat and you swat, but they never stop. Cursed things! Wild things! Damned natured freaks whispering death and crack pottery."

"Sir, p-please let me go!" Yuuta begged.

"No one believes. No one ever doe-Shut up, just shut up!" He shouted, shaking his fist in the river's direction. "Get out of here. He's just a boy!" The man looked quickly back at Yuuta. "They never stop. Their knowledge, it runs deep, as deep as the roots of a mountain, but…the price…It's too much…It's too much. They will corrupt you with decay and you will become like me. You'll be the ragged fiend! Everyone you love will be joined with the earth for harvest and you will be left a rotted-out trunk, pecked at by termites and choking dogbane," the man spat in a whispering growl, as he shook Yuuta aggressively. "Then they will come for you…to feed. They always come. That is their covenant." The man sealed his mouth and looked around fearfully, as if he expected to be attacked. He quickly shot his gaze back to Yuuta. "You must get out of here. You must go! They will come. Damned demons of the dirt. You must go! They will come for you too.

Go boy, get away!" The man pushed Yuuta. Yuuta stumbled backwards. He gaped. Saliva built at the corners of his mouth, but the words on his tongue were trapped.

The man returned to his motionless state, but his eyes were wide and crazed. Yuuta looked around quickly, wishing on whatever would listen for another witness to the rugged vagrant, but the street was silent and empty. He looked back at the man whose browned, wrinkled skin was like worn sagging leather. His lips were cracked and pasty. Yuuta backed away slowly. He kept his eyes on the man's face. He twisted and ran for home.

Yuuta reached the side door of his grandparents' rented basement without much recollection of the short run. His arms shook as he grappled with the backpack he tried to remove from his back. Once he successfully wrestled it off, he reached hastily into it and pulled out his key. He put the key in the lock and shoved his shoulder against the door to disengage it. He locked it behind him and put the chain on. He rested with his back against the wall, breathing heavily.

"What was that?" he whispered to himself. He tried to remember the man's darkened face and eyes, but everything had been a blur. "What is going on?"

His thoughts flipped erratically between the injured woman, Mr. Kaul's satanic stare, the nightmare, the whispering river, and the ragged man. The woman... The thought of her reignited a fire that was dwindling within him. Her pale skin and pink lips parted to show the tips of off-white teeth. Her fitted black dress and her white underwear haunted him.

He breathed deeply and descended the set of stairs from the door's landing. The basement hall was dark, but for a trail of light that snuck through from the outside. He quickly went down the hall, through the kitchen, and shut himself into his room. He threw his backpack with a relieving heave beside his closed closet.

The room glowed like a neon sign in the orange light that flooded through the sliding glass doors. The walls were paneled with an old flimsy wood panel board that his sofu said had been there since the sixties. A single bed was tucked against a wall, with the blue and white bedding made. A bulky TV sat at the end of it on a dark wood stand he imagined had been in the house before the wood panelling was installed. The room was large, but he made no attempts to decorate it. His only eye-catching source of decor was the bookshelf displaying hundreds of his beloved volumes. On his desk, a small stack of neatly organized math homework waited for his attention, and a copy of *Crime and Punishment* sat wrinkled and abandoned near the edge.

He walked past everything with targeted distaste and sat at the edge of his bed. He stared absentmindedly at the wall. Images of the woman clouded his mind. He wasn't as delirious as Raskolnikov, but within him a whipping flame stirred, lashing his insides. His eye caught a break in the panel where he had accidentally shot a mini puck during a period when he thought he could play hockey. He imagined he had stashed the woman's underwear there. Watching the hole, he fell into an unrecallable gap of thought.

A knock penetrated the hollow door, vibrating the panel walls.

"Yui-chan?" an elderly woman's voice asked, distinct concern in the tone of her pre-entry identification. Immediately following her inquiry into his presence, his sobo opened the door a fraction. She stopped as if about to accommodate his privacy and then immediately opened it entirely and stepped in. The apron she brushed her hands on was grease stained. He knew his sofu must already be home if she was preparing dinner. He could smell the pan-fried fish from the kitchen she stepped out of. "Everything okay, chiisana kuma? You left the chain on agai-Oh, Yuuta. You are covered in sweat and still have school clothes on! No outside clothes on your bed Yui, and your shoes. Take off your shoes Saito Yuuta! You walked through my kitchen with shoes on? How long have you been home? You don't come say hello to your sobo anymore? It's eight-thirty and I know you haven't eaten. Come, come. I have some fish for you and bread and tea and soup."

She quickly left the room following her barrage. He could hear the chinking of dishes and her annoyed murmurings through the bedroom door she left open.

His muscles fought him as he reached down to slip off his shoes, but he combatted his exhaustion and dressed into his home clothes and a pair of slippers. He left his room for the adjoining kitchen and sat across from his sofu at their scarred wooden dining table. He ate his dinner in silence, while his sobo and sofu talked about nothing. His sobo offered him green tea and frozen mochi, but he shook his head.

"Are you sick?" his sofu asked, as he squinted his eyes in examination. "Green tea will do you some good."

"No. No, I'm fine. We just…we had a very long day on our hike, and I'm-I'm just tired," Yuuta said, his gaze fell to his empty plate.

"Oh, today was the hike, Yu?" his sofu asked.

"Yes."

His sofu continued his squinting investigation while his sobo pretended to sip her tea nonchalantly. He could feel a cloud of concern dampen the small kitchen, but he tried to ignore it.

"Is it a girl, Yu? This ol' stud knows a thing or two about taming wild mares," his sofu chuckled with friendly eyes that looked slyly over a pair of black rimmed glasses.

His sobo choked quietly on her tea and shot a sharp glance at her husband, who quickly lost his grin and reworked his gaze to examine Yuuta.

"What? No? You-Stop! Everything is okay, don't worry about me. I'm just tired. Is it okay if I do the dishes and go to bed early tonight, sobo?" He forced the tight muscles of his face into a grin.

"Hmm, if I find you're keeping secrets Yui, I will make sure this Mr. Kaul knows you aren't keeping busy at home and need some more homework," his sobo said softly, purposefully ensuring that she didn't sound sincere. "Don't worry about the dishes though, I will do them tonight. Get some rest chiisana kuma, but I expect you up and ready to help your sofu and I tomorrow morning with some de-weeding: there's a nasty vine that's been killing the lilac bush your sofu has been driving me crazy about. Go on, Yui-chan, sweet dreams. Go." She shooed him out of his chair and into his room. She closed his door behind him.

He stood just inside and listened absently. The upstairs neighbours' footsteps groaned above him. The careful chinking of plates rang out of the kitchen. Pipes flexed in the walls. He heard a familiar laughter in the distance. He could feel a TV on somewhere nearby. The sounds distracted him, and he listened with his eyes closed as the walls of his bower shut in around him.

Yuuta woke up disoriented on his bed. He was still fully clothed, with his slippers kicked onto the floor. His bedding was wrinkled, but still made. The room's light was walled in by the opaque black outside. A feeling of troubled sleep weighed on him. His mouth was thick with spit that he struggled to swallow. A scraping sound made him jump. He quickly looked over to the sliding glass door from where he lay and saw a strange shape of flickering blue.

He shot out of bed and immediately turned off the light he had left on. He dove into a squat and turned around to look outside. A dog-sized stone figure was silhouetted against the unseeable backyard. It had layered skin, like large grey stone scales. Its eyes were carved pools of ocean blue. In its stone claw was gripped a once white towel or cloth. He hoped that he was no longer visible to it, but its blue eyes followed him in the darkness. A panic set in and he ran to hide behind the TV on its aged stand. The blue eyes continued to follow him, emotionless and icy. It lifted a rock-twisted claw and rapped at the sliding glass.

"What the heck is happening to me?" he said to himself, as he slapped his cheeks. "Is this real? Am I dreaming again?"

He peeked over the edge of the stand and saw the creature watching him. Its eyes like blue flames burrowed into him, analyzing him. He could do nothing but stare at it, as it did him.

It stopped rapping as they faced each other. He felt heavy from his lack of sleep and his fear. He slid back down behind the stand and rubbed his eyes.

Seeming to sense his hesitation, the creature rapped at the glass again. Yuuta breathed deeply. He prayed anxiously that his sobo and sofu didn't hear the racket. He stretched his eyes with his hands and brushed his hair in frustration. He didn't know what to do.

A clutching cold sent a chill through his body. He hugged his knees to his chest. Although his small basement window was closed, a whisper like a lake breeze blew through the room with the chill. It was an entwined feminine incantation that seemed to draw the creature as it began to rap with increasing intensity. The raps quickly became panicked knocks. The overlapping whispers matched the creature's gradual intensification, as the wave of female voices, like rushing rivers, flooded through his head. He stood up non-consensually, as the whispering chants drew him to his feet. He felt as if he was being carried with the current of the soft breaths, but not toward the creature, instead he was drawn toward the kitchen.

The creature hammered on the glass with both of its rock scaled arms. Blue eyes sparked in a torrent of panic. He shook his head, as if stirring awake. He looked back to see the strange creature's desperation, and he felt a natural inclination to go to it instead. The whispers suddenly hardened, and what was once a caressing blend of sensual female voices became an intermingled concoction of bird-like screeching and hissing slurs. As he approached the small stone creature, the deathly wails began to fade.

Once he reached the sliding door, the wails were gone, and the chill that erected his arm hair had vanished. He breathed heavily for a moment. His hand was on the door's lock, and he looked at the creature that looked up at him. The dirty towel was clutched in its claw. They watched each other. His heavy breathing lessened. He saw the blue waters of a mysterious grotto in its rounded sockets. It stared back at him without blinking. It lifted its towelless hand and rapped at the door once more.

He reached to unlock it but hesitated and pulled his hand back. The creature's small head moved with his hand. He looked past it and watched wind shake tall weeds that grew through cracks in the backyard's patio stones. The backyard beyond was cloaked in shadow, a backdrop of black staging the patio that was visible through the glass. The sidewall of a steel shed flexed, and the sound of cranking aluminum slipped through the doors. He looked at his sweaty, shaking hands and then brought his gaze back to the creature. It watched him expectantly. He shut his eyes tight, extended his hand again, unlocked the sliding door, and quickly opened it to let it in.

He opened his eyes and watched it pull itself easily over the cement ledge into his room. It stepped past him with short steps. It examined the room from right to left before it turned back to face him. He hastily shut and locked the sliding glass and swung quickly to face it, as it stood in the middle of the darkness. The towel hung like a lovey in its grip.

"Are-are you real?" he asked quietly. His hands twisted together. It didn't reply, but its blue eyes glistened and swirled in the contrasting darkness. Becoming aware of his worrying hands, he clenched them into fists at his sides. "Do you understand me?" He tightened his clenched fists. "I'm not scared of you! I'm not afraid of any of you…the man or the voices!"

It lifted the towel to him in response. Its eyes watched him, sparkling like a pool hit by the sun.

"I don't understand? What are you? What is that?" It shook the towel at him and took one step forward. "I-I don't understand." He stepped backward into the glass door and jumped at the coldness of it against his bare arms. "Please-please help me understand. Does this have to do with the woman?"

It remained motionless, but its cavern eyes appeared to tighten. It shook the towel in its claw grip.

"A towel?" Yuuta wrinkled his forehead. "How did you…? What is-"

The creature suddenly twisted toward the kitchen door, despite the silence. He didn't notice before, but the kitchen's light glowed in the cracks of the door's frame. Shadows wavered erratically in the light that slipped through the bottom.

Fear seized him. He tried to move backwards, but he met the cold glass again. The creature moved in a blur toward the kitchen door, its blue eyes left a trail of oceanic sparkles as it moved. It looked up to the brass doorknob and quickly turned expectantly back to him.

"It's just my sofu…" he told it, hoping that his assurance had convinced it more than it did himself. "He wakes up early for work and boils his tea."

Its blue eyes flared. Its snout-like face was free from expression, but he could sense its panic like a hidden vibration. It frightened him as he considered it, but he felt the need to help it. He moved toward the door and turned the doorknob.

Vines entangled the kitchen. They choked the furniture like a twisting hydra. The tiled floor was stained with dirt and mud dragged by the wet slithering creeper. It had slithered up the walls, coiling within its own thick extremities like mating snakes that drooled onto the floor. The blue-eyed creature rushed to the opposite side of the room. It followed the dragging trail of vines to his grandparent's bedroom. An unknown force pulled him behind it.

He danced through the twisted nature but lost a slipper in the process. His head thumped concussively; a thumping that beat with the life that flowed through the vines. It echoed like the banging of Congo drums. He covered his ears in hopes to suppress it, but it thumped and thumped.

His bladder was tight with his held pee. He craved to wake from the nightmare and use the washroom as he reached for a hanging vine. He missed his grip. He tripped onto his knees at the opened door of his grandparent's bedroom. Vines were dispersed inside the room, splitting like dripping veins along the floor and up the walls.

In the middle of the darkness, pungent with wet mud and a sickly sweetness, a bodily shape sagged grotesquely in the air. He flicked on the light switch with hands that shook. His sofu, stuck like a doll on a spike, was pierced from his rear and up through his mouth by a vine as thick as an arm. His sofu's eyes were hauntingly pale.

Yuuta gagged violently before he vomited. He emptied his guts. He choked and dry heaved as he tried to capture breaths of air. Blue eyes like raging flames watched him. They watched him sob like a child, kneeling in his own vomit and the other bodily waste he expelled onto the floor. He couldn't understand why the nightmare didn't end as he bathed in his fluids.

Chapter 4

A sensation of urgency blossomed inside Arjun. He had witnessed beauty and life spring up of the dust like a burgeoning flower. Honey-blonde petals with a hazelnut stigma. Natasha. Her name was Natasha.

He lay thoughtful in his bed as he waited for his morning wood to soften. The sun slipped through cracks in the blinds. Pages and worksheets were scattered in a partial circle on his apartment floor, a red pen and a crinkled rubric placed in the middle. He had left the kids' homework untouched and felt even less determined to mark it. He reached for last night's glass of water on his nightstand and baptised his tongue with the lukewarm liquid. It was a tasteless cleansing of his mouth and the grimy taste of morning. He considered staying in bed, but the vibration of his plugged-in cell phone convinced him to get up. He looked at the text from his mother and sighed.

He placed the phone back on the stand, slid out of the blankets to his feet, stretched, opened the damaged blinds, quickly examined the busy street, then walked over to the kitchen portion of his bachelor apartment. He grabbed the last cherry danish he had bought at the Circle K and sat casually at his small circular particle board table. The table filled most of the free space in the kitchen, but he didn't care.

He looked down at his stomach as he ate and analyzed the small gut hugged by what he thought was a shrinking t-shirt. Disappointed in himself, he looked back to the floor of papers and shook his head with a sigh. The sensation of solitude crept up on him. He shoved the last bit of danish in his mouth and wiped some of the sticking crystallized sugar onto his boxers as he returned to the window. He always found himself watching the street to pass time. A strange knock at the door sullied the idea.

"Who is that?" he mouthed to himself.

He wondered if it was his landlord, but he remembered that her knocks were always in three whipping taps, like Khatta ma'am's ruler across his ass after she pulled him out of his hideaway box. The door thudded four more times as if the person knew he was avoiding them.

He let a motionless moment pass. Silence hung in the apartment like sheets on a clothesline. He prayed that whoever it was would move on. He watched the door anxiously, unwilling to move.

Another thud-thud followed. He damned the person under his breath before he convinced himself to creep toward the peep hole. He licked his lips and dodged around the creaky spots in the floor as he crossed to the door.

"Erjun Kaool? Kall? Erjun...Kaul? My name is Chloe Blackleaf. I, uh, I'm a reporter for the, uh, City Star. I would love to come in and ask you a few questions," a woman behind the door said before he reached it. Her voice was velvety, and although muffled by the steel barrier separating them, he could hear her accent. He ignored her attempt to draw him out and stopped in place. "Sir, I just have a few questions I need to ask you. If you could please just let me in. I brought you a coffee?" She pleaded innocently. "Sir-Erjun, please let me in." She knocked on the door harder. "You really should get your side out before the police put out their lies."

He choked on the saliva he attempted to swallow and coughed abruptly, unable to quell the tickle in his throat.

"If…if this is about Natasha, the paramedics got her from Algonquin. She is probably at Huntsville Memorial or something. I haven't seen her since. That's all I know," he stated. Her name resonated in his head as he tried to consider what could have happened to her.

"Natasha? Natasha who?" Chloe asked. "This is about something that happened last night. Can you just let me in?"

He felt her desperation deepen. He took the moment to consider her accented voice. She sounded young, with a spritely tone, and a naive passion untainted by the entitled demands that came with age. He realized he wasn't clothed for answering the door for anyone, let alone a young woman. He looked sadly at his boxers now smeared with dried white crystalized sugar.

"I had nothing to do with anything that

happened last night. I'm really not dressed for an interview anyway," he called through the door.

"Oh, just pull something on!" she demanded immediately, as another thud vibrated up the wall. "Please Erjun! I know you don't know me…and this must all seem rather…abrupt, but I need you."

"Arre baap re! Just give me a second," he shouted. He pulled away from the door in frustration.

He grabbed an unfolded sweater and a pair of sweatpants from the top of his dresser. He pulled them on, then waltzed through his papers. Some of them stuck to the sweaty bottoms of his feet and he had to peel them off in a one footed dance before he finally reached, unlocked, and opened the door.

"I brought coffee," she said again, as she lightly shook the reddish-brown coffee cup gripped in her hand.

"Thank you," he sighed, and he allowed her to pass him with a gesture to the small kitchen.

He closed the door and re-engaged the bolt lock. He watched her slowly step over the now scattered papers. She wore casual black and white running shoes and tight-fitting cargo pants. She wasn't overly short, but she was shorter than his five foot eight, with straight dark brown hair that hung to her shoulder blades. She had childbearing hips that swayed. He figured his mom would probably love her.

She reached the table and seated herself. She placed the coffee cup on the side opposite to her as a clear indication of where he should sit. He walked toward the table and sat in the indicated spot. He realized that she had the benefit of facing the door. It made him feel unsettled, despite it being locked.

As he stroked his hand through his hair in a conscious attempt to make it presentable, his eyes caught her dark brown tilted ones, and he examined her more thoroughly. Her skin was an olive brown, and she had an aquiline nose. Her lips were plump, and she had a diamond face that was framed by her dark hair. Underneath her olive drab canvas jacket, and tucked between her cleavage, hung a rose gold necklace with a dangling silver leaf. His eyes settled on the necklace before he pulled himself back to the present.

"So…what is this about? I've never even heard of the City Star." He watched her reach into her cargo pant's pocket and take out a dirty notepad and a round-tipped pencil. She licked the tip, opened the word-filled book to a dated page, and put the pencil tip to the paper. She lifted her tilted brown eyes from the page and hesitated.

"Erjun," the sound of his name carried by her accent engaged his full attention, "are you close with your student, umm, Yuuta…Saito?"

The question stunned him. He felt his mouth hanging open. She squinted her dark eyes and he felt them on his face. They were sharp and smart but tightened by youth and curiosity. She had a woodland energy. As he watched her without blinking, his own eyes strained. His vision blurred and her eyes became three. The third eye faded in and out between her brows as his eyes watered until blinking returned them to two.

"Sorry I-… Is he okay? What happened to him?" he asked slowly, refocusing his gaze on her face. "Please tell me if anyone has hurt him! How do you even know he is a student of mine?"

"He's…missing." She continued her own watchful examination of him.

"What-what happened? What do you mean missing? Has he run away? What are you talking about? Yuuta?" He leaned forward; his face tightened as he clenched his jaw. She defensively put her back against her chair, as if startled by him. She dropped her gaze to his arms as if evaluating their value as weapons. "I think…you should–you should really go." He watched her hesitation. "I don't know anything. Yuuta was a quiet boy. He spoke to no one, and he kept to himself. I don't think anyone but his grandmother was close to him. If anyone has any answers, it will be he-"

"She's also missing," Chloe interrupted, her accent was heavy with each syllable. "Erjun, I shouldn't be showing you this but…well…you–you need to see this to-to understand the gravity of Yuuta's danger. I just want you to be umm, prepared for this, okay? It's sensitive and…unpleasant." She licked her lips. "It's quite violent."

She pulled out a cellphone, unlocked it, and placed it facing upward on the table. She turned it and slid it in front of him. He looked down at it cautiously and froze.

"What is that? What in the ajna chakra is that?

Arre baap re..." He swallowed a gag, pushed the phone away, and stood to his feet.

"That's Yuuta's grandfather." She held a loose grimace, seemingly desensitized to the macabre imagery.

"Get out of here! Wha-Why? Holy Deva! Please, just get out." He motioned passionately toward the door behind him.

"You don't understand!" she proclaimed.

"No, *you* don't understand. You need to go. I have nothing to do with this and I don't want anything to do with this-"

"Listen! Just listen for one second you stubborn Sauk," she shouted as she stood to match his aggression. Their eyes fused. He leaned forward and put his palms on the table for stabilization. The quasi-wood surface was cool despite the heat that emanated between them. "You need to understand. This-this wasn't just some murder of some old Asian man. This is something bigger. Yuuta's in danger. I...I need your help. Yuuta needs your help." She sighed. "I can explain more, but I really think you should come with me to meet my father. He knows more about what hunts Yuuta. He can explain this better than I can."

"Hunts?" Arjun questioned. He felt angry. He felt confused. "I really don't understand what is going on right now. Why have you come to me with this?"

"No... I, uh, I don't know much either, but he has no one."

"His grandmother, what did you say happened

to her? I mean…I think all I saw was his grandpa in that…thing." He gestured with the back of his hand to the phone, with no will to accept the contents. "Maybe she's with him? Maybe they're already on their way to the police. I'm just the Deva forsaken schoolteacher."

"I don't know either, Erjun. All I know is that they're both missing. It's possible they might be together. I don't know. We need to find them." Her desperation weakened her disposition.

"It's Arr-jun. And I don't even know you. What you're showing me…Is this some kind of sick joke? Are you even a real reporter? Don't you have some kind of ID? What the Deva can I do about it?" He gestured resignedly with his hands. "How do you even know all of this or have that?" He gestured again to the phone that remained face up on the table, the image of the gruesome execution still displayed like a casual family photo. "How do you know me and how did you find me? How do you even know Yuuta? Who are you, really?"

She shot him a look of scorn, as she slammed her clenched fists to her hips.

"You're sad. You really are truly sad, Erjun Kaul. My father was wrong about you. Look at you. Look at this place. You're a teacher? Yuuta is dead… Shit!" She punched her hips angrily.

"Dead? You don't make any sense. I don't know you. You haven't even offered to explain. You come into my apartment, of which I was coaxed into inviting you, threaten police involvement, insult me, argue with me, and show me…*that*, and then expect me to get up and pursue this insanity?" he argued, aware that irritation dripped off his face like the beading sweat that ran down his legs. Her eyes glared like his ex-wife's used to. "I just mean that, I'm not the person you're looking for. I'm a schoolteacher…"

Her twisted brow softened, and she returned her crinkled face to a neutral one. She sighed and shook her head.

"You really must understand, Erjun, you've already been pulled in. I know it all seems peculiar and inconvenient and grotesque and–and weird, but this boy is in legitimate danger and your life is tied to him. I-I'm not one for causes, but this is something real. This is something beyond borders. Beyond politics. Beyond flesh. Please come with me to meet my father…Please." Her remaining fire was quelled by her watery eyes.

He watched her silently and considered her plea. He searched his mind and reflected on the horrid picture and his relationship with Yuuta. The quiet boy no one spoke to who sat at the back of the class worrying his hands like a small child. The boy could've done something with himself; he could've been something, but his self-deprecations after the death of his parents turned him into an overloaded zebu. Yuuta was just another boy. School was their only bond.

Natasha. The name shook through his skull. The memory of the boy's coal black eyes flashed at him like black spots left from staring at the sun. The lightless, unblinking black holes that burrowed into the boy's head, creating endless pits, dug into Arjun's mind. He didn't understand the connection, but there was nothing else. She was the only link. He had to see her again and got answers. He needed to see her.

The room swirled as he staggered through his thoughts. He barely saw the woman at his table, who watched him with the eyes of a stranger. He hoped that he didn't appear as discomposed as he felt.

"I'm sorry," he said, as he bobbed his head with an apologetic twist of his lips. "I'm sorry, but I can't help you. There is nothing I can do for you. There is nothing that connects me to this boy, nothing large enough to commit me to something like that. Let the police investigate. Let them make their conclusions. I have nothing to do with this and I suggest you do your part as a 'reporter' and just report honestly, or whatever is expected of you as a journalist, I guess. Why would a journalist want her father involved anyway?"

"So that's that then?" she stated. A reproving look darkened her already dark eyes. She looked up at his face, forcing him to return the stare. "Your part in this is just over then, Erjun? You have no idea what danger this boy is in. What kind of man are you? A teacher of children? Pff, you're more the woman than I am. Rifle take you, you idiot!" She abruptly scooped up her notepad, phone, and pencil in a furious grip, and walked toward the door. He turned to watch her leave. The strange curse still lingered in his ears. Her pants were snug to her bottom, and he realised he should not be standing, as he felt an influx of blood flow to his groin. She quickly turned her head as her hand reached the doorknob. "If you change your mind, just…" She winced, as if struggling to speak. "There are stories of a voice: a beckoning. Just, uh, follow her whispers. It is said that she will bring the ganawenjige into her embrace. Do you understand?"

"Who are you?"

She released her grimace, turned toward the door, released the lock, and walked out. She left the soft clunk of the closing door behind her. His face flushed as he tucked himself into the band of his sweatpants and prayed his sudden stirring remained unseen.

He stood there in silence, unsure of what had transpired. He took a sip of the coffee that was left on the table. It was cold and black and left a bitter taste in his mouth. He shook his head disapprovingly before he abruptly realized that his bladder was full and returned the coffee back to the tabletop. He drudged through the scattered papers and nudged open the bathroom door that hung slightly ajar at the end of his bed. He switched on the light and attempted to relieve himself, but he struggled for a moment to empty his aching bladder into the toilet. He sighed in relief when the fluids eventually evacuated him, but a dark cloud shaded his thoughts. Natasha. Natasha. The name felt spoiled going through his mind as he shook away the final droplets of urine. He used a piece of toilet paper to clean the seat his piss had splashed on.

He walked over to the mirror and examined himself critically before he decided to brush his teeth. He flossed for the first time this month. He thought of her as he slid the dentine string between the off-white chicklets. He stretched his mouth open to look at his gums once he finished, but the distraction was fickle and the thought of her grew inside him. He took a quick shower; dressed; grabbed his keys, wallet, and phone, and left the apartment. The scattered assignments were left abandoned like children's bloody corpses on the floor.

Tiredness scratched at Yuuta's eyes like allergies, as they watched an olive-skinned woman enter the building across from their hideaway alley. The stone-skinned creature had allured him wordlessly through the evening's starless abyss to a point of numbness. The night's violence hung over him like a guillotine, dang-ling by a thread.

They absently waited in a soft blue shadow between two buildings and watched the apartment. The red bricked building was grubby and old. Surrounding apartments and stores were postered with local band flyers. Graffiti was sprawled in spiderwebs along the brickwork. Some troubled men wandered the street in the whiteness of the morning's light. He wondered if he looked as beaten and hopeless as they did. Despite his change of clothes, the taste of vomit lingered in his mouth and the shame of peeing himself sagged his shoulders.

He watched his stone companion from behind. He felt like a lost puppy stuck to its side. The troubled ones had passed them with undisturbed expressions. Glazed eyes on strange faces looked straight through them. He considered the value of the emptiness in the strangers' hardened cheeks. Their life and energy drained, ragged like corn husks, ugly like Goodwill mannequins.

The creature watched the apartment quietly. It breathed like a dog, but it never spoke. Its shoulders lifted up and down with each animalistic breath like the ventilator that had masked his mother's dying face. He remembered the dark hair that dangled across her forehead. He imagined that he used the back of his hand to brush it out of her eyes. He felt her warmth and her breathing movements. He jolted and realized that his hand was brushing the back of the creature's stone shoulder. The rock scales surprised him with their living warmth. It stirred from its intense examination of the apartment and turned glowing blue orbs onto him. He dove into the deep blue pools in search of understanding, but they only reflected the violent images that beat on his waking mind.

It turned back to face the apartment. There was no noise off the street. The unknown dominated his focus. He adjusted his backpack anxiously. Anticipation worried him. He said nothing. He shifted awkwardly, feeling the dirtiness of the unwashed pee on his legs. The sun rose slowly.

The sounds of the street seemed to arouse to life

as if a sudden pressure in his ears had begun to clear. He watched a coffee shop heavy with loitering guests. A mother and her baby waited uncomfortably for a bus beside a wild looking old woman who spoke to herself. He kept his eyes for an extensive moment on a trio of girls who dodged the homeless as warily as himself. Buses and cars were caught in a continuous cycle of stop and go traffic. Honking horns bounced off the low-rise walls that closed everything in. Distant power tools completed the mechanical symphony. The horrid music beat at him like a banging of cymbals. He tried to ignore the mismatched noise, but the shadows and the heat and the fear held his head under it like a bully drowning him in a toilet.

Flashing images of his sofu's distorted face ripped through his mind. A thick vine ripped between the lips of the beautiful old man's pained face in sprays of red. For a moment, the gruesome image of his sofu was suspended in his thoughts, until the floating picture was quickly replaced with the serene face of the woman-in-the-black-dress. He felt ashamed as the violent scene stirred something inside him. He watched as the vine penetrated bloodlessly between her pink lips. Her hazelnut eyes turned to him and watched him hungrily.

He started forward as the creature's clawed hand tapped his leg. He looked up to see the olive-skinned woman walking away from the apartment's front door. Her hips swayed in her cargo pants. He held his eyes on her with the sensation of the woman-in-the-black-dress still vibrating between his legs. He took a moment to breathe to himself and returned his eyes to the creature. It looked anxiously from the woman, who quickly became a distant shape mingled in the lightly crowded street, to the apartment she came out of. He wondered at the creature's erratic head movements.

Without warning it abandoned the alley and maneuvered its way like an ape to the opposite side of the street. The stained towel was clutched in its other claw like a snake in an eagle's talons. It stopped at the apartment's unmarked entrance door and motioned for him to follow. He sighed as he wiped his sweaty palms on his pants, but before he could move forward a slimy grip enclosed around his wrist.

He tried to pull away in a panic, but the grip was wrapped like twisted roots. He was yanked back into the alley. His eyes were forced to look into cold dark ones. The frightening man from the bridge held him by his shoulders. Sweat glistened the matted forehead of the man. His beard was crusted with earth. He stank of soiled cabbage.

"Boy, you must listen to my words...." the man whispered through unwashed teeth. "It will consume you. It is of a corrupt master...I can show you, but you must come with me. We must flee!"

Yuuta struggled feebly to break the man's grasping fingers, as he punched wildly at the man's arm with his free hand.

"Let me go! Let me go! I don't have anything. Just let me go, please," Yuuta fought.

"Boy, listen to me! I can see them too. They have

taken from me too, but we must go *now*," the man spat. Yuuta watched the man's bold eyes seek out the creature he slandered, then turned to look at it himself, but it was no longer there. The man pulled Yuuta back to face him. He gripped the neckline of Yuuta's sweater. "This isn't a game, boy. You have already seen their power, their value of human life. You will see again and again as their games devour everything you are and everything you love…If you follow it, it will bring you to its master. You must run. We have no more time. We must go!" The man tried to pull him again.

Yuuta mirrored the man's stubbornness and attempted to pull himself away. The brute's grip was iron to his childish pleas. After an awkward struggle against the man's strength, blue torches flicked past him. The man was suddenly ripped away. There was a moment of shuffling clothes, a thud, then a groan. The creature stepped away and the man was struggling to his knees.

"Boy…boy, don't make my mistakes…These beasts…they will blacken your eyes. They will tap you like a maple. You will become a slave…a slave to the antler-crowned master." The man breathed heavily, coughing between breaths. Fear dribbled from his dried lips like spit, as his left arm cradled his ribs. His dark eyes reflected the blue flames of the creature's. The creature was like a poised snake, but its blue flames were swirling torrents of fire.

"Who-who are you?" Yuuta asked. "What's going on? What have you done to my sobo? Where is she? Where is she!?"

"Boy-" the man started, but the dragging of heavy feet forced them to look back to the street.

A disheveled, old, tan skinned man stumbled into the alley. Filmy eyes looked passed them. He leaned against the wall as he dragged himself forward, mumbling.

"The whispers...they call to me. I'm no waagoshi -akiwenzii...I'm just a man. Not a fox, just a man." The new man stumbled toward them, his slow and deep nonsense no longer distinct.

A heavy black and red plaid jacket hung off the man's shoulders. His face was obscured by dangling long black hair that was striped with a silver streak. His darting eyes peeked through the blinding strands. He dragged himself past Yuuta, reaching out to the creature, as if witnessing something wondrous.

Yuuta followed this new man anxiously with his eyes. He suddenly realized that the ragged man from the bridge was gone. The creature watched the stumbling man defensively, unaware of the escapee.

The man with the plaid jacket reached for the blue-eyed creature but tripped forward and fell to the ground like a weak child. He laid there in a puddle of his own moans and ramblings. The creature turned its blue flames on Yuuta and hesitated. He felt aggravation emit from its sapphire stare, until it returned its eyes to the apartment across the street. Yuuta adjusted his backpack and turned to watch the man whispering in the dirt of the alley.

"Are…are you okay, sir? Is there someone I-I can maybe…call for you?" Yuuta asked.

He felt disturbed by the troubled soul of the city. The man's milky eyes turned his stomach. He feared him, despite him lying like a decrepit stray. He had never seen a drunk stranger before, but now that he was reminded of the lack of control and the lack of being, he couldn't help but feel the burden of the man's unpredictability. He saw a drunk father getting home with a posture of guilt and unconscious remorselessness. He shook at the thought of his own father's sinewy hand.

The man mumbled slowly, chanting nothingness under his breath. Yuuta and the creature watched him. They stared like witnesses to something shameful.

The man reached out weakly to the creature, but his hand fell limp to the ground. He looked frightened. He looked alone. Sadness trickled through Yuuta's churning stomach and mingled with the embarrassment of his disdain and his fear for the man's state. The man was another victim. He was another soul dumped on the street like shameless litter. He was a man. He was nothing but a man.

"I-I don't think we can leave him here. I think we should, uh, I really think he should come with us to…to wherever we're meant to be," Yuuta suggested to the creature.

The creature turned from the apartment to the mumbling man then to Yuuta. Its blue eyes flared. They stared unblinkingly at him. It made a sighing noise through its nose. A moment blew by with the soft breath of a city breeze, before it nodded.

Chapter 5

Natasha awoke abruptly. Pristine dropped ceiling tiles and covered fluorescent lights filled her vision. The lights were off, and the room was dim despite sun beams breaking against the window to the right of where she lay. A docile blue curtain hid sources of hoarse breathing and instrumental beeping. She adjusted to pull herself up from her back, but an IV leash mentally halted her. She returned her gaze to the ceiling to find comfort in its institutional security. She blinked dreamily at the dotted ceiling tiles.

As the angles of light changed with the position of the heavens, a silent daytime slithered away. People entered and left cyclically like the movement of clock hands.

After countless empty turns of the hands, a purposeful shuffle in the room disturbed her. She watched as her curtain undulated from side to side as it was adjusted by an unseen figure.

"Oh, you're awake?" asked a spritely, south Asian girl in scrubs who poked her head around the unsettled curtain. She had a bright, youthful smile, with a vulture-like sternness to her jaw. She was short, with ombre deep brown shoulder length hair. Her anemone scrubs hung from her, too big for her petite frame.

"Yes," Natasha replied. She watched the young nurse without lifting her head.

"You should definitely eat some of your lunch," the girl nurse said, smiling. "You have here some beef, rice, carrots–"

"Where am I?" Natasha interrupted.

"Huntsville Memorial. You were brought here last night," the girl said, seemingly unphased by the rude interruption. "As I was saying, you should really eat the food that is there. You've had nothing to eat since you've been here. Are you vegetarian, or vegan, or have any allergies?"

"What day is it?" Natasha continued.

"June twenty-first. Saturday," the girl nurse said after a hesitation.

"June twenty-first..." Natasha whispered to herself. "June twenty-first. June twenty-first? Something... something was today... June twenty-first? Something was that date...? I-I can't remember. It's like-like I'm a few days out of touch." She struggled into a sitting position before she brushed her hands through her hair in frustration, wary of the tube that dangled from her wrist. "Why am I here? Huntsville Memorial? How did I get here?"

She looked around in fearful confusion. She examined her hands. She shifted her head erratically from side to side as she attempted to analyze her surroundings behind the curtain. Her hair spilled from behind her ears.

"It's okay. It's okay, just relax a moment. Take a deep breath. Come on." The girl breathed in and out deeply, as if she was coaching a woman in labour.

"Stop that! Just tell me…why am I here? Who brought me here?"

The nurse watched her with a look of unspoken workplace exhaustion.

"I wouldn't quite worry about that just now. I left you your meal on the tray there." The nurse indicated with a gentle hand gesture to a tray that hung over Natasha's legs on a mobile stand. "I'll let the Doctor know you're awake and she can update you on what happened after you've eaten, sound good?"

The nurse gave an insincere smile and returned behind the curtain. Her footsteps were soft against the floor, but Natasha was satisfied when she heard the door close. The satisfaction quickly faded as she soon ached for someone to talk to. She was a manic mess. A bed ridden donkey with a semblance of amnesia. Her stomach felt like a bloating mass. She was cold. She wanted to escape. She clenched her teeth in anger before she shoved the hair that spilled out from behind her ears back into place. She pulled at the instruments latched to her, but fear suspended her left hand over the IV in her right wrist. She gripped the inserted needle. She held it for a moment. She stared at the crevices of the tape that held it in place. She pulled her hand away without removing it.

Accepting the leash, she began to maneuver out of bed, but hesitation anchored her. Her damaged feet hovered above the ground. Anxiety flooded her fearful hesitation in a thousand speaking thoughts. She felt the abuse of a collage of sound and blurred memories.

"Why did you treat her that way?"

"What is wrong with you?"

"You're afraid."

"You *are* crazy. Why else would you be here."

"She could see it in your eyes."

"It's not just you that thinks you're crazy."

"You're just like her."

"You're just like her."

"He sees you...."

"He's coming."

"He's coming."

"He's here!"

"Run!"

"Run!"

She compressed her temples with her palms and began to scream.

"I'm fine! I'm not crazy. I'm not like her! I'll never be like her...I'm not crazy..." She swayed and fell off the bed to the floor. Her drip bag dragged down on top of her in a tangle of tubes. Laughter washed over the voices and the noise intensified her nausea. She coughed with the sensation of vomiting. A blur of anemone rushed in beside her with a larger mass of azure. The faceless figures held her hands and felt her forehead. The skin to skin was a forgotten comfort.

"It's okay...It's okay," she heard them chant. "Breathe...Come on, breathe with us."

She heard their soft, deep breaths and mimed them blindly. She felt herself lift off the ground. They returned her to the bed gently. She watched the blue curtain as if staring into a cloudless sky. The faceless nurses rerouted her machinery. She blinked out a small tear. A light hum resonated in her ears. She accepted the embrace of her heavy lids.

Natasha opened her eyes to a room bathed in fluorescent light. The room was silent and the blue curtain that enclosed her before was gone. A woman in a white medical coat stood beside her bed. The woman scraped a pen across a clipboarded sheet.

"I'm not dead?" Natasha asked the woman softly.

The woman chortled. "No," she said, as she continued to make notes on her sheet, "but if you are rude to one of my nurses again, we will have to have a serious talk about that."

"I'm sorry. I…It's not like me to act like that."

The woman in the medical coat stopped writing and gazed at her. The woman didn't smile, but her presence was a welcomed comfort.

"I am Dr. Mardin. I typically do not work with mental trauma patients, but Dr. Kovalcik is…indisposed," Dr. Mardin said with a light sigh.

"Mental trauma? What mental trauma?" Natasha's tones of insecurity peaked at each syllable.

"I do not mean crazy, if that is what you are thinking. Sometimes victims of trauma can experience short-term and long-term cognitive effects. These may be memory loss, lack of awareness, irrational fears of confinement, or feelings of restriction. Post-traumatic stress disorder is not simply a function of flashbacks and nightmares." Dr. Mardin paused for a moment and analyzed Natasha's face. "What is your name?"

"It's Natasha, Natasha Wyntr. With a Y and no E."

"W-I-N-T-Y-R or W-Y-N-T-R?"

"W-Y-N-T-R."

"Thank you," Dr. Mardin said softly, as she noted something on her clipboard.

Natasha watched the woman as she wrote. She had pale skin, and though her face was lined with age, her hands were as smooth as untouched snow. She was tall and her brown hair, streaked with white, was tightly pulled back into a bun. Her eyes were wrinkled with expression lines and were small and close together, but she emanated a familiar warmth.

"How old are you?" Dr. Mardin continued.

"Twenty-seven," Natasha replied.

"Why did you not have any identification on you, or shoes, or a jacket?"

"I'm not sure. It's all so…absent. I remember work, and a-a life…but there's a gap between that and—and some forest. I remember a face. Do you mind if I have some water?"

Dr. Mardin looked up from her clipboard again and analyzed her. "Of course," she said, as she reached for an unopened bottle that had already been waiting there and passed it to Natasha. "How do you feel? Do you have any pain that you are able to pinpoint?"

"Umm...sure, yeah." Natasha sat up to take a drink. She swallowed quickly and looked down at her blanketed body. "My ankle and...my feet in general, they burn quite a bit. The nausea and bloating have lightened, but my head is pounding. My arms itch, my throat burns. I don't know, I can't explain it, but I don't feel right all over, really. Something feels wrong inside me...and with my body. I can't escape this feeling of discomfort. I don't know..."

"How much do you remember from the forest?"

Natasha hesitated. "I remember the whispers of trees, the emptiness of the night sky...Faces and shapes of familiarity. I can picture falling snow and—and black water. A vague feeling of my mother." She thought of the laughter, its faint echo in the back of her mind.

Dr. Mardin watched her in silence. The woman stopped taking notes.

"Maybe you do need Dr. Kovalcik." Dr. Mardin tucked the clipboard to her chest.

"I'm not crazy! I-I can't explain it."

"I am not calling you crazy, Natasha. I just think that it is more practical to see the specialist on such matters." Dr. Mardin sighed. "I suppose in light of Dr. Kovalcik's absence, however, you should go on."

"You don't understand. I have my memories. I see them like—like pages in a book I once read or scenes from a movie. I remember...I remember that everyone called her crazy -- my mom, but I get it now: she could hear things. Things that talk to us. She could-We can listen to the voices of…of something beyond, but here. We can hear the river's song, feel the anger of the trees. We can see nature and we can…smell it. I know. I'm not crazy, I know this sounds insane, but it is obviously genetic, whatever this is. Right?"

"Where is your mother now?"

"I-I don't know," Natasha said. "Something inside me says she's…gone."

"How, Natasha?" Natasha didn't reply. She watched Dr. Mardin make a hasty note on her sheet. She could see that the boxes on the page were almost completely filled with small, black, and barely legible chicken scratch. "How did your mother die?"

"I don't know…" Natasha repressed the urge to search her mind for the memory. She suddenly realized that she had no memory of her mother's face. The realization didn't pain her.

"Do you have someone we can call? A number?"

"No one I can think of…" Natasha said after a quick search of her mind. She suddenly couldn't even remember her boss's name. It all seemed like a strange sight in the distance.

"I see. Well, I believe this is a good start, Natasha. You should rest. We will be monitoring you for the remainder of the afternoon and into the night, so do not be worried about anything. Nutrients have been provided through an IV, and you have a catheter and a bed pan below you. Try to just relax and sleep your remaining lethargy off. We can speak more tomorrow."

"Please don't go…I'm afraid to close my eyes

while alone." Natasha shied from the shame of her fears.

Dr. Mardin sighed with a saddened twist to her lip. Her face was otherwise composed.

"Some battles have to be fought alone, Natasha. One day you will face the truth of being a woman. The struggle of natural inclinations to be a beast of burden. You will have to choose to carry the weaknesses of your mother, your own regrets, and the sins of your child, or you will have to opt to be an unmanned vessel needlessly ovulating for twelve weeks in a year while men fawn over you like some prized dumpling. The choice haunts each one of us. How could it not? Every month we are reminded of how we are failing our natural purpose. It is a sick joke...God must surely be a man: no mother would impart this burden on her daughters. You are young and healthy, Natasha. Embrace your loneliness. Close your eyes and face it. You cannot allow the world to convince you that being alone, that embracing some ugliness, is some kind of spinster evil. This is not a Charles Dickens novel. Now rest. Close your eyes, or I swear I will have Gail in here telling you about her titas and kuyas."

"I don't know...Mothers are women, and women can be evil too," Natasha said.

"Hmm..." Dr. Mardin nodded. "There is wisdom in that, sure."

Dr. Mardin winked at Natasha and walked to the light switch on the wall. She hesitated before flicking the lights off. She walked out of the dim room into a brightly lit hallway. The door shut behind her. Silence was the only thing that she left behind.

Natasha wanted to return to sleep, but her mind was a maddening entanglement. The memories of who she was seemed like the reflections of a stranger's diary. The image of her mother was filled by a black shape she didn't recognize. She remembered dark eyes and poisoned souls; images of men and women like shifting movements in a strobe light. She felt the burden of their presence in her head, but she had no feelings of love or concern for them: they were shadows of a patchwork past. She twisted a stranded bunch of her hair between her fingers. The craving for a cigarette dried her mouth.

"A clever woman, this…Doctor," a soft feminine voice whispered from across the room, struggling with the word doctor as if she had never said it before. "I wonder if her lack of beauty was the inspiration for such a conclusion to the nature of women." Natasha focused on her breathing, convinced that the voice was another symptom of her slipping grasp on reality. "It is quite alright little flower, you are not there yet, but I must say, your mother was sturdy in her self-assurance. You seem to have embraced the madness from the onset. She was much stronger, determined to prove the song of bimaadiziwin singing through her. Such a peculiar woman. You do not seem to resemble her. Pity…" The feminine speaker sighed with a soft breath like snowflakes brushing against a frosted window.

"Who are you?" Natasha whispered. She released the twist of hair she had pincered between her fingertips and sat back up. The shame of her visible habit forced her to blush. "You knew my mother?"

The corner she looked to was shrouded in darkness, as the light from outside was hidden behind opaque curtains. The shape of a slender figure sat lounging, a black shadow in the unlit room. A void of silence draped over them.

"Me? Who am I? Little flower…I am the sound of rain drops on dry boughs. Giiwedin's whisper at the beating of butterfly wings. I am the master of mesh-kwadoon, great daughter to the sun and moon. I am the mother of the earth and of all things."

"But what is your name?" Natasha demanded, as resolve returned to her.

"Look to your feet and you shall see, little flower, for the land is of my body," the woman said. Her voice was pure.

"What do you want with me?"

"I am here to teach you," the woman advised.

Natasha squeezed her eyes aggressively and rubbed them in circles with the palms of her hands.

"I just want to be normal. To be happy. Without this pain or the rashes or the fear. I want a husband and maybe a career. A family…A cat. I want to know who I was. I want to know who I am. Can you tell me that? Oh my God! Now I'm here, talking to something created by my mind. What the hell is going on?" She began to cry. "Where does this end? I'm caught in the middle of this spiral. And you, how do you play in? Are you the mother my mind has conjured? A feminine shadow that speaks in code. I know she's there, like a word I seek in the back of my head. She-she's just a nameless, faceless figure haunting me."

"Breathe little flower-"

"Stop telling me to breathe!" Natasha yelled. The shadowed woman remained motionless; her face masked behind the darkness. Natasha wiped away tears with her arm. "Why am I crying? I can't seem to stop with these. Just leave me alone, please. Leave me alone! I don't need your help. I was fine without you. I am fine without you!"

The woman stood to her feet, a looming blackness that grew in the corner. "I will return to you, little flower. We have many things to discuss. Many things. Although I assure you, I am not an imagined spectre of your mother, I can tell you of the woman she was. Once you have bloomed and ripened, fed by the burrowing roots of your understanding, I will bestow upon you the truths of your world. The world within a world. A world cloaked by rock and willow."

"Truths? Which truths? What are you-" The door to the room creaked industrially. Natasha broke her gaze from the corner and examined the sound, as the opening door split the dim room with light. The girl nurse and one in azure scrubs entered. Natasha's head swept back to the dark corner, decorated now with an empty sofa chair.

"We didn't mean to startle you, love," the nurse in azure said. She was a blocky woman, with short hair that accentuated her large jaw. The soft white glow of the hall made the light concealer on her dark face look like a discoloured paste. The young girl in anemone followed closely behind, her smile strangely large. Both women had deep black pupils, like strange holes in their sockets. A flickering memory of a man holding her flashed across her mind, as she recalled coal-like eyes that asked for her name. The nurse in anemone closed the door behind her, and the shadows of the room rapidly stretched and vanished in the dimness.

"I-I think I'm feeling better," Natasha lied, as she watched the women walk towards her through the curtain of darkness. She held her posture and rubbed her blanketed legs. "N-no need for any medication or anything. I'm really doing much better. Can I speak with Dr. Mardin?"

"It's quite alright, love. We're here to help you. Don't worry, we're RNs," the woman in azure scrubs smiled jovially, her eyes unblinking black masses. The tan skinned nurse held her youthful smile, but her gaze never broke from Natasha.

"I don't know how much begging I have left in me. Please, I just want to go home. I'm not crazy, I'm just-I'm just tired. Please..." Her eyes were dry and burned like a volcanic ash.

The nurses licked their lips as they reached the side of the bed. The heavy one in azure walked around to the opposite side and Natasha was left in the middle of them, forced to look between the two sets of raven eyes.

"He wants you. He hungers for you," the nurse in anemone whispered.

"You must take his seed. Meshkwadoon must be fulfilled, he said," the nurse in azure smiled.

Their eyes were wide and wild. Natasha didn't fight them as they gripped her shoulders and pushed her into a lying position on the hospital bed. She felt as if she was being ritually prepared. Her mouth quivered, but she couldn't summon the resolve to repel them. Their fingers gripped her like those of a defiling fiend's. She prayed internally for a quick and painless death, with her sexuality intact. Their eyes delved into hers. Her head spun. Their faces leaned over her ravenously.

"Please. P-please! I'll do anything!" she cried tearlessly.

She tested the hands that restrained her, but they held her solid to the bed. Panic sent spasms to her feet, and she began flailing her legs. The nurses managed to hold her in place with ease while they wrapped a strap across her shins. She felt the leather grip her through the blanket as the nurses tightened it. Once they tested its security, they tucked her arms tightly to her sides. She winced at the moist warmth of their hands, as they held her arms against her body. They used their free hands to wrap another strap across her chest. The air was forced out of her lungs as they tightened it. She could feel the rough edges of it dig into her through her shirt. Her breasts were compressed painfully. She clenched her teeth and shut her eyes. The room was silent but for the creaking of the brown leather straps straining against her pitiful struggles.

"It's okay, Natasha. Breathe. Breathe," the anemone nurse whispered.

She felt a sharp pinch in her arm as a tingling burn flooded through her veins. The room spun. She felt as if snakes wriggled inside her limbs. She blinked away blurring droplets to watch black eyes and barely white teeth hypnotically stare back at her. Her muscles numbed, as the burning sensation spread through each ligament. Saliva built up like sludge in her mouth and she struggled to swallow. Her spotted vision caught a small hand with a tube as she felt her mouth wrenched open and the tube placed aggressively inside. She could feel it begin sucking out the excess fluids her burning throat couldn't swallow. Her throat tickled and ached in discomfort, but she felt nothing below her neck. She was like a floating head whose body was an immovable weight. She mentally pleaded to her limp limbs to show any sign of life. Her mind couldn't comprehend the loss of feeling. The nurses forced her head to the side and suddenly puke spilled out. She never felt her gag reflex engage as she vomited violently into a bucket the nurse in azure held. A rough cloth was swept across her face and the tube hooked back into her mouth. Through painful blinks she watched as the nurses left the bedside and stood by the window like videographers facing her with insincere expressions. The sucking tube hooked in her mouth was a waterfall in her ears.

A soft breeze kissed her cheek, as a face hovered above hers through the darkness. It was suspended like a floating nightmare. It was indistinguishable as it shifted in colour and shape from a reptilian scowl to a handsome man.

"Who is this being that speaks the tongue of the Oziisigobiminzh?" he asked. He blinked softly. He had black diamond pupils in a stir of yellow. "A sacred cycle has passed since the shame of Nanabozho. The cloud sea has broken. The Great Father's eye lightens the turtle's burden. Men pillage the being of beasts and flora. You must be one with me. Our seed must be joined with oeh-da." He had an eerily soft masculine voice.

She stared at the apparition. She didn't blink. She couldn't blink. His face hovered within inches of her own. She attempted to speak but the words wouldn't escape her feelingless chest. Her mouth opened without sound like a fish's silent screams out of water.

"These mashkikiiwikweg, touched by your taint, shall be your guide. You shall follow them to the gichimitig," he demanded.

"Wha-I—I can't. I can't. Help! God, someone help me!" she called into the darkness of her mind. Her eyes reached soundlessly to the drones by the curtained window.

The man's eyes tightened. He watched her, as if unsure of her.

"Your seed must be joined with oeh-da. I sense your fear. I taste it through the sweat that dribbles like dew down your face." He closed his eyes as if focusing on a sudden pleasure.

She tried to pinch her eyes shut.

"It's the meds. None of this is real. You're fine. You're not crazy. None of this is real. This isn't real. I'm not crazy. Close your eyes, and it'll be gone. Close your eyes. Close your eyes," she repeated in her head.

"To exist in such a state. Do you not rot inside? Your mind is wilted like an unloved flower. Sadly, it appears that we must move by rule of pain to remind you of your duty to meshkwadoon, and to *me*," he growled.

She shifted her eyes to see the small tan skinned nurse approach reverently. The girl unsheathed a needle that was tucked into her pocket and injected it into Natasha's feelingless arm. The sound of the sucking tube disturbed the unsettling moment of silence. She choked as searing pain flooded her body. No nurse was there to catch her sprays of vomit, as she puked and dry heaved onto the pillow and her shoulder. The tube fell out with the contents of her insides. She gagged aggressively as she struggled against the restraints. She cried out as pain flushed throughout her body. The being's voice reverberated through her head. Her suffering blackened any sense of awareness.

As the pain slowly became manageable, she realized she was no longer in the room. She was being pushed through the hospital on her strapped stretcher. The nurses were both pushing and guiding from the head of her bed, while she looked up to the ceiling like a lobotomized child. Their black eyes glowed in the rich white of the hallway lights.

Chapter 6

Unremarkable music played on the radio as Arjun backed his car into the hospital parking spot. Once he was satisfied with his distance from the black van parked beside him, he turned the ignition off. He sat for a moment and took slow deep breaths to quell a spontaneous onset of nervousness. His loosened bowels were a reminder of his body's shaky nerves. As he approached equilibrium, he pulled down the visor, opened the mirror, and examined his teeth and the widow's peak that slowly receded up his scalp. He flipped the visor back into place, exhaled slowly out of his nose, then stepped out of the car like it was his first step off a cliff. A sweet smell of pine accompanied his first inhalation. He felt Natasha's presence like a visitor that lingered in the back of his head. He had to see her again.

When he dreamily found himself at the ticketing kiosk, his numbed fingertips struggled to pay for his parking pass. Once he had successfully paid and placed his parking ticket back on the dashboard of his car, he double checked his doors were locked, then walked across the parking lot and through the front entrance.

The hospital smelt like the bottom of a bleach bottle. The stench of sterilization burned his eyes and he wondered at the severity of its quarantine cleanliness. The strange quiet and inactivity seemed to preserve the odour. The foyer was filled with natural light, but its vacancy made it lifeless. A gift shop sat empty and visitor booths were unattended. An aged man and woman stood in a near hall like anchored ghosts in flowing gowns of light blue. Folded wheelchairs lined the wall to his right, their steel frames sparkled immaculately.

He looked around curiously before he followed coloured posters to the front desk, where a time worn clerk watched her computer screen. The clerk's gray hair was cut to her ears and looked hardened by years of product. She wore a pink cardigan that aged her more than her suffering strands of gray. A TV behind her played the channel twenty-four news soundlessly.

"How can I help you?" the woman croaked, as she peaked over her computer screen.

"Natasha. I'm here to see Natasha. She, uh…she would've come in last night," he said, as an uncomfortable sensation of heat ignited his cheeks. He cleared his throat.

"Okay…What's your name, sir? What's your relationship to the patient? Do you know which unit she's in, sir?" the clerk asked investigatively. He could feel her stern eyes analyzing him in a manner consistent with the possibility that she had been in that chair and in that role for timeless decades.

"We're…friends," he said, with an attempt at confidence.

"I see…Well, do you have your *friend's* last name, sir?"

"I…No, I don't."

"Mhm…Sir, you will need to provide some information on the patient in order to request a visit, otherwise, you will have to wait until she is discharged, okay? Do you understand what I'm saying, sir?" The clerk was conspicuous with her suspicion.

"Okay…uh, thank you, I guess. I'll see if I can, uh, get something…" he said, stumped by the sudden hurdle.

The woman returned her gaze to her computer monitor and began to type. He tapped his fingers thoughtfully on the desk and sighed. He turned and looked to a directory on the wall. He felt her. He felt her presence like a bass drum in the distance. She was there. He knew she was there. As he stared at the directory, a pair of running men bumped into him. He made an annoyed grunt and turned to scold them with his eyes. All he saw were their backs with the word 'Security' shifting in the light.

"Maybe I shouldn't be here," he whispered to himself. His confidence dwindled. "Why do I think this feeling is her? She could've been discharged hours ago…This…this could be-"

"Sir, do you have another question?" the clerk wedged between his thoughts.

"Arre baap re, I'm sorry. Was that out loud?" he laughed, burningly embarrassed. "Don't mind me, I'm just…I'm just talking to myself."

The clerk squinted her eyes, as she reanalyzed him. Suddenly he felt ashamed for being Indian under her stare.

"Sir, I suggest if you are going to wait, you do it in the waiting area over there," she suggested, as she indicated with her hand a bench that sat close to the entrance.

He ignored her as he felt a shift in his gut. The pulsation gradually pulled away, like the music from a stereo moving further and further out of ear shot.

"It must be her. It must be her," he repeated to himself.

He followed the fading sensations out the entrance way and back outside. An ambulance left the hospital down the visible driveway, but he saw nothing else. Greenery whispered around him, and a murder of crows wheeled above the facility like a black halo in the blue sky. They called out in a barrage. The thumping inside him dwindled until it was no longer there. He watched the crows circle above the hospital before they flew westward and were no more. A faint presence in the back of his mind remained, like an unwelcome intruder hidden in his home.

He returned into the hospital, where the void left by the vibration's sudden absence was heavier on him. He eyed the clerk warily. He turned his eyes to the elderly pair in gowns as they continued to haunt the hall like erect corpses. He walked back to the directory, examined it again, shook his head, and followed the path he saw the men in security jackets take.

The maze of halls was vacant except for the accompanying sounds of elevator dings and the ricketing of beds on wheels being pushed unseen around unwatched corners. He walked past similar waiting areas where parents attended sulking children who mindlessly watched the channel twenty-four news, which seemed to play silently across the hospital like telescreens. Either no one talked, or if they did, they whispered. There was a present fear in disturbing the institutional tranquility of the facility.

Eventually his path led him to the Emergency Room. He was no longer sure if this was the destination that the security was destined for, but a residual pulse lingered there. It was quiet. A grim intensity permeated the air. The elderly that waited in the open room looked uncomfortable and distant, loneliness and dissatisfaction soured their wrinkled, veiny faces. Partially hidden behind a curtain was a child that cradled her wrist with her mother beside her. The mother had her face buried in her phone. Whispered discussions between victims of injuries and attending medical staff filled the halls of the triage facility as he walked past curtained cubicles. The news, again, played without volume at a corner TV for those who waited in chairs for treatment. He listened patiently. He looked for a sign of anything that could indicate her presence. He smelt the air softly and prayed silently that he could smell her, but nothing broke through the enduring scent of disinfectant.

"Sir, are you lost?" a woman asked pointedly, startling him.

"Err, yeah-Yes, of course, I'm fine. I'm just looking for my friend, Natasha. She, uh, said she was here," he spouted, as he turned to the woman. She held a clipboard and wore a white smock. Her face, hair, and eyes were wizened, but she had stern shoulders.

"Natasha who?" she asked, her tone softened while her small eyes tightened. She pulled the clipboard to her chest and crossed her arms.

"Yes-yes, I've been trying to find my friend Natasha…She's a young woman, with, uh, dark hazelnut eyes, a mole on her nose, white skin…Have you seen her?"

"Friend?" she questioned, as she weighed him much like the clerk at the main reception. "Notwithstanding your purpose or relationship, she is no longer here. In fact, if you have any idea where she might have gone, I would appreciate it if you could disclose that information to us…and the police."

"I-I don't really know anything…I was the one who called her an ambulance, or well, was involved in it. My class and I found her at Algonquin. I just wanted to see if she was okay. Myself and-and my class, we were worried for her. It's not everyday something like that happens. I would like to, uh, give some reassurance to my students," he lied.

"You felt it was necessary to visit her? A woman you randomly found unconscious, let alone claim you are her friend?" she questioned with squinted eyes.

"I-I don't know," he stuttered.

"Dr. Mardin, the Inspectors are here, are you

still okay to meet them?" a tiny woman in turquoise scrubs asked as she approached the pair of them. "We can look after Mrs. Hedrick…She's in here once a week now that her husband has passed away. I think she's just trying to dodge her daughter-in-law."

"Indeed…Well, sir, you can either have a seat and wait for Natasha to come back or you do as I suggest and return home. If Natasha feels the need to make arrangements to contact you, she can do so herself. Otherwise…your pursuance of this woman will be highly suspect in the circumstances," Dr. Mardin said smartly, as she looked at the digital watch on her wrist. He felt his cheeks darken as frustration flared internally. His hands were sweaty, and he eyed her angrily. "Now please, I have things to do."

"Saala kutta!" he cursed, as he grabbed the collar of her smock. He locked her eyes with his. "You must help me find her! I-I need to find her…Please."

She tried to pull away from him, but her resistance was weak.

"Dr. Mardin!" someone squealed from behind the old woman he strangled in his grip.

Panic stirred around him as nurses and patients rose to spy the commotion. The child cradling her wrist poked her head around the curtain while her mother pulled up her phone to begin recording. An elderly woman in the background shouted muddled obscenities at the general disturbance. The small nurse in turquoise filled the room with shouts in her intent to calm the commotion. Her voice was high with anxiety.

He loosened his grip when he saw Dr. Mardin's fearless eyes. As he did so, a thick arm like a tentacle placed him in a headlock. Gasps followed him as he was dragged away from her. He struggled against the aggressor stubbornly. Screams and sharp cries populated the blurred space. His sight became spotted as the flow of oxygen was blocked from his head. He attempted to flail in defence, but the attacker restrained him professionally.

"That is quite enough! You can let him go, Daryl," Dr. Mardin's voice pierced through the cloud that shaded his vision.

He choked as air flooded into him; the branch-like limb unravelled slowly around his collar bone. He no longer attempted escape, instead he leaned for comfort into the mass that held him in place.

"Sir…this is a hospital, not some backwater Lindsay pub," she said, as she approached the pair. "Daryl, again, please let him go. I will have none of this in my ER."

The tentacle arm unraveled from around Arjun's neck. The brute pulled him upright, leaving behind two large hands on his shoulders.

"I-I'm so sorry… I don't know what came over me. I just really need to see-" Arjun began, but he was interrupted by Dr. Mardin as she hastily lifted her open hand in a silencing bong motion. She welded his widened eyes in place with a piercing stare.

"What is your name?" She inquired calmly. Curiosity calmed the room. Everyone respected her peace.

"It's Arjun...uh, Arjun Kaul."

"Okay, Arjun," she stated after a moment in which she sought patience, "I believe it is in your, and our, best interest if you came with us to discuss your interaction with Natasha. Let us talk privately and in a more reflective state of mind. Our current atmosphere is not conducive to healthy discussion." She turned and began to walk through the gallery of curious glares, but she rotated her head to confirm his acquiescence. "I do not have all day, Arjun."

Daryl gave him a soft nudge toward her, as she walked purposefully out of the triage. More nurses swooped in like high perched birds to re-establish order, as they guided the elderly in hanging gowns and concerned parents with their excited children back into their curtained mausoleums.

He followed the confident woman as she led the way through a staff only door. The hallway on the other side was quiet and windowless. White, fluorescent light bathed it. He could feel Daryl's presence behind him like a wall at his back. After a couple of turns into adjoining halls they stopped outside of a door numbered one-oh-eight.

"We will talk in here, Arjun. I only have forty-five minutes or so for this meeting so lets please not waste any moment," she expressed before she quickly entered.

He hesitated outside of the open doorway. The room was dim but clearly disheveled. Documents, supplies, and bedding were splayed like a Kandinsky painting on the floor. After only a moment, Daryl guided him in with his large hands. Two police officers stood together; their hands waved in discussion. Dr. Mardin stood beside a set of unhooked machines and a side table. She crossed her arms.

"This was her room," Arjun said to the pensive Dr. Mardin, as he settled inside. The sudden smell of Natasha filled him. His eyes closed in hidden ecstasy as he inhaled deeply.

"Indeed…" she nodded slowly, "this was her room. Mr. Kaul, please meet Inspector McClinton and Inspector Waynebeck. They will be involved in our discussion."

The police officers respectively nodded their heads in a non-verbal greeting, as they ended their animated conversation.

"Daryl, thank you for your help. Although I am but a frail old woman, I think we should be able to handle it from here," she noted sarcastically.

Daryl left without any notable indication of annoyance. His shoulders were held back in a show of presence. He closed the door as he exited.

"Very well, I would like to discuss some peculiarities with you, Mr. Kaul," she began. "What do you know of Natasha?"

The police officers watched him quietly, their faces uniformly carved and unlined.

"I don't know anything, really. My class and I - I'm a schoolteacher - were hiking a trail at Algonquin Park as a field trip, just around Oxtongue Lake. We were just leaving to take the bus home when we found her curled up in the middle of the path. Umm, she was dressed kind of fancy, but she had nothing else on her. Her feet were bloodied and covered in mud. Her ankle looked swollen. That's really it. I carried her from the trail to the bus and met the ambulance that took her here."

"How did you know her name?" Inspector McClinton asked, her hands casually held the neck of her bullet proof vest.

"Oh…I asked her for it. I asked her for it when we were by the bus. She woke up…She was crying. I wanted to comfort her…so I asked her for her name. It seemed harmless," he explained.

"Do you believe that that is her real name? She didn't offer any other information?" Inspector McClinton continued.

Dr. Mardin kept her inquisitive gaze locked on Arjun as he hesitated. The room's silence made him nervous as he sought an answer internally. A faint whistle escaped Inspector Waynebeck's nose. The inspector sniffed to clear his nasal passage and the room became an utter quiet.

"I can't really say whether…whether it was her real name or not, it is not something I considered immediately significant, you know?"

"You touched her?" Dr. Mardin asked, as she continued to search him with her eyes.

"I believe so, yes, but I didn't do anything… foul? I just cleaned her feet and carried her out. I did wear gloves. I also didn't think it was appropriate to leave her abandoned on a trail like that. That's why I carried her. Listen, I didn't do anything…I-I just came to see if she was okay." A droplet of sweat ran down his cheek.

"Perhaps." She pulled away from his eyes and closed her own in thought. She uncrossed her arms and interlocked her hands. "Mr. Kaul…Arjun, what did you plan to say to Natasha when you saw her?" Her eyes were still closed.

"I, uh, I didn't specifically have a plan. I just felt that it was something necessary for me to do…To come see her, and I guess see if she needed anything."

"If she needed anything? Is that kind of charity typical for you?" she inquired.

"I mean, that is how I'm saying it now…being put on the spot like this, of course it's going to sound weird. This whole thing is weird. I just felt the need to see her…I wanted to see her. I'm here now without her, so clearly that must be some kind of indication that I was not involved in her disappearance. I don't understand what is going on here and I could be, and I should be, out there looking for her." He wiped away the sweat that collected in his unshaven stubble.

The Inspectors' eyes hardened. He felt the nerves of the interrogation. Dr. Mardin nodded.

"What would you have done if she turned you away?" she continued.

"I never really thought about it," he replied.

"How did you know she was here? I am struggling to make the connection between you and her. What about her drew you here?"

"I don't-I don't know what you're referring to? Was it an urge or desire like I'm some kind of pervert? No, come on. I'm telling you; I'm not involved in this… I just…I, uh…I just saw something in her eyes…She was like someone looking up to me for an expectant shoulder. I felt a sense of her. A vibration that still wiggles along my skin like a colony of invisible ants. I felt like I knew her somehow…That I know her."

"Arjun, was there any other that made contact with Natasha that you are aware of?" Dr. Mardin opened her eyes and watched him as if she rested a conclusion on his response.

"No…Umm, yes, a boy. A boy named Yuuta… Yuuta Saito." His gaze was on his hands, as he examined white dryness in his brown knuckles, when he shot his head up at a sudden realization. "I-Arre baap re! Holy Deva." The curiosity of Chloe's search bloomed into a revelation.

"Is there something else?" She asked, as she lifted her gaze back to his face. "Why does this realization disturb you?"

"I-It's nothing. I just think that…he might be in trouble, but I don't know how that relates to any of this." The desire to look for Natasha twisted inside him like an unsustainable craving.

"What kind of trouble?" She held his gaze.

"I don't know…Forget I said anything."

"We'll entertain it, Mr. Kaul," Inspector Mc-

Clinton interjected. "Go on."

"Umm…there was a woman. She came to me. She said she was a reporter. She said her name was Chloe Black-something. I don't know, it sounded fake to me…but she mentioned him…She said that Yuuta was in trouble…In danger, really…"

"Danger?" Inspector Waynebeck pursued. "What do you mean? What kind of danger?"

"Listen…I'm not sure. I didn't get the details."

"You didn't get the details?" Inspector McClinton pushed. "Was your student's 'danger' not significant to you? This is highly unusual…"

"I…You're right, but…I don't know. I didn't think it concerned me."

"Natasha does concern you?" Dr. Mardin's eyes were unwaveringly penetrating.

"I don't know what to tell you…"

"Well, whether he is in danger or not, I estimate that he must be seeking her too. Inspector McClinton, I think this boy is involved somehow. It may be in our best interest to seek him out," Dr. Mardin concluded.

"I don't follow, El," Inspector McClinton said.

"Nor I," Inspector Waynebeck followed.

"It is just a theory at this point. Therefore…I think it is best we do not pursue any argument in its favour until we can piece it together. I believe Natasha is connected to both this man, the boy, and now both Gail and Cheryl in the same way. I don't know what the outlook of the investigation precludes, but my recommendation is to seek the boy, Yuuta," Dr. Mardin said.

"Arjun I must ask one more time: if you do find Natasha at this point, what is your intent?"

"Intent? I'm not sure I understand. I suppose the feeling is–What I feel now in my desire to seek her, it's like when you have been gone for a long time from home on a trip, or for work, or because you moved somewhere…and that gut feeling, that something inside you, that tells you that you really need to go back, you know what I mean? I just have this void that senses her absence…like a blurred shape in the back of my mind that will only be clear when she's near." He bobbed his head in consideration of his thoughts.

"I see," Dr. Mardin pensively noted. Her fingers were still interlocked. She looked through him like a window to a peculiar landscape. "I think it would be appropriate if you went home now, Arjun. I understand the futility of that statement, but I anticipate the command of these Inspectors will weigh more heavily than my recommendation. The inspectors will look for Natasha. They will also seek out Yuuta. I suggest you find an intense mental distraction until such time as this can be resolved."

He looked between the interrogators. He sought clarity in the silence. Each thought snapped back to Natasha like an elastic band. A hazelnut whirlpool grew inside him. He felt it begin to consume his ability to reason as the need to find her overcame any instinct of self-preservation.

"I, uh, I understand. This *is* odd, isn't it? Me being here at a time like this? You're right. You're absolutely right. I should go home. I have an excess of work to do, and it is not in my best interest to get mixed into this mess. Nor as an educator is it respectable...is it?"

"Excellent," Inspector McClinton stated dryly. "Now, unfortunately, we will need much of this, including your personal information, in writing. This will allow us to seek you out if anything further is necessary. Please complete this form and you are free to go, indefinitely. Please don't take my candid manner as an indication that I feel no sense of shame in knowing you sought this woman over reporting on the knowledge of this boy in danger."

Inspector McClinton handed him a form and a blue pen that was tucked inside her vest. He took the writing documents without another word and filled them in.

Arjun rediscovered himself with the glow of white fluorescent around him, as he mindlessly wandered the halls of the hospital consumed in his focus to feel Natasha. He felt nothing but the empty spot she was supposed to fill. He stumbled awkwardly through the sliding doors and forgot the moments that lead to him sitting behind the wheel of his sedan.

The late day was quiet except for a set of melodic songs that came from the treetops. The sky was a vivid and clouded purple. He sighed softly as he turned the ignition and pulled out of his parking spot.

Highway signs were soon dotting his rear-view mirror as he drove westward. Sunglasses barely shielded him from the unblocked rays that cracked the horizon. The conversation and guidance of Dr. Mardin slipped away with each farm-viewed kilometer, as hazelnut orbs continued to spin like hypnotic disks in his mind. Hunger reminded him of his corporeality, but the long-sought idea of her shadowed over his stomach's desire to eat.

Hours crept past until he pulled into a gas station off the 69. Night dawned and he walked into the gas station store. He grabbed a bag of gummy candies and a vitamin juice. He paid and asked for the washroom key. Once he urinated, he returned to his car and entered another lapse of blackness until he realized night had consumed the sky.

His air conditioning ran softly. The radio was off. Streetlights in a trail above him flickered passed like meteors. The pulsating inside his skull grew more violent with each kilometer. He knew he was close. He could feel her edge forward like a distant image slowly coming into view. It was only moments before the pulsating became a sloshing wave. He could feel her. His stomach churned with the mites of nervousness. His fluids brimmed like a roughly poured glass of Coke. He pulled off at the next exit and took the ramp onto the 17.

A city's orange radiance lightened the sky to the North and hid any evidence of the stars. His driving became indistinct. He had been caught in a ceaseless autopilot that pulled him onward. He made an instinctual left turn off the highway and followed the road that arched southward. His vision was flecked with specks, as his temples began to tense with the strain of the intensified vibrations behind his eyes.

He didn't get much further southward before he had to pull over to the side of the unlit road. His head throbbed. He went to get out of his car for air, but instead was overwhelmed by a blast of noise.

Trees creaked and groaned in distinct displeasure, whispering unknown curses. Wordless screams, carried by a soft wind, permeated the blackness. The thumping in his head became a deep synchronized chant. He stumbled and gripped the side of his car. The chant intensified as he weakened. He knew he had to go on. She was close. He could feel her. He took a swaying step. She was so close. He took another step. He could feel her. He could feel her like a warm embrace wrapped around his chilled body. She was so close. He stumbled to his knees. Laughter evaporated the evening's groans, a shrill that deafened him.

"Your ivory flower seeks a mortal salvation. Are you to be the harbinger?" a hollowed-out voice ripped through him. The laughter echoed around him. It ceased suddenly as a pair of gloved hands pulled his eyes from the ground to a pair of troubled pools of gray. "To see the flames of man so dimmed by her curse...You are nothing but rot, mutt. A shell destined to servitude. Taste the flesh of the dirt as you prepare to bear witness to the sowing."

The being laughed. It stuck cold, earthy fingers into his mouth. He gagged but was too weak to fight back as it probed aggressively inside. It laughed louder. Its brown teeth, gnarled and nasty, were visible between its crusted lips. Its face was chalky white and freshly scarred. It removed its fingers from the back of his throat with a jerk. He gagged as it left behind something that he was forced to swallow. He choked it down, while he attempted to regain focus.

"What are you? Why…Why?" he spluttered through aching breaths. "Where is she?"

It broke away from his frightened gaze. It sniffed the air greedily like a dog searching for its subject.

"I am a servant of life. One with meshkwadoon." It looked back to him; his head still clamped between it's fingerless-gloved hands. Its eyes swirled in a tempest of shadowy grey. "I am fear by association. I am destiny's design. I am the burden bearer of man's most unwellcome enemy: truth. I am the hated son. Where is she? She seeks death, for death is all she knows…Such is the flaw of her design. Such is the flaw of all Anishinaabeg."

The being shrieked hysterically. Its laugh was a wave of winter frost that chilled him to his bones. It laughed until it spluttered up an insect's slimy corpse. The bug fell abruptly down the being's chin, like a child's dribble, and rolled soundlessly to the ground. Silence followed. The trees sought hungrily for the being's next words. It stared unblinkingly into him, each breath a December wind that rushed out of round, unpainted, tanned nostrils. As it watched him, a pair of yellow lights flared in the reflection of its swirling eyes. The beams emblazoned the image of the being like a spotlight. It smelt the air hastily and growled.

"Smell her, dog. Taste her tingling beads of being in the dust. Feel her. She calls to you. Dog! Dog? Are you there?" It laughed.

"What are you?" he demanded again. Fear was swung around his neck like a noose's hoop. "Why are you telling me this?"

"The ganawenjige must know the way, mutt," it said, as it pulled him by his chin. It smiled again, abruptly released him, then turned with the wind. It faded into the trees that beckoned it.

He heard a car approach from behind him. He struggled to look away from the brush that hid the frightening being, until he heard the squealing of worn brakes. The voices of the world returned to their whining as the car came to a complete stop beside him.

"Erjun…? Is that you?" a familiar accent called over the car's roaring engine.

He turned reluctantly and saw Chloe's shocked diamond face looking out her passenger window. She stared at him. Her dark tilted eyes were the last things he saw before he hit the ground.

Chapter 7

The afternoon fled as Yuuta watched for the day's third bus. His motley trio sat in a corner of the station as kids and people filled it. Everyone continued to ignore the blue-eyed creature kneeling beside his chair. Their eyes lingered instead on the mumbling old man that sat on his other side. The old man's long and greasy black hair, with its vivid silver streak, was fingered behind his ears. He had a strange appearance of open-eyed unconsciousness.

Mixed noises filled the station. Groups of older girls laughed tauntingly behind painted nails. A rugged woman in a reflective vest, with a hardhat clipped to her backpack, leaned on a pillar with her eyes on her cellphone. Older boys shouted obscenities with disruptive intent. He felt like an alien. He looked at the passing groups shyly. He twisted his hands together as he eyed them, envying the strange guys all the girls chose to be with. Bared midriffs and curled locks flushed him. He tried to resist the flashing image of the woman-in-the-black-dress' white underwear in his head, but she consumed his undistracted thoughts. A shower thought perversion that teased him, despite the barrage of his sofu's horrid death face.

He chased the thoughts away as he tried to piece the day together. The silent trips had left him unsure of himself. The attendants at each station had eyed him and the man suspiciously, as he paid for the both of them each time. Their eyes always hung on the man.

Yuuta had allowed the creature to guide them to its intended destination based on silent gestures, but the money he stole from his sobo's sewing box wasn't as much as he thought it was. He looked at the man beside him. He would've thought the man was sleeping deeply if not for his open eyes.

"Sir, are you okay?" Yuuta asked, as he worked up the courage to address his dishevelled companion. He appreciated the solace of not having to talk, but he feared the man would think he was strange if he said nothing. The man said nothing. His mouth sat open, and he breathed heavy warm breaths like a dryer exhaust vent. His large tan hands, crusted with dry and bloodied skin, rested limply on his knees. "What's your name? I'm-I'm Yuuta. I'm usually pretty quiet myself, but you both have me beat…Do you, uh, do you see it too? The-the thing that's with us?"

The man showed no sign of understanding. Yuuta looked around to see if anyone watched them. He felt his hands twist faster. He shook his left leg without thought. To his immediate relief, a PA announced the arrival of their Ontario Northland bus. Neither of his companions stirred.

"Well, uh…" Yuuta said, standing to his feet, his knuckles gripped. "I suppose that is us?"

He removed a pair of crinkled tickets from his pocket and analyzed them. The typewriter-type text was jumbled and almost unreadable. He looked at the man. The man didn't move. He looked at the creature who kneeled at his feet. It twisted its head to look at him. Its eyes were expectant, like a dog awaiting command. He sighed, grabbed the man by the arm and tried to pull him to his feet.

"Come on, sir. Our bus is here…We have to get on it." He struggled against the man's dead weight. He was relieved that no one seemed to notice his plight.

The bus unloaded its contents, and a crowd of people came in through the sliding doors of the station. He let go of the man's hand and turned to watch. An old woman was slowly taking each step, holding the railing while she used her cane as a guide. The bus driver watched her with impatience. Yuuta shook his head then shuffled hastily through the crowd. He scolded the strangers who watched the old woman's feeble struggles wordlessly. His mother's sympathetic eyes flickered in the back of his mind. A group of expectant travellers were lined along the side of the bus waiting for her. They looked at their phones and watches impatiently.

"Come on, we don't have all day," a man yelled from the back of the line, as Yuuta reached the bottom of the steps. "Tell the kid to wait his turn, for Christ's sake."

"I'm sorry mam, uh, would you like my help?" Yuuta offered, as he stretched his hand to the struggling woman.

"Get your scrubby hands away from me. I am not some decrepit invalid!" the old woman spluttered through loose teeth. Her cane slipped off the last step, as she waved away his hand. She stumbled forward and into his silent companion, who waited like a stone block behind him. "G-get-get this drunk Indian off me! Get off me!" She weakly pushed off the silent man's middle. "This is outrageous…I'm an old woman. Help!"

The old woman obnoxiously moaned and carried her complaints to a pair of chit-chatting attendants who stood near the entrance of the bus stop. Yuuta looked between his two companions that stood silently together, sighed defeatedly, and guided them to the back of the line. Everyone else turned indifferently back to their devices; their viral hunger extinguished.

They boarded after only moments of waiting. The bus had consumed the line greedily, and its driver's face looked as if he suffered indigestion as a result. As they boarded, the driver's squinted eyes widened for a flicker of a thought when Yuuta advised him the tickets were for himself and the old man. With indifferent approval, they followed the aisle to the end.

They sat two seats from the back. The man followed without Yuuta's indecisive guidance. Yuuta removed his backpack and placed it under the chair. The creature kneeled between his legs on the floor. He thought it looked like a small person preparing for some form of prayer. The man sat in the aisle seat. He looked relentlessly ahead, but his filmy eyes darkened with brown substance. He breathed quietly with his mouth closed.

Yuuta looked out the window of the waiting bus and watched life flow in and out of the station. Hunger pained his stomach, and the heat of the creature between his legs reminded him of the fluids he needed to pee out, but he sat in stubborn silence. Quiet chatter carried throughout the aisle of seats, as the vehicle lurched forward with a rumble.

Night came without warning. Strip malls were replaced by highway signs. He watched taillight trails as he rested his head against the glass window. The cool familiarity tricked him into retrospection as the horrific images of his sofu's impaling soon followed each red taillight through the tinted glass. The lights' trails were like the blood red smears of dragged bodies. The woman-in-the-black-dress, in only her underwear, quickly replaced the image of his sofu.

He breathlessly lifted his forehead from the glass where droplets of sweat pooled. The image of the woman impaled in her nudity remained like a Poeish phantasm. He breathed deeply, mitigating the nausea, but the abusive imagery strangled him. He began to hyperventilate. He focused on the sweat that dripped down his nighttime reflection. The sound of his sofu's wheezing laughter filled his head. The feminine incantation he had heard at his house swallowed the laughter. He felt an urge to stand to his feet, but the weight of the creature resting on them held him in place. The feminine whisper, like the soft calling of his mother in the distance, grew louder. He couldn't help but wonder if it was his mother calling to him. He perked his ears to listen. A hand softly gripped his vibrating leg.

"Ye'll drown, ye know," a deep voice whispered slowly beside him. Yuuta investigated the man's sun beaten face. "Ye must come back up for air, or ye'll take the suffering into yer lungs…Yer final breaths will be choked by yer fear. Ye must breathe. Leave the deep pools to the summer pike, eh?"

Yuuta stared at the old man. The man maintained a soft grip on Yuuta's leg. The wordless feminine whispers quietened, but his mother still occupied his thoughts. The old man's hand vibrated lightly with his grip. Yuuta wondered if he was nervous. The old man seemed to realize his shaky hand and pulled it back to his own knee.

"What is your name?" Yuuta asked. Shyness unintentionally softened his voice.

"My name…Yes, of course…my name," the old man mumbled slowly, as he licked his lips in thought. "They call me, Ogi. That is, the people I know call me Ogi."

"What is a wahgoshi…umm…acheywhensie?"

"That's a curious question-"

"You said it…Earlier today," Yuuta quickly interrupted.

"I don't mean to scare ye, friend, but I don't quite recall anything before getting on this bus here. I'd blame ol' Daniel…but we haven't danced for years, if ye know what I mean. I'm really just here because it seems like the right place to be, ye know?"

"So, you don't remember anything from earlier today?" Yuuta's voice cracked awkwardly. "I-I don't think you should be on this bus…We might be taking you from your family, or maybe you should visit the doctor or…Do you even see the-the blue-eyed thing here?"

Ogi crinkled his eyebrows, his gaze hesitated on Yuuta before he dropped it to Yuuta's feet.

"I don't see anything, friend," the man stated matter-of-factly. The old man's jaw tightened. He turned his eyes to the back of the seat in front of him. "I can only assume ye mean waagoshi-akiwenzii?" Yuuta nodded reflectively. "Well, it means old man fox, if that's what yer referring to," Ogi's gaze was thoughtfully locked on the chair ahead. "The waagoshi-akiwenzii is a kind of calm in…unwieldy chaos. The reverential - which means, uh, admired - tribesman, whose guidance empowers the spirits of the Anishinaabeg…He's a figure long forgotten, replaced in form, they say, by the great mother of Aayaash, Waagoshii-Mindimooye."

"You said you weren't…that, I think. I didn't really catch much else of what you said…I don't know, it's okay. I-I was just curious."

"Ah, it's no bother. I suppose knowing what I say and do during these black outs is prudent in its own way, eh?" Yuuta watched the old man curiously before he returned his gaze to the darkness outside. Highway lights illuminated grassy plains, sparse woodlands, and farm fields. The evening's ghouls were a misty dream that faded out of his memory. The creature at his feet breathed softly against his legs. "What's *yer* name, friend?"

"I'm Yuuta." Yuuta looked back at Ogi. He dropped his gaze to Ogi's chin.

"Utah? Like the state?" Ogi asked, still looking to the front of the bus.

"No-no, I'm Japanese."

"Japanese? Ye're born there?"

"Well...no. I was born in Canada...but my parents and grandparents are Japanese. They were all born in Japan."

"I see. Do ye feel Japanese?" Ogi continued. Yuuta saw the corner of the man's eyes tighten.

"I...I'm not sure what that feels like."

"Hmm...good point. Yer not one of those Bobcaygeon fans or hockey players, are ye? My people have lived here for many generations, and I'm not sure sometimes I know what it is to be Anishinaabe either..."

"Who are the Anishinaabe?" Yuuta lifted his eyes to Ogi, who now watched him with imperious brown ones. Any sign of the filmy grayness was gone.

"What that means is that I'm supposed to be a member of the Anishinaabe tribe. I mean, I hunt, I fish, I snowshoe, I ride ATVs...I live a quiet life surrounded by good spirits and nature's wild, but...my people are a people whose beliefs in themselves seem to be commonly outweighing any ancestral belief in nature's spirit. Hard to have strong cultural autonomy in a melting pot where the cross is raised higher than the sun, I suppose…Anyway, I'll let wiser ones answer that question for ye. For among the wise, I am but a man."

"Oh, you're a Native?"

"Hmm? Where are we going anyway?" Ogi asked. He turned from Yuuta and examined the seats around him.

"I-I'm not sure. To Sudbury, according to the tickets, I think…After that, I'm not sure…" Yuuta twisted his mouth, unwilling to re-indicate the creature at his feet whose guidance he followed. He couldn't release the insecurity of the old man's potential concern for his state of mind. He held his eyes shut. He prayed to be free of the silent eruption that brewed inside him. He felt his hands twist together without restraint. He tried to pull them apart, but he was convinced that once he had those final twists in, he would never need to do it again. He felt Ogi's large hand grip his shoulder.

"Steady, friend. Steady. We're still a few hours away from Sudbury. Why don't ye get some shut eye?" Ogi suggested, concern clear in his deep whisper.

Yuuta released the tightness of his eyes but kept them closed. Ogi patted Yuuta's shoulder before he returned his hand back to his knee. Yuuta silently wished that the old man had held it there. The idea of it reminded him of his mother. His mother's jet-black hair tied into a bun was a standard morning comfort. Her trail of coffee fumes always greeted him like a friendly neighbour. He sniffed his nose and twisted his head in the direction of the window. The memory of her hospital bed was a black cloud in his mind. Residual whispers clung to him like an unusual frost on an early Spring morning: a ghostly aura that mumbled in his ears. He tried to breathe through their feminine chants, but they called for him.

"Ogi, sir, do you have anybody you need to get back to…or is maybe looking for you?" The whispers stopped as if they listened. "A-a wife? Or elderly mother? Or child?"

Ogi hesitated and twisted the left side of his mouth. "I have a daughter. She's a bit older though, so I don't expect she's waiting for me…My wife, well, she is of the spirits now. She was a smart woman, and her daughter is much the same…but Chloe, well, she sees me more as an Elder than a father, ye know? So ye can say that I've really been quite alone for some time…but I make do. I'm a busy man, and a household ain't a home without a busy man, as they say," Ogi noted with a wink, as he turned to Yuuta. He was calm and cool like a lake breeze.

"Your wife…what was her name?" Yuuta asked, afraid to reveal his ignorance of commonplace condolences. He shivered as he suddenly felt penetrated by Ogi's gaze.

"Dawn. Her name was Dawn," Ogi eventually said, as collected as he was before. "Friend, why are ye here, alone, and seeking to accommodate the presence of a strange old man? Where is *yer* family? What is there in Sudbury that ye look for?"

"They're all gone…and, uh, you're going to think I'm crazy, or just being a weird kid or something, but there is a creature at my feet that I see who is guiding us. It came to me the night my sofu-sorry, my grandpa, died. It doesn't speak, but it seems to be protecting me. It has blue eyes like…like Christmas lights. It isn't very tall, and it's strange looking, with rock scales like a knight's armour. I don't think it's…from here, but it comforts me, in a real kinda way." Yuuta eyed the creature that rested dreamily against his right calf like a lounging pet. A new energy twinkled in Ogi's eyes. He leaned over to double check the spot between Yuuta's feet but said nothing as he pulled back.

"Ye don't say…Ye don't say…" Ogi hesitated, before settling back into a sitting position. His hand was on his chin. "Have ye ever heard of the bagwajiwinini? Or maybe ye've heard of *The Deetkatoo*…ye know, the book?"

"I don't think so…I mean, I do love to read, and I do love books, but I haven't heard of either of those things."

"No, eh? White man gibberish anyway…Well, the bagwajiwinini are said to be sprites of nature. There are three kinds, they say. The apa'iins' were said to be the invisible kindred of men, who fought both blight and disease. They were guardians and shepherds of harvest, but on the wings of colonization came resentment and hate, they say. It is said that they now serve a vile mind. Puk-wudjies are of rock and water, with the burning hunger of a bear. It is said that they served Nanabozho, the Great Hare, in defiance of the Horned Serpent who bred them…and that they have distanced themselves from men, despite once being great teachers and mystics. The pai'iins are said to be watchful warriors. It has been spoken that the primary nature of these mysterious bagwajiwinini is to keep the beasts of the deep from surfacing…An eternal task that has kept them distant from people, and…well, I imagine they must still be serving this task, eh?"

"I don't understand…" Yuuta said.

"I speak of the little ones, friend. And they say the eyes of the puk-wudjies are like windows into a great sea. Ah, never ye mind. Maybe there is a reason why the Anishinaabeg are a history lesson and not a civil affair's one, eh?"

"What do you mean?"

"I mean…Well…Ye'd say it's not all quite so sad for me as yer own story, eh? How did yer grandfather pass? A young kid like yerself should not be wandering alone, ye know."

Yuuta's chest tightened. He gripped his hands into fists to prevent himself from worrying them. "I-I'm not a kid…" he whispered, as he rocked his head from side to side. "I'm not a kid."

"Friend, if ye want to keep that to yerself, I don't mind. It's all a matter of small talk. There's no obligation to tell me nothing," Ogi said calmly, as he patted Yuuta's leg. "Do ye have a drink for yerself? Maybe a nibble of chocolate or some chips, or something to calm yer spirit?"

"No, I-I haven't eaten since yesterday. Was that yesterday? Time is…it's kinda foggy. I don't know…I don't know." Yuuta put his face in his hands. He felt Ogi's concerned stare.

A gradual twist of violence turned inside his head. Vines, like slithering tree roots, wriggled slowly inside. Drums thumped somewhere in the distance. Their soft echoes were accompanied by the resurrection of the whispered incantations. He heard a poignant dinging sound. A warmth at his feet began to rise along his leg and he lifted his eyes from his hands to the creature pulling its shoulders back. He straightened himself and looked out the window.

The bus pulled into a small parking lot off a main intersection. Lights were orange spotlights in the night. They highlighted the bus depot like an important thought in a book.

A crow flew off the building to a lit spot on the ground where it pretended to pick through food garbage. It cocked its head for a moment, then flew into the darkness. Its sudden flight brought Yuuta's gaze to a single shape of an extremely tall figure standing in the darkness at the side of the depot's traveller center. Eyes like oblong white rocks accompanied the figure like children peeking from behind its skirt of shadow. The strange eyes watched the bus.

Ogi stood calmly into the bus aisle. He stretched his arms with a groan. The creature at Yuuta's feet looked around like a dog lifting its startled head from an unheard noise. It climbed onto the spot Ogi had risen out of. It sniffed the air, then jumped to the rails of the overhead baggage rack. It crawled like a wild monkey to the front of the bus, where it swung out an open window.

The feminine chant whispered to Yuuta seductively. It urged him to follow. It was a soft whisper like the moist sensation of fog. She called to him. He needed to go to her, but Ogi stood in his way like a cement barrier. Yuuta felt reasonless anger brew inside him, as he looked at Ogi's thick form, but once he caught the old man's brown eyes it washed off him. Fear filled the gap left by his abandoned anger as the bus shook from the weight of something crashing against its side. He joined others to look out the windows to watch a swarm of beady eyed beings excitedly circle the still shadowed figure. Their white eyes were like ivory garden stones, misshapen and chalky. The other passengers craned their heads to the wheels, oblivious to the demons.

"Come to us, sweet child. She is with us…the woman you seek. We will bring you to her. She calls for you…She needs you. Come…Come…Come to us," the feminine voices whispered. The chant ran like a stream through his head. He felt the warmth of his mother. He pushed between Ogi's form and a passenger who stood in the aisle. All thoughts of his mother were replaced with the image of the woman-in-the-black-dress.

He slipped desperately between the stretch of seats to the front of the bus. The door was open, and the driver was outside yelling obscenities to the figure in the shadow. Yuuta sprung onto the pavement, and as his feet hit the ground a naked pale creature stepped into the light. The bus driver froze in horror. Its milky skin was etched with scars. A red stain encircled its mouth. Its eyes were like clouded red gemstones. It bent down to examine the man frozen in shock.

"I was promised flesh," it said, as it leaned over the man, "and I shall have it."

The man-creature pounced in a blur onto the driver and bit into his neck. Dark blood sprayed along the monster's face. The bus driver's shock ended in a violent scream. His screams were quickly replaced by a hideous gurgle that became the only sound to accompany the thumping of the creature's clawed hands against its lifeless prey. Yuuta heard mixed screams from behind him, but he couldn't look away. The beady eyed creatures began to vibrate and then they ran like a pack of wild pygmies toward the blue-eyed creature that was splayed like a dog's rag doll at the side of the unmoving bus.

The pack of wild demons took only seconds of charging, claws of their four limbs clicking off the ground, before they got to the unconscious creature. They slashed at it animalistically. The vulgar sounds of chewing were overtaken by the manic scratching of nails on stone.

Yuuta's chest clenched as he watched. The pale monster lifted its head to examine him. A shrewd and familiar laughter filled the depot.

"So potent..." a deep spectral voice spoke, as if

blown through a tube. The pale nightmare returned its bloodied face to the opened corpse that was a man only moments before. "Come, child. I can take you to her." The beady-eyed creatures continued their barrage on his lifeless companion, but his need to see her grew wild. He swore he could taste the earthy sweat that soaked her hair in the air of the depot, like a mist floating down upon him. "Yes…Yes. Taste her in all things. Smell her."

Yuuta felt an urging to go to the feeding monster, but he didn't move. Fear and disgust strained him. His eyes bulged as he watched helplessly. The moment suspended in his mind, until it was interrupted by the last sounds of mixed panic from behind. He turned to see people fleeing from the bus in terror. A man with a briefcase tripped after a pair of women who ran toward empty cars in the lot nearby. Ogi walked off the bus last. He leaned into the handles as he stepped down. He stared around with milky eyes. He stumbled forward. The pale beast laughed, a demonic sound that tickled down Yuuta's spine like a spider's nest cracked over his head.

"To taste the rich flesh of an old fox. Too many moons have passed since one of your kind's blood has basted my throat," it growled.

"Be gone, worm," Ogi spat through his teeth. His eyes were a swirl of milky grey. "I'm sure the only thing to baste yer throat is pig's milk."

The pale creature snarled. Its inhuman face contorted with instinctual disdain. It stood to its feet and towered above them.

"Silence, fool! I shall not be pestered by the asinine words of a mortal man," it growled. Blood dripped off its chin. Each drop made a clicking sound as it hit the ground in a puddle at its feet, distinguishable through the sound of ticking slashes off stone.

"Friend," Ogi nodded to Yuuta, handing him his black backpack. He swayed as he pulled his arm back to his side. "Take it, and flee from the toxic fumes of this ugly, old blow pipe."

In the same moment, the beady-eyed beasts whipped like debris in every direction as a great stone bear, with eyes like raging stars, lifted from the cement ground. It looked around, a primal rage visible through its gnashing jaws. Claws as long as fence spikes pincered one of the little creatures. The little bark-like creature dangled limply, a sticky sap oozed on to the pavement from its body. The blue-eyed bear whipped the limp creature out of its grip, like a cut of spoiled meat thrown away in disgust. It roared in a stunning boom at the pale monster.

"Maamakaadakamig! What a beast my brother has bred," the spectral voice spoke in excited hysteria.

The beady-eyed puppets returned to the pale monster's side, and from the darkness, between the orange lights of the depot, stepped a man-like being. The figure was shorter compared to the pale fiend, whose red eyes glared through the night, but was still taller than a normal man. It had a masculine face and black hair like a great lion's mane. It had a chest like a woman's, that covertly looked out from under a red leather vest. It was strangely feminine but had the shape and ugliness of a man. It stopped and watched him. Its face was chalky white, as if painted for ritual. Its eyes were like misted grey clouds.

"Run, child. Run, run, if you must. Find the ivory flower. Find her, or I shall find you and force you to watch your elder drained into the ever-thirsty earth," the being's voice threatened across the wind.

It laughed hysterically. Its high-pitched shrill opposed its cavernous tone. It stepped forward with a hideous smile, but a gust of a brisk breeze blew its body into a million particles of dust the wind swallowed.

Yuuta looked at the bear-like beast that was silenced by the figure's presence. It suddenly roared furiously into the air. The beady eyed creatures scattered. The pale monster laughed horrifically and licked its stained lips. Its hideous red eyes sought Yuuta's soul, but as the blue-eyed beast roared again it snarled, turned, then fled on all fours like a lanky doe. Calm followed. The stone bear brought its eyes down upon Yuuta, blue blazes raging like supernovas in its head. Ogi stumbled to his side. The filmy grey that fogged his eyes already began to darken.

"Where…Where am I? Are ye alright, ye look like ye've seen an aniwye?" the old man said.

Yuuta watched as the bear sat, satisfied with its work, and scanned the now empty bus depot.

"I-I'm okay. Yeah, I'm fine, I think. Are you sure you're okay…?" Yuuta asked, as he stepped over to hold the disoriented man up.

Ogi didn't respond. Yuuta struggled as he felt the man's weight leaning into him. He stepped away once he was confident in the old man's posture, then swung his backpack over his shoulder. He turned to the docile stone beast. It breathed in great bellows through its open mouth. Ogi stumbled as he saw the violated corpse.

"Creator! W-what happened…?" Ogi kneeled over the indistinguishable body. Yuuta realized a warm dampness in his pants and looked down to see his returned shame. He considered using the towel tucked away in his bag but didn't. His nausea cramped his stomach. He watched Ogi begin to whisper to the body, opened like an omurice. Ogi turned back to Yuuta with a frightened look and shook his head. "What happened?" the old man repeated. His eyes frothed like twisting rain clouds as he looked at Yuuta. Yuuta saw the chilling horror of the man's fear.

Chapter 8

The sluggish sound of a ceiling fan accompanied Arjun's slow waking. He lifted heavy lids into the face of a pillow. He sleepily tilted his head to a wall wallpapered with pink flowers on white. He swallowed the distasteful morning saliva that had collected in his mouth and sought his nightstand for his cup of water. He immediately pushed himself up and turned to face the room as confusion followed his goalless search. A faint blue slipped below a set of black curtains and outlined furniture shapes. He considered checking the door just beyond the edge of his bed, but a fear of the unknown held him in place.

The strange being's chalky face was trapped in the mangled images of his thoughts. He remembered the cool pavement, the rumble of an engine, and car lights like glowing eyes. He got caught in the contemplation of his memories. The thought of Natasha pulled him back to reality.

The room gradually brightened as the sliver of light grew large enough to enrich the space with a soft blue glow. Birds chirruped ecstatically through the curtained window. They carried energy into the lifeless room. A knock interrupted his thoughts. He lifted his eyes to the closed door at the end of the bed.

"Erjun? Erjun, are you up?" an accented woman asked through the door.

"I-Uh, Chloe? Wha-Why?" He felt the confusion of a hangover without the pleasure of the evening before. He tightened his posture.

"Yes. I'm coming in, okay?"

"Of course-sure, I mean…it's your place, isn't it?"

She opened the door impatiently and stepped into the room. She walked quickly to the window and whipped the curtain open. Light consumed any remaining darkness. He shielded his eyes from the sudden brightness.

"We've been waiting all morning for you. Come on, Erjun, get up," she said, as she rounded on him.

"What do you mean? Who? Who's been waiting on me?"

"Just get your clothes on and come have something to eat. You've wasted the whole morning," she snapped.

"Is it Natasha…Is she here? She's waiting for me?" The thought of her burned in his chest like acid reflux.

Chloe glared at him, shook her head, turned, and exited the room. He followed her with his eyes. She wore a loose tank top tucked into a snug pair of black cargo pants. Her brown hair was tightened into a braid. He felt no desire to call after her.

He smelled the air, and his nostrils were immediately filled with a moth-ridden staleness. His posture slackened. He sat quietly. The sounds of muffled voices carried through the floor, but his mind had no interest in listening. He took a deep breath, slipped out of the blankets, and dressed himself in the wrinkled and unwashed clothes that whoever undressed him left unfolded beside the bed.

Natasha consumed his thoughts as he stumbled over a mustard yellow ottoman in the middle of the room. He swore under his breath. He wondered at the yellow object's resilience despite the weight of his body colliding with it.

His socked feet were soundless on the shaggy carpet that led into a hallway. Closed brown doors darkened the windowless hall, which was smothered by the same pink flowered wallpaper. A heavy smell of old books and dust clouded the air. An opening at the end wrapped down to the floor below.

He took the stairs warily, as they moaned under each step. Sets of shoes clogged the small space at the bottom. His own pair were tossed just inside, as if kicked off hastily. A spider's aged web hung from the corner above the door. Talking carried through the adjacent sitting room. He listened cautiously. A man with a deep voice dominated the conversation. Chloe's irritated tone was distinct. Arjun struggled to catch the words in his lethargy. The clinking of silverware on glass dishes accompanied the talking.

Arjun walked through the musty and aged sitting room. A pair of couches, torn like cat towers, sagged against joining walls. Blankets and pillows with no pillowcases hung in a dishevelled mess off the furniture. A vacant fireplace sulked against the wall on his left, dust occupied its unadorned mantle. A sagging backpack leaned against the side of one of the faded brown sofas. He walked to the closed door on his right and listened.

"Dad, you don't have to stay here. We can bring Yuuta to my place," he heard Chloe say on the other side.

"Chlo, this is my home. Ye grew up here. I grew up here. Can we leave it at that, eh," a man replied.

"No…No, we can't leave it at that. The others look down on us. They think you live in squalor. They say we shame Anishinaabeg. They say people don't need further excuse to shame Anishinaabeg." Chloe argued. "People are sensitive lately, you know that."

"What do they know of shame? They're too focused on reconciliation handouts and coloured Pow Wows for TV commercials and school posters…Chloe, just…let the weight of my spirit be unburdened by this nonsense. Yer once were happy here…little girl dancing in the radiance of the mother. My little daughter… don't leave me far behind…." the man said.

Arjun put his hand up slowly to turn the doorknob to realize that the door was knobless. He poked it with his finger, and it shifted lightly. He rubbed his sleep crusted eyes then pushed his way into the adjoining room.

His sudden presence coerced the room's eyes.

The curious breakfasters watched him as he froze in the door's frame. His gaze fell on Chloe, but his examination ended swiftly as he spotted a boy in his peripherals sitting shyly beside her. The boy's face was sunken, with dark bags under his green eyes. He looked sickly pale.

"Yuuta?" Arjun exclaimed. "Arre baap re, Chloe! Why is Yuuta here? Do you know how old this boy is?" Chloe's glare was persistent, but she didn't respond. Yuuta's stare was lifeless. "Yuuta, are you alright? You look sick. Have they done anything to you?"

The room held its silence. A flickering blue suddenly caught his attention, as he spied a strange animal creature sitting on the floor cross-legged on Yuuta's right side. Its back soaked in the rays of the sun that flooded through a set of glass sliding doors.

"What the f...What is that?" Arjun exclaimed, as he stepped back into the door that had just settled from his entry.

"We don't see it, friend," said a man who sat placidly across from Yuuta.

They all sat in dark chairs at the sides of a dark stained, wood slat, rectangular table. A dried-up bouquet drooped in the center, its dark purple flowers dominantly browned. A plate of partially eaten strawberries, blueberries, toast, and rice sat in front of each of them.

"Have a seat. Would ye like some toast?" the man asked, as he motioned to the chair beside him. "Try some of this lavender jam, friend. It's quite enriching at this time of day."

Arjun remained standing; his gaze locked onto

the blue torches that burned relentlessly inside the sockets of the strange creature.

"Why-why can't you see it? What do you mean?" he asked. Before anyone could respond, Yuuta pushed himself hastily to his feet. The boy went to speak but twisted away from his chair and ran out of the room through a door to Arjun's right. A slam inside the other room was followed by the suppressed sounds of vomiting. Arjun turned his head to the pair at the table. Chloe moved her food around with her fork. The older man ate his food with an unphased look. The strange creature's eyes watched the door Yuuta fled through. Arjun rounded on Chloe. He fought for words to overcome the noise of the young boy puking. "What is this? Why is he here? What is that… thing? Holy Deva." He massaged his temples aggressively.

"Have a seat, friend," the man said sternly. His voice commanded acquiescence, like a no-nonsense Principal. "Let the boy be. He is shedding the shock and trauma of too much, in too short a time. His spirit will require some mending."

"I-I don't know what you mean," Arjun stuttered.

"I tried to tell you, Erjun," Chloe rose to her feet confrontationally. "You said nothing of this had to do with you, and now look. Look! You show up here, kneeling like a wounded animal on the road. Stinking of fear and…desperation. Did you actually come by Memegwesi's call? How did you know to come here? What are you doing here?"

"Chloe," the man said deeply, the depth of his voice silenced them. His head trembled slightly as he licked his lips. "Sit. It's quite alright…We can all talk cordially, eh? There's no need for shouting or anger. Ye know he knows nothing of the truth, Chlo. Ye can give him that. Sit."

Arjun sat beside the man and Chloe returned to her chair. She crossed her arms with a wifeish stare.

"Arjun, I am Chloe's father, Ogichidaa. Ogi. I understand a man's reservations considering what is before him, but please listen to the words of this old goat." The man stopped talking to take a bite of his toast. "I have spent many years in communion with the spirits of this world. I have borne the spoken tale of the wind; by the fox, I have found guidance; from the rivers, I have obtained resilience. I feel the stirring sensations of Hahnunah's great burden. I hear the voices of the children of the sea. My knowledge is old…and its roots dig deeper than the shovels of man. My people are the bearers of this learning and I ogimaa of the craft." Ogi breathed in deeply and released the captured air into a long sigh. His head shook slightly. "I know that means nothing to ye, I know…but ye'll get where I'm taking ye in due course. Now understand, my people are no longer relevant, I'm sure ye've seen. The man of the East has claimed the land and our way of being. We hold fleeting tradition for the sake of our dwindling children. Now my people are underlings, and the youthful North American man is one of investment firms and spiritless worship. Reconciliation has proven our demise, with each dollar given to us a hammer that splits us into smaller bits from our whole. We have retained the image of the colourful aborigine seen from a window in passing cars, or on screens that capture a moment of nothing, like zoo animals on parade. Nothing but tax funded reserves of alcoholism and decay to them, but they don't know nothing about us. We simply seek communion with a land that is burdened by the weight of our being. Are we but an eyesore other? My people are caught in an unspoken war that will rage until our inevitable end. Now, my friend, I shall get to my point. The land - *our* land - it speaks to us with its dying breaths on the wind like a Jack Vance novel. It has called to us as it grows pallid. It suffers to sustain the spirit of being, while it awaits the sown seed of the daughter of Muzzu-Kummik-Quae. The Anishinaabeg are left as handtied waabange, with power to hear, but not to speak." The old man's head never stopped vibrating as he spoke. He took a drink of his water with unsteady hands and set the glass back down with a clunk. "The descendant daughter of Muzzu-Kummik-Quae is the paid price of a bargain struck to separate that which is of the spirit and what is of flesh. This boy, Yuuta…his story is no longer that which concerns the flesh. He is spoken for…as are ye."

Arjun hesitated in the silence, unsure if Ogi had finished. The quiet was broken by the sound of Yuuta re-entering the room. The boy dragged his footsteps lazily across the ceramic kitchen floor, until he reached his chair and slid weakly into it.

"Yuuta, why don't you go lie down for a bit," Chloe suggested as she watched him with sad eyes. "I'll get some manoomin harvest naboob ready for you. It's great on the gut."

"No-no, thank you," the boy whispered softly. His eyes were tilted toward his untouched plate of food.

"Yuuta? Yuuta, have they hurt you? Have they... coerced you? Let me take you home. These people aren't right. They're-they're dangerous," Arjun pleaded.

"You Sauk! You don't listen. He doesn't have anybody. Did you not see the picture?" Chloe argued.

"This is...wrong. You should've taken him to the-"

"What picture?" Yuuta interrupted, as he lifted his solemn gaze to Arjun. "What-what picture?"

"And what will you do? You're going to dump him into the system? Who knows what your true intentions are? Something brought you out here and it was nothing of our design," Chloe continued. She stood up again to face Arjun.

"He's just a kid!" Arjun shouted, as he slammed his fist into the table.

"Exactly! The system isn't designed to take on a non-white pre-teen. He'll be forced to experience things no kid should go through. He may never find a home..."

"Things aren't the same as when you were a kid. He's not going to be forced into some Residential School."

"How dare you?!" she shouted, as she waved a finger toward him.

"What picture? Please…What picture? Please tell me. Please…" Yuuta whimpered. He grabbed Chloe's arm.

Chloe swung her elbow up from the surprise of the sudden touch and clipped Yuuta's jaw. The boy fell backwards into his chair. Before any follow up reaction could be made, the blue-eyed creature was already standing on the table with Chloe's neck gripped in its claws. Blue, like the flames of a gas stove, whipped violently off its face. Their glow reflected in the perspiration that dampened Chloe's tan forehead.

"Enough!" Ogi shouted. The room immediately fell into silence.

"It's okay," Yuuta whispered to the strange creature. "It's okay."

Chloe's feet hit the ground. She panted with rough breaths and rubbed her throat. The creature stepped off the now shattered dish and spilled breakfast remnants. It hopped to Yuuta's side. It investigated the boy, as he stared with empty eyes at the broken plate.

"How-What was that strength?" Chloe breathed out hoarsely. Her eyes looked down at the broken glass as well. Lavender jam was sprayed across the tabletop in a painter's splatter of pink. Ogi sighed. His right hand, gripped around his fork's handle, vibrated like he was signing his name. He put down the clutched fork and irritably gripped his wrist.

"Now is no time for this," the old man said quietly, as he stared down at his hands. "Arjun, it is Yuuta's choice to stay with us."

"He's a child, he doesn't have any right to a choice," Arjun said.

"M-may I say something?" Yuuta inquired softly. His eyes lifted to Arjun's. "Mr. Kaul…she calls to me. I hear her voice like a song playing in my head. I have to go to her. I felt it before, but the pain- I have to go to her."

Yuuta paled whiter as he spoke. His eyes darkened. Arjun could see the boy mouth words to himself silently.

"Yuuta…Her name…her name is Natasha," Arjun revealed, understanding the ceaseless urge that floated inside the boy's head.

"Natasha? Natasha. Natasha…" Yuuta repeated.

"The boy, he can't be part of this," Arjun stated, summoning his obligation of authority. He kept his eyes on Yuuta.

"I don't make any choices on the matter, friend. I simply do as the spirits bid," Ogi said softly.

"Natasha…I-I can do this. We can do this," Yuuta resolved as he looked down to his companion for support. "It's too dangerous out there for her. We…we must help her."

Arjun watched as black consumed Yuuta's eyes like a comic book symbiote. It frightened Arjun, but he felt it too. The light that bathed the room was richer. He could hear the bouquet's wheezing attempt at life. He knew she needed him. She was desperate for him. She would die without him. She was close.

"Let me find her, Yuuta. Let me do this for us,"

he offered, just short of begging.

"It smells her - your towel, Mr. Kaul. I-I didn't understand at first, but it was...confused by the mix of smells." Yuuta hesitated. "It took me to your apartment. I saw Chloe. I saw her there. It didn't understand and I didn't understand, but it's because your sweat is also on the towel."

"My apartment? What…?" Arjun tried to piece together Yuuta's mumbles.

"I smell her too. I just want to keep breathing it in. I must find her. It must be *me* to find her," Yuuta demanded.

Arjun watched the boy, pitying his decline. He knew twelve-year olds and he knew the hold Natasha had over himself. He understood the chaos that stirred unconsoled within, a rakshasa that haunted the boy's unfiltered thoughts. He knew this old man and his reckless daughter didn't see. They didn't know Yuuta's suffrage. They couldn't know.

"No…I will not allow this to continue. I have to bring him home," Arjun determined.

"No! I must see Natasha!" Yuuta yelled.

"Yuuta isn't yours to take," Chloe continued to argue.

"Enough. I said enough, Chlo," Ogi sternly interjected. The man's deep voice was amplified inside the small kitchen. Chloe opened her mouth to protest but closed it quickly. "Arjun is right. We cannot keep Yuuta here."

"I won't go. I won't go. I won't!" Yuuta released

in a tantrum. He began to sob. The realization that he was a child showed in Chloe and Ogi's eyes.

"It's okay, bacha. It's okay," Arjun said, as he reached out to the boy across the table.

Drippings from the boy's nose splashed off the table's surface. His eyes were black and swollen.

"My sobo…I miss her. Where did she go? Why did she leave us?" Yuuta attempted to wipe the tears out of his eyes as he sobbed.

They let the boy cry quietly into his hands. Arjun felt an unconscious need to check his phone. He remembered obtrusively that he didn't respond to his mother's text. Before he determined to reach into his pocket, Yuuta looked up. He sniffled, wiped his face, and looked between them. He wiped his face again.

"I-I'll go…" he whispered and sniffed. "I'll go with you, Mr. Kaul."

He locked green eyes on Arjun. Chloe shook her head. Ogi sighed.

Chapter 9

The backyard was a mess of junk that fanned out into a field of dirt. The sun that had energized the morning was clouded over. A soft breeze made much of the unusable machinery crank and groan. The breeze grew into a heavy gust and the stretch of rusted equipment and vehicles echoed like a workshop filled with hammering. The wind carried over the yard and stole the sound of banging metal to a near line of trees. The backyard became silent. An unwelcome cold remained.

Yuuta attempted deep breaths to control the nausea that bubbled in his stomach like a shaken carbonated drink. He hated vomiting. He feared that the dry heaving that followed each experience would end in his choking death. His ribs ached from the earlier expulsion of his insides.

He watched a white butterfly flutter out of the smashed windshield of a rusted car. The sound of the house's sliding glass door opened behind him. He lost the focus of his breathing. He twisted to watch Ogi walk through the opening. The old man directed himself toward where Yuuta stood. The old man walked slowly, as if his muscles were stiffened by hours of gardening.

"No appreciation for the classics anymore, eh?"

Ogi said, as he stopped beside him.

Yuuta looked the car graves up and down. He didn't believe that any of the blocks of rust were ever anything interesting.

"This red one here, she's a 1987 Acura Integra. That girl there got Chloe between dance and school," Ogi chuckled as he smacked the paint peeled hood. "That forest green truck beside the Integra there is my 1977 Dodge Warlock. She was my baby. I picked up Chloe's mom in it. Her old pops thought I was riff-raff, ye know."

Yuuta looked between the scraps of metal. Both vehicles were on blocks with yellowed grass and weeds growing through them.

"How are ye, friend?" Ogi asked through the following silence.

"Uh, she's in pain. She suffers and is…alone," Yuuta admitted. "What could I do anyway? Mr. Kaul is right; I shouldn't be here. I should…I should…I should be in school tomorrow. I should have friends…My sofu and sobo are dead b-because of me. This is m-my fault… All they did was try to love me when my parents…l-left… When they left me I…I…I miss my momma." He sobbed into his hands. He felt Ogi's arm wrap around his shoulders. The old man said nothing. "Why did they leave me? I-I'm nothing without them. I'm just some orphan now. How do orphans even go to school?"

"Ahh, friend, it's quite alright. Come on. Let it out now. No harm in a spiritual release, eh? Flush them out, my friend."

Yuuta's crying dwindled into sniffles. He dragged his sleeves across his eyes and nose anxiously.

"I-I'm sorry, sir. I shouldn't be…I shouldn't be crying like that in front of you." He brought his eyes to Ogi's chin.

"Nothing wrong done, friend. Ye wouldn't think it with the wild nature she exhibits but Miss. Chloe in there could fill a couple biskitenaagan with the amount she still cries," Ogi laughed. Yuuta met Ogi's smiling gaze. He felt his own cheeks crack. He stretched his mouth out and wiped away the last remnant of tears from the corner of his eyes. The old man patted his shoulder. "Come on now. Let us pack ye up and get ye on yer way, friend."

The old man pulled his hand back to his side as Yuuta shrugged under the affection. Ogi turned and walked casually back to the house, and through the sliding glass door. The yard of scrap was empty of life.

Yuuta made his own way back to the house after a few moments of conclusionless self-reflection. He stopped to examine a set of garden tools that rusted in a bucket under a doorless wooden shed. Something about the sharp edge of the rusted hatchet that leaned inside the bucket sent shivers down his spine. He picked it up and tucked it into the band of his pants. He looked around to see if anyone caught the fiendish theft. The scrap was a silent spy. He turned back towards the house and walked through the sliding door and into the kitchen. He wiped his bare feet on the rug as he stepped inside. His mute companion waited for him. Mr. Kaul and Chloe turned similarly frustrated eyes onto him as he interrupted their continued bickering.

"Mr. Kaul, I am okay to go now," he said softly.

"Sounds good, Yuuta," Mr. Kaul replied. "Do you got everything?"

"Yes, I do." Yuuta turned to the puk-wudjie. "Are you...coming with us?" The creature nodded its head a single time. Yuuta smiled. "Cool. Really cool."

Its blue eyes twisted and sparkled despite the cloud coverage outside. Yuuta felt the urge to pet the creature, but he held his hands at his sides.

"Chloe said that my car is sitting at the side of the road a bit from here, so she'll be taking us," Mr. Kaul noted. "After that, we'll be on the road for a bit, so make sure you use the washroom and fill that stomach with some-"

"Okay, thank you," Yuuta interrupted. He watched Chloe and Mr. Kaul shift their eyes toward each other. He tightened his fists and focused his mind away from the sudden embarrassment. His body clenched at the thought of just running. He wondered to himself why he stood there, as the thoughts of leaving it all behind urged him on like a chatter in the back of his head. His nausea stirred. "I, uh...J-just take me home, please. I can make my own way from there."

Mr. Kaul nodded his head. Yuuta felt his teacher's understanding.

"Okay, bacha, let's get out of here. Grab your things. You're right, no point wasting precious minutes," Mr. Kaul affirmed, pleased with himself.

"Are you sure, Yuuta?" Chloe said. She stepped forward and lifted her hand, but she stopped. "Yuuta, you can stay with us? We can really help you."

"Chloe. Enough," Ogi cautioned. His tone was deep, but not harsh.

Chloe stepped back and shook her head in annoyance but said nothing else. Yuuta took the opportunity to walk past them all through the door and into the sitting room. He picked up the backpack that leaned like a squat goblin against the side of the couch, quickly snuck the hatchet inside, and threw it over his shoulder. The puk-wudjie followed him to the front door and watched as he put on his socks and shoes. Mr. Kaul came up slowly behind the little creature. The man slouched as he stepped methodically from the swinging kitchen door.

"Alright, lets roll out of here," Mr. Kaul recommended as he slipped on his shoes.

Mr. Kaul led the way outside. Yuuta was forced to shield his eyes as clouds broke with a shower of sun-driven arrows. Natural life sprawled across the front yard, unkempt and invasive. An army of twisted weeds, over arching trees, and untrimmed vines crept up the porch railings like a slithering horde. The air vibrated with an unseen energy. He and Mr. Kaul simultaneously inhaled. He heard the melodic call of Natasha like a whispered sonnet as he exhaled. The nature pulsated in harmony like a beating heart. He felt the vibrations through his soles like the footsteps of an approaching titan. He suddenly realized Chloe had joined them on the porch. She had been watching them.

"Ready?" she asked.

Before either Mr. Kaul or he could respond, she stepped down the front-step and walked a skinny gravel path through the overgrown yard. The path opened into a dirt patch that ran down to a single lane street. A red car waited for them. Chloe entered wordlessly into the driver's seat. Mr. Kaul wrapped around the vehicle to the passenger side. Yuuta took the rear driver side seat and his companion crawled across him to sit in the middle. He watched Mr. Kaul flinch and eye the creature warily from the side of his eye.

Chloe started the vehicle and pulled onto the street. She drove for a few minutes before she was forced to take a right onto a wider road. Trees watched them knowingly. He caught the sound of their whispers through the open windows. The beating heart of the world intensified as they approached a silver car abandoned on the gravel shoulder on the opposite side of the road. Mr. Kaul rubbed his forehead. Yuuta wondered if Mr. Kaul felt it too. Chloe made a U-turn after she passed the vehicle and pulled in behind it.

"I would feel better if you let me smudge your car," Chloe said as she turned to Mr. Kaul. "It's a…a purification ceremony. We practice it to cleanse the body, mind, and spirit... The beautiful Earth stirs, Erjun. You must feel it? She's like a waking child crying for her mother. I fear for you. I fear for you both. Please let me do this." The thumping echoed in Yuuta's head like the hammers of Hera's revenge. "Erjun, are you alright?"

Yuuta struggled to decipher any more of her words as he watched the pair through squinted eyes. He tasted pennies in his mouth. His vision was spotted, and the pounding resounded through him. He tried to block the sound as he covered his ears, but it was like the crashing of waves in his ear drums. The puk-wudjie watched him with sparking blue eyes. "Yuuta? Yuuta? Are you okay? Erjun? Yuuta doesn't look so hot."

"I smell you," a hauntingly deep voice spoke inside Yuuta. "The flesh of abinoojiinh…such is the craving of inini-mamiidaawendam. Pure and untested, like a fresh apple. I do not hunger for such things."

Yuuta screamed. The voice of the demon sank deep into his bones. Whispers whipped him, and the great heart of the earth molested him with its concussive drumming. He felt himself lift off his seat. He had risen into the air, as if the sky pulled him into her embrace. A pure blue floated heavenly above him. He felt himself seated against an object. Mr. Kaul sat weakly beside him. Sweat dripped down Mr. Kaul's face. Yuuta heard Chloe's quick steps leave them. She returned with a small stone bowl and a box of matches. She kneeled on the ground between them.

"One life. One creator," she whispered as she struck a match.

She twisted the match against something in the bowl. An herb store smell followed a continuous cloud of white smoke. She waved out the match, before tossing it in with the burning substance. She placed the bowl onto a flat patch of grass at Yuuta's feet. She bathed her hands in the smoke. She cupped them and threw fumes into her face. She repeated the action, but instead brushed the smoke toward her chest and waved it down her body.

"Yuuta, before you, I kneel in the brilliance of Creator. My body clean. My soul purified. Please join me in this smudging to purify you, to balance you. Use your hands to bring the smoke into your eyes and you shall see what is good in yourself and others." Chloe's eyes were closed. She picked up the bowl and held it within his reach. The smoke curled like a spiral staircase into the breeze. He mimicked her and cupped his hands to bring some of the smoke into his eyes. She kept her eyes closed and made no gesture to ensure he followed her guidance. "Yuuta," she continued, "smudge your ears, so that all things that you hear will touch your heart." He carried the smoke in an attempt to bring it to his ears. "Smudge your stomach to cleanse you of your nausea and of those illnesses yet to come." He followed her guidance. "Smudge your feet, for you use them to walk upon our mother earth and should always do so gently." He waved the smoke to his toes. "Smudge your being and you shall find stability and humility in your spirit."

He took a handful of smoke and waved it around his body. Embarrassment reddened his cheeks as she opened her eyes to watch him complete the action in his own way. Before he could say anything, she pulled the bowl away and brought it to Mr. Kaul, who had been watching silently with heavy breaths.

"Erjun, before you I kneel in the brilliance of Creator," she repeated to Mr. Kaul. "My body clean. My soul purified. Please join me in this smudging to purify you, to balance you. Use your hands to bring the smoke into your eyes and you shall see what is good in yourself and others."

Mr. Kaul followed her guidance as she led him through the same closed eye mantra.

Once he had smudged his being, she plucked away the smoking bowl and stood to her feet. She inhaled deeply and began to walk ceremoniously around the car that Yuuta realized they leaned against. She waved the twisting fumes toward the vehicle as if she guided a large paint brush. Her slow steps off the grass and onto gravel were loud in the quiet. The beating heart of the world was soothed. He felt immediate relief from the suffering. The internal torture was a dream he couldn't quite put together. An Atlassian weight lifted off his shoulders. He turned his head exhaustedly to Mr. Kaul. Mr. Kaul rubbed his eyes with his fingers and then wiped away the sweat that dripped in beads down his face.

"Yuuta…What happened? Did you feel everything…shaking?" Mr. Kaul slurred.

"I don't know," Yuuta said, lost in the clarity that cleared his mind.

Chloe finished her circle of the car and placed the burning herbs between them. Yuuta heard a faint crack in the trees, which seemed to form a wall of the forest, and glimpsed blue eyes like lamp lights shifting through them.

"I think he's watching us," Mr. Kaul murmured, his gaze turned similarly in the direction of the flaming orbs. "How does he know to trust her?"

Chloe sat cross-legged in front of them and watched the bowl with adoration.

"I don't know," Yuuta repeated in a whisper. "I trust her too."

"I know…I know," Mr. Kaul nodded.

The peace carried for many minutes. The smoke swirled in a slow trail of white that soon began to thin. Chirping birds brought music to the quiet. A soft blow from the sky, like the breath of a god, lifted the last remnant of the fumes. Chloe watched the bowl for a moment before she picked it up and dumped the ashes at the passenger door of the car, beside Mr. Kaul.

"Erjun, go with peace. Keep him safe. Please… just keep him safe," she urged.

She sighed with one last look at Yuuta and returned to her car. She opened the trunk and placed the bowl inside and wrapped around to the driver's side where she got in. She started the ignition. The low rumble from the engine filled the roadway. Yuuta watched her stare through the windshield. She idled for a few moments then pulled off the gravel. She returned the way they came.

"Well, I guess that's that. We should probably get going," Mr. Kaul suggested as he stood up with an aged moan. He did a tap of his front pockets and his rear right pocket. His relief was clear at his discoveries.

Yuuta stood to his feet too. He brushed the back of his pants off. "You should call your thing back. It's time to get out of here."

"Yes…uh, Puk-wudjie! Puk-wudjie?! We're leaving!" Yuuta shouted, as he curled his hands around his mouth. He and Mr. Kaul listened. He heard nothing. "Puk-wudjie?!"

Only birds answered.

"Do you think it'll follow?" Mr. Kaul asked.

"We're not leaving without him!" Yuuta panicked.

"It could likely keep up with the car, no?"

"We're. Not. Leaving." Yuuta felt his face heat up with the realization of his anger.

"Alright yaar," Mr. Kaul yielded, "keep it together. We can wait for the thing. I'm not trying to aggravate you; I'm simply trying to get us going…You know what, I'll wait for you in the car."

"Mr. Kaul please, I'm…" Yuuta started, but he quietened himself.

Mr. Kaul shrugged his shoulders. He dipped into his pocket and pulled out a black rectangle. He pressed the rectangle and the car lights flashed as the doors clicked. He mimicked Chloe's actions but didn't start the vehicle. He stared at something in his lap instead.

Yuuta took a moment to appreciate the calm. Nothing spoke. Tree leaves shifted in the breeze, but only the wind carried through their branches. He considered the absence of his companion in light of the clarity. He watched the trees cautiously. The sound of

the automatic car window opening behind him distracted him.

"Yuuta, we should get going soon. I can probably grab you something to eat along the way if you like," Mr. Kaul called out.

Yuuta ignored the man. He watched the forest's edge with a sense of purpose. He heard the automatic window close and looked back to see Mr. Kaul looking down the road with a look of frustration. The man was foreign to him. His dark face was shadowed in a dark scruff. His eyes were unkind. He didn't smile or joke. He was no more than a bound servant of Circe. Yuuta distrusted the man's intentions.

Yuuta heard a rustle beyond the forest's edge and returned to watching the spots of light between the trees. There was no sign of the creature. He looked back one more time to confirm Mr. Kaul wasn't watching him, then stepped across the grass and into the forest. An unseen vibration reminded him of the life that ran through each twisted root.

"Puk-wudjie!" he called. "Hello?" He leaned forward and listened. A crow's caw killed the toted silence borne by the trees. Rays of daylight pierced through branches to illuminate the forest floor. A white butterfly fluttered around him and settled unseen into a bush. "Where are you?" His voice echoed. He felt fear like a flame too close to his skin. Its warmth boiled his stomach like a troubled sea whose waters cast up mire and dirt. He wondered at the faintness of his spirit which fought him with each step; a feather weight pinned by what was left of his sanity. "Who am I?" He spiraled inside himself. "I have nobody...I have nothing."

He began to twist his hands. Everything seemed blotchy like an art history painting. He felt the death of his parents like a toxic waste poured over him. A faint whisper fell from the treetops, as leaves rustled in the breeze. He couldn't bear it. The sounds. The pain. The death. It was all a nightmare he carried each day as he dwindled into something wicked. He couldn't understand a sensation of love outliving the burdens of his heart. Everyone was gone. Everything punished him.

"Natasha," a slithering whisper placed in his ear.

Natasha? Natasha...She was his refuge. Her hazelnut eyes were the saviour of his contrite and lowly soul. She was his Jesus.

"He seeks her too," he whispered to himself. "He's desperate...I see the hunger in his black eyes like a rabid dog. He sickens me...He sickens me!" He clenched his hands together and repressed a scream. "I must have her. I must have her for myself."

He lifted his fists and released their grip. He knew Mr. Kaul wouldn't be taking him home. He knew Mr. Kaul would be taking him to her, a witness to the man's twisted fantasy. He knew he had to end it before he could let him get to her. A cold breeze brushed his hair. He shivered.

"Oshikinawe, she is closer than you know," the soft voice of a man whispered in his right ear. He spun to face the hanging limb of a tree. "Come for her...She is in need," it whispered in his left ear. "I can guide you, oshikinawe."

He began to hyperventilate. The peace of the smudging lifted like a sheet pulled off him. Trees bent inward, their whispers like belittling taunts.

"Stop! Stop, please!" he yelled.

"A-a-are you okay, love?" a woman stuttered unseen from somewhere behind him. "I-I-I c-can help you."

His bulging eyes sought for the invisible speaker. He twisted his hands. The whispers were silenced.

"I'm-" He licked his lips and swallowed. "I'm not afraid of you. Please, I'm just lost…Can you help me?"

"Lost?" the unseen woman squeaked. "Oh n-n-n-no, you can't be lost. You're exactly where he wants you t-t-to be, love."

A large woman in a dark blue nurse's outfit slipped between a pair of trees. She slouched her left shouldder. Her short brown hair was a tangled mess of leaves and dirt. Her skin was exposed to the cleavage of her thick chest. Mud was smudged along her chin.

"Are you okay?" he wondered with sincere concern.

'Oh y-y-yes, love." She smiled eerily as she slowly limped toward him like a child of Eurydemus. "I-I-I-I can help you, love. I know the way. C-come with me. I can take you to h-h-her."

"Is she cl-No…No," He tried to shake her out of his head. "I can't. I'm waiting for someone."

"Don't c-cry, love." The woman was only a few long steps away from him. "I can help y-y-you find your friend."

"Do you live out here?" He stepped backwards "Are you a lost doctor or nurse or something? Were you attacked?"

The woman hesitated for a moment and lifted her eyes as if to delve them into her mind.

"I-I-I remember a ch-child. He had black hair… A-a child. My-my child," she stuttered softly. "Only him…I o-only see him. I-I-I can only see him." She began to rock from side to side. She held her stomach as if something was pushing out from the inside. "Him. Misiginebig…Misiginebig…Misiginebig. He is here. H-h-h-he- I serve him. I m-m-must serve him." She grew uncomfortably erratic. She dropped to her knees, then fell to the dirt pleading to the air with her hands locked together. "I serve you. I serve you. I s-s-serve you," she repeated into the flattened plants below her. "I c-can take him to her, p-p-please. Let me take hi-hi-him."

He looked around. No one else was there. He didn't know how far he had gone. He wasn't sure if Mr. Kaul was looking for him or had abandoned him. The deranged woman frightened him, but he pitied her. He saw the pain that stirred inside her. His indecisiveness held him in place. He couldn't move.

"Do you hear him too?"

"Y-y-you hear him? He s-speaks to you?" she mumbled from the ground. Spit flew from her mouth.

"It's more like a…a haunting. He's like a nightmare that keeps slipping into my awake mind. What is he?" Pity softened him. She said nothing. She stared wildly into his eyes. "You don't have to - Just don't worry about it."

"Y-your eyes…Tell me what he s-s-said!" She spat. "I must know n-now. You must tell me. You m-m-m-m-m-must t-tell me." He stepped back. He felt suddenly alarmed by her animalistic stare as she pushed herself onto all fours. "I-I'm sorry. Don't look at me… Don't l-l-look at me. I'm a m-m-monster. Oh God!" She moaned, as she curled her face into her arms. "He-he-help me…Help me please."

"I can't do anything. I'm-I'm just a…I-I don't even know where I am or how to get home, or what to eat or what to think. I have nothing left. I can't give you anything. I have nothing to give you. I'm…I'm just… scared." He stumbled backwards.

"W-we must go to her, love," she whispered suddenly. She quickly stood and stepped toward him until she was inches from his face. "I-I-I can take you th-there? She isn't f-far. She's to be l-l-l-laid in the embrace of the weeping willow." The woman's breath smelt like turned soil. Yuuta was comforted by her. He felt an odd sensation of safety and loyalty, like a time grown relationship between a master and their pet. He said nothing. She watched him with excitement. "I c-c-can take you there? I-I-I can, love. Th-th-that's exactly what he wants."

"Doesn't he frighten you?"

"Oh no no no no. N-n-no, frighten m-me? He i-i-i-i-is everything. He sees ev-ev-everything, love. He is the Lord like my grandma used t-to tell me of. Th-th-

the voice that g-guides all. S-spirit of the sun, s-stars, sky, earth. We n-n-need him," she extolled.

"Do I frighten you, abinoojiinh?" the masculine voice spoke from behind him. Yuuta turned quickly. There was a man who leaned against a thick tree. His hair slithered in great black strands behind his shoulders to the back of his knees, like tamed roots. He had a handsome square face. His eyes blazed like a swirling yellow nebula. He had a twisted necklace of black shimmering stones around his neck. His chest was bare. His arm was wrapped in a black tattoo. He wore snug black pants that were decorated in colored scales. "Do you fear me, child?" the man asked again. His voice was alluring. "You are a seedling. Do you think she has a need for such an undeveloped pod? Although, she could give you great power…" Yuuta felt the ground shift as if snakes twirled at his feet. He looked down to watch damp roots unravel from the dirt like the tentacles of a kraken sloshing out of an ocean. Branches creaked and flexed as they came to life. "Do you fear me?!"

"L-l-l-lord, bless me. B-bless me," the woman released in adoration. She lifted her hands to the man behind Yuuta. "I-I-I s-serve only you, Lord God."

A branch swung down and swept the woman away. She landed against a waking tree. She slid slowly down its vibrating trunk. She didn't move as she balled at the bottom. Blood added to the stains of dirt along her chin as it dripped down her face.

"Bagwanawizi gichi-mookomaan," the man chuckled, breaking his square face with a suave smile.

"W-who are you?" Yuuta choked out.

"You know nothing of who or what I am?" The man held up and examined his necklace in a ray of the sun. "This is the flesh of my flesh."

Yuuta watched the ominous figure. He pulled his arms into his chest as a damp breeze misted him.

"Yuuta?!" Mr. Kaul yelled from behind the man. "Saala kutta! Get away from him!"

The man sighed, and before Mr. Kaul could break through the trees, he was grabbed by hanging branches. The man smelt the air.

"He stinks of her, as you do," the man snarled. He waved his hand as if casually swatting an insect. The trees groaned angrily. Roots locked Yuuta's feet in place. Mr. Kaul yelled. "She does need you, abinoojiinh, but...I suppose a man would be best. May Nimishoomis take your spirit and bless the land with your ashes, to be spread like falling snow across the shoulders of the turtle." The man bowed his head.

He dropped his hands in an orchestrative motion and Yuuta felt the roots pull his legs in opposite directions. Searing pain shot through his groin as he tried to resist himself being torn in two.

A great growl suddenly echoed across the trees as rapid thudding grew closer. The man scolded something behind Yuuta and slithered like a flitting shadow into the treetops.

A thrashing of movement and sound encouraged Yuuta to look to his left where a hairless bear battled swaying tree limbs. Each limb it shattered sprayed the earth in water, like blood across the dirt. The beast roared at the sky as it bouldered a large tree over with an impact from its shoulder. Yuuta's peripherals caught a movement of slithering black and returned his pained stare to where the man had stood. In the place of the man, a shimmering black spiral of glistening scales uncoiled. An enormous snake with the torso and head of a reptilian-man stuck out a forked tongue. Its other-worldly stare locked Yuuta's.

"I am giiwanaadingwaam that will haunt you and your ancestors until the demise of your line. To the dirt like frightened mice shall you return," a demonic voice hissed through the trees.

The bear maneuvered beside Yuuta, through the strangling roots. Nature's debris scattered the forest floor, muddy from the water that drained from each wooden limb. It snarled wildly and sliced the roots that stretched him like a doll in the hands of a toddler. He tripped awkwardly as he tried to stand upright.

The great, black man-serpent recoiled as if to strike, but it stopped and held its celestial eyes on the beast beside Yuuta. The bear roared. Its eyes slashed and sparked. The blue flames flared like wind whipped torches out of its eye sockets and across its face.

"Yuuta, come on!" Mr. Kaul hissed through his teeth. The man-snake whipped its head around and considered Mr. Kaul. There was a moment of hesitation. Mr. Kaul was held in place as if prepared for sacrifice.

His eyes bulged. He suddenly clenched his face. "Fuu–uck!"

The blue–eyed beast roared violently. Trees and earth shook. Yuuta was late to covering his ears as the explosive noise deafened him. The man–snake turned its head back to face them.

"Dare not trust the servants of Nanabozho," it hissed angrily.

It suddenly collapsed to the earth as hundreds of smaller, black serpents. The snakes scrambled through the labyrinth of twisted roots and vanished.

A strangely soft breeze shook the leaves of the statuesque trees whose limbs were entangled unna-turally. The beast beside Yuuta breathed heavily, as it investigated the ground. A pointed branch protruded from a gap between two plates of its rock-like skin. A green mossish fungal infection swelled like dry blood out of the wound. The moss grew along the embedded stick until the brown bark was replaced by the green coating. It walked slowly to Mr. Kaul and shattered the roots and branches that wrapped around his arms and legs.

Yuuta looked to the base of nearby trees for the woman. He found her limp, with the roots of a tree curl-ing over her like frozen claws. The earth drank the blood that ran off her swollen face.

"Mr. Kaul! She needs our help," he called out. He turned to see the beast sit down, its eyes now quelled flickers of lapis lazuli. Mr. Kaul limped over to him. His teacher had bags under his eyes and massaged his left shoulder. "Mr. Kaul, we should take her to a hospital."

"Yuuta…we need to get out of here. This whole crap show…It's gone too far," Mr. Kaul sighed.

They both lifted their heads as another breeze blessed them.

"I-I think we should take her to…*her*," Yuuta suggested after the breeze had passed.

"Natasha…" Mr. Kaul said absently to himself. "Yes, I mean, uh, of course. That…that seems like the right thing to do, I think."

Yuuta watched Mr. Kaul curiously. He knew the torrent that flushed through the man's veins, as it pumped like wriggling insects through his own. There was a shame in seeing this man as he was: vile eyes and twisted thoughts. A man with vivid intentions, with a reliance on the steppingstones that paved his way. Yuuta knew the monster that grew inside Mr. Kaul. He also knew that Mr. Kaul had to die.

Chapter 10

Natasha looked up at the ropes that scraped like sand-paper across her wrists. She breathed shakily. She strained to look down at her body. Blood painted her breasts. The dry bark was like pointed gravel at her back. The flat surface of the ground was just within reach of her toes. She struggled to support her bandaged ankle on her opposite foot's heel. Her calves ached in exhaustion. Her wounds burned.

The whipping sound of a stick switch was a metronome in her head as it came in random slaps against her. She tried not to resist, as each movement was a torturous friction along her slashed body. She cried softly instead. She internalized a prayer that it would end in her death. Endless fire-smoke blinded and choked her. The crackling of a flame filled the silence between each whip.

"It's okay. It's okay. Just keep breathing. Shh, Shh, he'll be here soon," the tan skinned nurse con-solingly smiled, breathing heavily.

"Stop! Christ...Please!" Natasha cried. "Why... Why are you doing this? Please-"

"You must be cowed, bitch," the nurse growled with a flick of the stick. Her face quickly returned to a childish grin.

"Why are you helping him?" Natasha pleaded. "You don't need to do this…Please. I-I won't say anything. Just let me go. Whatever he is, he's using you. You don't need to do this. You don't need to do this…"

"Don't you know?" the nurse smiled. "Don't you know?"

"Know…what? I don't know anything that's going on…" Natasha cried. "I don't even know if…if this is even…real. Where are we? Why are you doing this? Please…Nothing…Nothing is worth this."

"It's okay. Shhh, shhh, it's okay. Just breathe through it. Just breathe," the nurse muttered sincerely, as she whipped Natasha across the thighs. Natasha sucked in between her teeth as the pain seared through her. "I can't stop. I'm sorry." The nurse giggled strangely. Natasha felt the slash of the switch again and again. She spluttered in pain. "It's okay. Shhh, shhh, shhh. It's okay." Natasha could feel the nurse's eyes looking at her chest.

"Please don't…Please, no more. Please," Natasha groaned.

The nurse's face looked innocent, but her eyes were lightless voids. Natasha felt the nurse trace the stick in a trail of blood that dribbled down toward her groin.

"Don't be scared…It's okay…He said to keep you alive…Yes, yes, I'm sorry, but you must be prepared. I… I said I would prepare you for the sowing. And once… once the seed has been planted, he will need me. He will *need* me. Don't you know?" The nurse stopped the point of the stick just below Natasha's belly button. The fire's flames silhouetted the nurse in orange. The nurse suddenly screamed as she lashed Natasha along the side of her buttocks. "And this is all because of you. You brought me to him. Thank you! Thank you! You have no idea…He…he is empowering…He's a god. You can see the universe in his eyes. His…his golden-brown skin in the moonlight. I need him. I need him!"

"He'll kill you…He'll kill you, whatever he is," Natasha breathed. "He is…nothing…You…you will be killed."

The girl laughed and slashed Natasha across the breasts. Whatever was left of her resilience broke. She released her final energy in a pained howl. She slouched like a dead animal against her restraints. She prayed that the girl would just do it. She blinked through gaps of unawareness. A blur of white teeth was etched like a burned TV image under her closed eyelids. She gagged and spluttered as her mouth was forced open and water poured into her throat.

"Don't you dare die, bitch," the girl spat angrily, her stern jaw clenched. "I need you for him. I need this!"

The nurse lined up the stick against Natasha's side and whipped her in a continued succession. She took the blows lifelessly. She felt the abandonment of faith, as if she was being nailed to a Caucasian mountain. The nurse grunted with each slash to her skin.

"Savour the tender bite of mortality, forsaken daughter, for you shall be my blessing to Oziisigobiminzh," a masculine voice said. The nurse imme- diately stopped whipping her.

"My lord...I-I have her here, as you asked," the nurse said. "I have prepared this ugly cow for you. How can I serve you? Let me serve you."

Natasha opened her eyes reluctantly. The nurse was on her knees. At the edge of the fire stood a man cloaked in darkness.

"Animosh! Come!" the man demanded as he waved at the nurse with irritation. The girl scrambled up and dashed to the shadow's feet. Her anemone scrubs were covered in dirt and droplets of blood. The blood shimmered in the firelight.

"Thank you...Thank you, I shall serve only you," the girl praised.

"Stand, worm," he demanded. The girl listened without hesitation. Her scrubs hung loosely off her. She was significantly shorter than him. The shadows of the flames made him appear as if great black wings spread from behind his back. "Speak no more," he stressed slowly, as he penetrated the girl with an unforgettable stare. He gripped the girl's hair and pulled her head back in an aggressive wrench. She squealed but didn't contest his assault. "Open." He tapped a finger to the girl's lips. The girl opened her mouth. Natasha couldn't look away. He lifted his other hand and pulled the bottom of the girl's jaw open. He shoved his hand into the open mouth. The girl choked and gurgled as he removed his hand with a jerk. The flames glistened off the saliva that glazed the tongue he pincered between his fingers. The girl collapsed hysterically to the ground. Blood spluttered out of her mouth like thick black oil. The man stepped over the wriggling girl and walked slowly toward Natasha. "I have no need for such swine." He lifted Natasha's head with his fingers. He held the tongue at his side nonchalantly and cracked his face with a charming grin. "What is your name, oshki-niigikwe?" His voice was disgustingly affable. He pulled her stare into his own. "I feel the blood pulsing through your body...Oh my, what has this beastling done? Tsk tsk tsk tsk tsk." He dragged the girl's tongue along a trail of blood between her breasts. "So sweet."

"Stop it!" Natasha spat. She was too weak to struggle. "Stop!"

The man blinked slowly and licked his lips.

"You shall submit to me," he snapped. He whipped the tongue to the ground. The girl screeched behind him like a frightened pig.

Natasha felt tears bubble in her eyes. The restraints prevented her from wiping them away.

"Get the hell away from me!" She screamed. "Please...God, please."

The man slammed his large fist beside her head. The shape of his angered face was reptilian. His eyes tossed like stormed waters under a yellow sky.

"You must..." the man seethed. He slowly calmed himself. "You must come with me willing to Oziisigobiminzh."

"Who are you? Why...Why...?"

"I am but a slave to meshkwadoon," he waved;

his anger suppressed. His face was handsome again. His black hair had a crystalline sheen.

"I don't understand…" she wept. "I don't understand…

"Neither do I, ikwezens," he confessed, as he smelt her hair. "You are much more flowered than is usual, but maybe more ripened is sweeter?" He stooped to pick up the stick that dripped with her blood. She pinched her eyes closed. She refused to acknowledge the fiend's words. "The thought of man's youthful appetite disturbs me. What is he but a ravenous and sickly fiend that strikes the most vulnerable? Beasts consumed by a need to be sexually gratified." She looked up at him, but he was staring beyond her. "There is no need to resist, ikwezens." He fingered the stick and brought his unearthly gaze back down upon her. "Be one with me. Our seed will free the land of the ticks that feed off Hahnunah like a wounded sow. We shall be unburdened by the foulness of the proud and the profane. Let us feast on the flesh of life, ikwezens."

She restrained herself from following his exotic deep voice but failed. She hung to every word. His yellow eyes twisted, and she felt his spirit reach into her. Her thirst was satiated as if each inhalation of his soul could sustain her from death. He abruptly broke the invisible bond and turned away from her. His head faced the darkness beyond the dwindling flames.

"Three come now. Two will die. As from a cycle must be raised the seed's ganawenjige. Death will come easy for this one…I saw it in his eyes," he foretold.

A horrid choking squeal behind the man ended with a voiceless gurgle. The man turned back to face Natasha. He edged forward and his bronze skin touched her. She winced.

"It's not real…It's not real," she insisted to herself. "It-it's just too much…It's just…It's-it's too much."

"It is very real, ikwezens," he sneered. "It is more real than the blood that drips down your navel."

"I-I can't do this. Please, you have to listen," she begged.

He laughed. The sound lifted like a bird's call into the dark sky.

"To laugh! What a thing!" he shouted then breathed in deeply. "Internal and glorious. A pig rolled on its back. A chariot of truth. A brother's zhawen-jigewin and his lash. It is of the voice of *He* beyond the sky. The pleasure of akiwenziiyag. It is the spirit of life. Laugh ikwezens! How do you bear such burdens without laughter? There is much darkness in you, ikwezens…Are you truly the daughter of Muzzu-Kum-mik-Quae?"

"It's just too-"

A snapping of branches screamed through the trees. A murder of crows tossed into the air and flew away like ink blotches against the patches of visible night sky.

"A familiar scent?" the man taunted with a smile. He threw the bloodied stick to the ground and stepped backward. The dying orange glow behind him made his shadow press against her. A moist and cool mist soothed her naked body. "Strange is the allure of snakes on women, strange is the disdain of men," he said, as he spilled into an unraveling pile of black serpents at her feet.

"Oh shit!" she shrieked as she made painful attempts to lift her toes off the earth.

The snakes slithered into the darkness. The unkept fire wavered, as the last burning log crumbled with a silent spray of sparks. It left behind a soft glow of embers.

A dark shape broke through the blackness of the trees beyond the dying fire. She squinted to distinguish the lumpy figure. A second shape came in behind the first. A pair of unilluminating blue lights hovered in last.

"It's her…" a youthful voice noted.

"Yuuta, wait," a man snapped.

She erected her head to the shadows coming toward her. She felt the need to plead, but she couldn't summon the strength. She felt burned and choked. Her body felt flayed and damp. Her muscles were seized. She shivered. She was freezing. Cold bitten like a child pulled out of an icy lake.

A man stepped into her vision. His bulk was explained by a hidden person he supported. The embers provided no assistance in revealing the shadowed figure leaning into the man's right side. The man's dark hair was disheveled. He had a round nose and a soft chin. She could feel him watching her, though his eyes were hidden.

"Who…who are you?" she asked weakly.

The man said nothing, as a boy shyly came in beside him. The boy was tall, and his face was pale. He twisted his hands together nervously. His eyes looked black in the darkness.

"I'm Arjun," the man offered cautiously.

"I'm-I'm Yuuta," the boy stuttered.

"This woman…I'm not sure who she is," Arjun said, indicating the huddled shape he supported with an awkward shrug.

The blue lights sparkled at Yuuta's feet. She broke from their stares to examine the flickering glow. She gasped as its face lit up in the radiance of its own dying light. She shivered again.

"It's real," Yuuta said. "We can…we can see it too."

"C-can you please help me?" she begged.

Arjun and Yuuta quickly looked at each other, then the boy rushed to her. He kept his eyes to the side as he reached for the bonds around her wrists. The man grimaced, hobbled the unnamed woman to a spot in the darkness, and limped in beside the boy. The man's eyes dragged from her chest to her eyes, then to the bonds Yuuta worked at. She saw the boy side eye the man with unsaid aggravation and then stop, as if struck abruptly with a thought.

Yuuta went into a backpack he twisted off his back and removed a small hatchet spotted with rust. He looked at it quietly. He said nothing as he maneuvered to her side and began slicing the blade along the taut rope above her wrists.

"Deva! Where'd you get that, Yuuta?" Arjun inquired with concern.

Yuuta whispered to himself but said nothing distinct. He sliced back and forth with focused determination. Arjun watched the boy before he turned his concerned eyes to her. She stared at a droplet of sweat that twinkled down his cheek.

"Don't mind him…he's a bit shy," Arjun said. "It's Arjun…Arjun, like I said before…not just Arjun, but Arjun Kaul, I mean."

"Why are you here…?" she asked through her pain.

"We….umm, well–"

"You're the face…That man…That man I saw," she said with a start.

"Ahh, yes. I saw you. Really, we saw you…in Algonquin," he revealed slowly.

"Why…Who–"

The bonds that held her snapped. She fell like a rubber dummy into Arjun. He struggled to hold up the dead weight she rested on him. The boy slipped his arms under hers from behind. They held her with an awkward struggle. She winced. Her wounds raged with a spiking fury. Her ankle felt like a numb bowling ball hanging from her shins. As Yuuta and Arjun directed her to the dead fire, they both stopped as they suddenly realized the curled corpse twisted into itself like a beetle.

"Arre baap re…" Arjun coughed with a gag.

Yuuta said nothing.

"She was…It wasn't me…Some kind of man…"

she tried to explain. Arjun's sweaty hands vibrated under the strain of holding her up. Her body pulsed as it flushed blood through her fiery extremities. She envied the peace of the corpse. "Can you close her eyes?" No one moved. They watched the disfigured shape quietly. "Someone…please close her eyes. Can she not have the dignity to leave this shit behind, rather than having it stained on her soul?"

The two moved Natasha awkwardly to a nook in a large tree. She clenched her teeth from the pain of the cold earth against her mauled skin. Arjun stood to go to the corpse, but Yuuta quickly set to his feet to look upon it. He crouched down at its face. After a few odd seconds he reached into its dark shape and pulled his hand back. He stood up. His gaze was still on it. Arjun walked over and gripped Yuuta's shoulder. The boy flinched from the sudden touch. He looked up at Arjun, then turned his angered face on her. His distinct black eyes caught her breath.

"Natasha…I can help you. Something in me tells me I must. It's so strong. I need to be with you," Yuuta vowed as he walked toward her.

"What–what do you mean?" She grimaced.

He didn't respond. His skinny, tall form towered over her. He removed his hooded sweater and draped it over her chest. She pulled it over her enough to cover her breasts and blood mopped pubic region. Yuuta look-ed away considerately. She caught Arjun with the side of her eyes openly watching her.

"We need to leave here," Arjun worried, seemingly unaware of his shame.

"T-t-the willow tree…" a muffled voice from the darkness squeaked. "We n-n-n-need to get her to the w-w-willow tree." The forgotten shadow shuffled by the base of the tree where Natasha had been tied. "H-he will b-b-be back."

As the hidden woman struggled forward, Natasha recognized the large shoulders and dark blue scrubs.

"How?" Natasha breathed. "The other one… She…"

The nurse limped closer; her left shoulder slouched. Her face was swollen and covered in dried streams of blood and patches of dirt.

"We must b-b-be gone by the time h-he gets back," the nurse stuttered. Natasha's eyes stretched at the site of the woman's limping form. She tried to yell, but nothing came out. Her thoughts reached out to Arjun desperately. "It's t-t-too late. Too late. It's t-t-t-too late. He's here," the nurse stuttered, as she looked around like a crazed woman.

They all looked around. There was no wind. There were no birds. No animals called or whined or wailed. The trees hearkened to the night's desire for quiet. The sagging nurse in torn azure breathed heavily. Her shaking form radiated fear.

"Natasha…that is your name? Na-ta-sha. Beautiful," a whispering wisp emanated from a distant spot in the darkness. "I said there would be three, Na-ta-sha, and three there shall be."

"Don't listen to the beast!" a ragged voice shouted. "He's a forsaken devil!" The shape of a curl-shouldered man stood by the dark orange embers. His hidden face was matted by long hair and a thick dark beard. "You must run. You must all run now!" The man was frightened. Yuuta sucked in a quick breath of air. Arjun jolted his head to look to the newcomer. Neither of them moved. "This creature…We must go now!" The blue-eyed creature puffed its shoulders weakly. A green and rotted stick protruded like an additional limb from its abdomen. The man turned his head onto her and froze. "By Odin…" he croaked. "You...you look just like her...Natasha, you must go." A cackle reverberated like a whip of thunder across the rainless sky. "Feikinstafir!"

"Maamakaadakamig! We have found you all, as one," a malevolently deep voice spoke. Its tone seemed pleased but for its monstrous hollowness. She recognized its earthy sound.

"It's here…" she breathed to herself.

The blue-eyed creature growled weakly. A shadow stepped forward, darkening the space it filled.

"Do you still seek death, ivory flower?" the deep voice asked. Its words filled the air like a cold breeze.

Her wounds felt a semblance of soothing from the coolness against her burning body.

"Please..." she prayed.

She begged for absolution from the twisted fantasy that spun like a widow's web in her mind. She was exhausted of will. A shiver shook her bones. Despite the cool relief, her body burned in a flaming rage. Her ankle violently twinged. The earth vibrated with the essence of an unseen energy.

"This? This is nothing. A flitting fly life." The figure stepped into a stray moon ray that broke through the branches. Its hair, like a lion's black mane, swayed in the breeze of its presence. It had a four-lined scar across its cheek. "Yesss. Yesss. You are but a sprout."

"Stop!" Yuuta yelled. "No more…Look at her! Look at her!"

The being laughed.

"Holy Deva…" Arjun cursed under his breath.

"Jiibayaabooz, you join us?" the handsome man said as he stepped beside Natasha from an unknown hiding place. He squatted and placed his warm hand on her shoulder. Yuuta stirred on her other side.

"You are zhaagwaadizi, snake," the hermaphroditic being said. Its voice frosted the air. The leaves on the trees curled inward as if seeking warmth. "I have not come for you, dirt dweller."

"Are you not of my blood?" the handsome man snarled. "Take your unsightly maji-manidoo and be gone."

The hermaphroditic figure laughed. Its frosted essence chilled her spine. The burning of her body was replaced with the discomfort of her vibrating limbs. She couldn't move. She was trapped. She felt herself becoming one with the earth like the fungus that infected the blue-eyed creature's wound. Death would be a beautiful release from the burden of this suffering. She closed her eyes.

"Where is she?" Yuuta demanded of the man whose hand was gripped like warming stove elements on her shoulder, "My-my sobo…Where is she?" The being and the handsome man laughed as the boy's voice cracked. The twisting of their putrid noise was a swirling black maelstrom of horror. "Where is she!?"

The living webs of the world vibrated. Trees trembled and whined. The earth creaked like an unlubed machine. The blue-eyed creature stumbled to its knees. All things were synchronized in their discomfort.

"Maamakaadakamig!" the scar-faced being bellowed.

The handsome man lifted from his squat. He considered Yuuta.

"What do you know of meshkwadoon, abinoojinh?" the handsome man pursued mysteriously. He stepped around her and toward the boy. Yuuta didn't move. His dark eyes were hate filled.

"Where is she?" Yuuta demanded. "The vines… It was you."

"Ah…such is the tragedy of the ganawenjige," the handsome man explained soothingly. He brushed the boy's cheek with his hand. "So warm. So full of life."

"You sickening serpent," the ragged man growled. "Your scaled hands are the truth of your words. He's a child. Take the man."

"Arre baap re…" Arjun breathed.

"No!" Natasha released. Her voice lifted out of her like a wood-instrument's cantabile screech. "Stop this…This is…this is crazy. The world isn't this…It can't be this…"

"Yes, oh yes," the scar-faced hermaphrodite laughed. Its shrill sound was haunting. "Oh, to taste you. What a treat. Feast, windigo, feast on their flesh and on their fear!" A massive shadow slunk out of the darkness. Hauntingly red eyes motioned with each step it took until it stopped beside the strange figure. The smell of turned raw meat filled her nostrils. "Smell them. Taste them. Feast!"

A large, pale, and lanky shape walked toward them. Its white skin separated it from the surrounding darkness. Its red eyes looked between them all animalistically.

"You are a beast, Jiibayaa…" the handsome man hissed. He turned away from the stunned Yuuta to confront the strange figure. The hermaphrodite's chalky face was wrinkled in crazed excitement. "You dare give passage to the waabiiganaandam?"

The pale creature did not abide the hesitation and it sprung like a four-limbed milky spider at the ragged man. The ragged man dodged to the side. He maneuvered around trees as the beast continued its barrage. Its long-clawed hands were like pincerless crabs spraying chunks of wood each time they missed.

The blue-eyed creature pushed itself onto its hind legs. It swayed but clenched its little fists and solidified its shoulders. It looked no more threatening than an anxious rabbit.

"Run, boy! Natasha, run!" the ragged man's raspy voice called from the forest darkness.

"Fool!" the handsome man yelled at the hermaphroditic being. "She is mine."

"No, no, no, nooo, nishiime. You are mistaken. Oh yes, you are mistaken. What power do you have, water serpent? Hmm? You believe Anishinaabe see only Anishinaabe beauty? They see a lidless pest of the earth." The scar-faced being listed its hands and the trees shook as a deep blackness spread like opaque smoke among them. She felt someone lift her and pull her into their sweaty embrace. "Flee children! Run, run, run, children. We smell you. We taste you. Run for your lives!" Its deep voice bellowed through her mind.

The person carrying her stumbled. She knew it struck him too, like a sudden debilitating blast. She saw nothing through the black cloud. Her eyes were heavy. A lashing branch slapped her, but she didn't feel it through the numbness. She felt nothing through the numbness.

Chapter 11

"Holy Deva…Holy Deva…Holy Deva," Arjun breathed heavily as he stumbled through the forest.

The world of darkness vibrated. His arms quaked under the weight of Natasha's naked body. He felt Khatta ma'am's whippings with each swiping branch.

The black smoke had faded like an overstretched cloud, and he suddenly understood that he had abandoned Yuuta to the madness. He slowed his pace as the boy's face filled his thoughts.

"I have to keep going," he breathed to himself as he looked down at the woman in his arms. "I must save you. I have to save you."

He stumbled as he requickened into a trot. He felt his arms weaken under the strain of the recovery. His limbs demanded respite. He prayed continuously for relief, until suddenly the trees opened in response to his zealous calls. He ripped through the natural doorway as if he was rushing for a washroom to release his muddy bowels. He stumbled from the grass and dirt to the gravel shoulder of a road. He fell to his knees and his arms almost gave out.

He breathed exhaustively as he lay his porcelain

bundle onto the rocks. Each deep breath felt like his last. He craved water, as balls of saliva filled his mouth like moist cotton swabs. Sweat soaked him. He coughed aggressively. He struggled to compose himself. He couldn't spit the coppery taste out of his mouth. He looked down to the closed eyed woman. She was just like he found her the first time. His eyes drank in her naked body. She was covered in crusted blood and shallow slices.

"Those little fff-" he spat furiously as he examined the wounds. "Fuckers." She breathed softly. She looked peaceful. He shifted. Her breasts moved. He examined her body thoroughly. "This is crazy, isn't it?"

The trees swayed quietly. They no longer seemed to show conscious concern for him. The blanket of silence reassured him. He felt the residual tranquility of Chloe's smudging. His breathing found the lightness of equilibrium. He put his hand on the pale woman's stomach. Its warmth intoxicated him. He traced a slash along her hipline with his finger. He pulled his hand quickly away at the distant sound of an animal's bark. He somehow felt its excitement as the trail it sought became stronger. He felt it sniffing for him.

"This way! She's got something!" a voice called.

A more distant bark joined the first dog's. Trees rustled across the road. He could see moving shapes through the dark, then a quick flicker of a roving flashlight. He knelt without moving as a single dog on a leash and its handler slowly crossed the road to them. The dog tried to pull the handler right on top of them, but the man quickly heeled the beast.

"You! Get on the ground! Put your face in the dirt!" The dog reignited with the handler's sudden aggression toward Arjun. "Get the fuck on the ground!" Arjun slid weakly to the rough gravel. He dragged his gravity restricted arms to his front. "Stretch your arms out in front of you. Stretch them out!" The dog pulled wildly at the leash. The white light of the flashlight blinded Arjun. "Face in the dirt. Don't look at me! Look left! No, my left! Look left!" Arjun tasted the dust of the rocks that were kicked up by the commotion. He stretched as much as his body would accommodate him. His muscles were driven by fear. "Stretch your feet out! Stand up! Come on!" The dog's barking added to the abuse. Arjun tried to stand. "Stop!" the handler demanded when Arjun was back on his knees. He stretched his hands out desperately toward the man's black boots. "Turn! Turn! Was there a stutter? Turn your fucking body!" The handler was dragged forward, and the dog's gnashing was inches away from Arjun's nose.

"I'm trying, saala kutta! I'm trying…" Arjun spat. He shook with anger and felt the sweat of his anxieties leaking from every pore.

"Did I say speak, Babu? Put your face in the fucking dirt!"

"Derrick. Derrick, it's all good," a female's humoured voice said. "We got this one. We need to find the boy."

The dog's ravenous attempts at Arjun quelled

instantly as the slobbering beast was pulled toward the forest by the handler. Its barking continued into the trees.

Arjun turned to the road to watch one of the Inspectors from the hospital approach from the other side. She was trailed by another handler, the handler's searching German Shepherd, and Dr. Mardin.

"No one touch them," Dr. Mardin stated as she ran to kneel beside Natasha. "What happened to her? Tell me, Arjun."

"They…they tortured her," he lamented. He tried to keep the fear and anger from showing on his face.

"Who? Who tortured her?" she pushed.

"I, uh…I don't know. Saala kutta, I don't know," he swore.

"Call it in," the Inspector delegated to the dog handler that arrived with her.

"Yes mam," the handler said. He pulled away and engaged his radio.

"Gloves on, Naydeen," Dr. Mardin said. "We need to make sure that no one touches either of these two…"

"W-will she be okay?" Arjun asked through his panting.

"Mr. Kaul, we warned you," Naydeen said, as she stepped forward. "We trusted you would go home and stay away from this. Now look what the hell we find…"

The trees shivered. He could feel their troubled spirits like a tingle on the back of his aching arms. There was no wind. The night was calm. Stars spread across the visible sky like a spilled bottle of glitter. A crow cawed from somewhere close by. The words of everyone around him were mosquitos in his ears. Disdain grew in his gut like a malignant cyst.

His internal smoldering was interrupted by a deep pop that echoed like a concussive firework from inside the forest behind him. A series of distinct cracks followed in quick succession. The remnant of their echo held in the air with a soft ringing. The Inspector shot a look to the handler fingering the radio at his chest.

"Mark, radio Derrick," Naydeen commanded.

"Romeo two-four-one - Romeo two-four-one, this is Delta two-one-one, report, over?" Mark spoke into his chest.

Everyone was silent as they anticipated a response. The trees bristled with an ecstasy. They bristled with the taste of life. Another two pops followed. They held their silence.

"Ten-twenty-four, wait out," a barely audible voice crackled over the radio. Another pop rang.

"Shit!" Naydeen cursed. "Call it in, Mark."

Mark stepped away with his canine in tow and became distracted by conversation with his radio.

"What's going on, El?" Naydeen asked Dr. Mardin.

"We-we should go…She must be protected," Arjun cautioned, sensing their fear. "They're coming. The weird shit…It's all coming. We have to go."

The two women stared at each other. Another

three low and heavy pops filled the air. The permanence of the sound chilled him.

Aggressive rustling announced something rushing toward them from the forest. His vision was suddenly filled by a frightened black faced German Shepherd. It dove rabidly at him. He felt its jaws wrap around his arm like a crushing weight as he shielded his face. It wrenched him like a caught rabbit. The clenching teeth were like a vice-grip. The darkness was blurred around him as he weakly tried to fend off the snarling beast. Barking and yelling intensified the blur. A crackling snap was followed by the dog's squeal as it jolted into the forest.

"That's not-How?" Mark fretted.

The officer's hands were wrapped in the leash he struggled to maintain. The dog bit at the air wildly, as if snapping at something flying around its head. He pulled the dog away to calm its nerves. Naydeen tossed her used taser to the dirt.

"I got Natasha. El, help Mark with this idiot when the canine is heeled. We need to get the hell outta here. Shut her up, Mark," Naydeen hollered over her shoulder.

Their panting encroached upon the roadway's quiet as they trundled along its gravel shoulder. Arjun's arm burned under the makeshift bandage wrapped by Dr. Mardin. It pulsed with heat. He didn't trust his mind to gauge its functionality. He cradled it to his chest. Naydeen carried Natasha in her arms. Natasha was nestled against her like a child. The Inspector glistened in the dark from the sweat that bubbled out of her, as the light of a flashlight swung with their hasty movements. Arjun limped with the aid of Dr. Mardin, who breathed unathletically. The handler trailed behind, his dog's barks a beacon of sound.

Blue and red light rolled off the trees around a bend in the road like vibrant strobes in the darkness. Three OPP vehicles and a blue SUV blockaded their path. A pair of uniformed officers talked as they manned the block. One of the officers spotted them approaching and turned to confront them. He hesitated with his hand hovered by his waist, until he realized Naydeen and her burden.

"Ambulance is on the way, mam," the officer called. He broke away from the other officer to help Naydeen. "We've got APS setting up blocks."

"Don't worry about me…just…don't touch her," Naydeen said to him through light gasps.

Suddenly Arjun smelt it. The death. It hungered. The canopy above recoiled. He tried to break free, but Dr. Mardin stubbornly held him erect.

"We… must… go," he breathed. "It's coming… We have to leave…now. Listen to me! Arre baap re, there's something coming…I can feel it."

The air thickened with its stench. The police officers ignored him. Dr. Mardin stopped.

"What is coming?" she inquired.

"Pale death…" he warned.

Laughter split across the blockade with the force of a bugle. Darkness crept toward them like stretching fog. The lit spaces were consumed by blackness. The stars were blanketed as if clouds suddenly blew across the sky. The others seemed to see nothing. The flashing blue and red were consumed by it. It was a murky lightless mist that consumed all things.

"Do you fear the darkness? Why…why do you think all Anishinaabeg fear the utter blackness of night? Do you fear the darkness of your own soul?" the demonic voice of the red-gloved figure spoke. It was like a deep howl carried by the shadows.

"It's-it's here," he panicked. "Here…among us."

He broke free of Dr. Mardin, his body rejuvenated by the fear.

"Arjun? Arjun, you need to calm down," a muffled voice spoke through the dark, as if the cloud was a wall that separated him from the others. "Arjun, relax…Sit down. We are right here? Can you hear us?"

"Yes," he spoke excitedly, as he reached out for someone to guide him. He couldn't see anything. "Hello? Natasha? I-I can't see."

There was nothingness, until a set of scarlet glowing embers stepped into clarity. They were like sparkling droplets of blood suspended in the air. They vanished with a blink and re-emerged closer. He had to crane his neck to them. They moved toward him at a consistent pace. He smelt its rancid vapours.

"I need to feed. I was promised flesh and bone. Blood like nectar on my tongue. I need to feed. I need to feed," the evil spoke.

He backed up slowly until he bumped into an

unseen object. The deep red floating orbs hovered feet from him. He felt each step it took. Strange deep head shaking echoes vibrated through the blackness. He could hear a dog barking savagely somewhere in the distance. The red orbs flicked out of site. He spun to follow their darting trail, as they swiveled from left to right through the black like a waltzing pair of insects. He swore he could hear screams in the distance. He felt his shoulder pulled away from the red eyes, but he resisted and pulled back aggressively. The invisible force pulled at him again, but he swung away from it. The eyes vanished. He couldn't retrace them. He spun desperately to find them. There was only black.

"See now the feast of my beast," the deep-voiced fiend laughed with a banshee's shrill.

The blackness drew backward like a reeled cable to reveal the gruesome demise of the two officers and the dog. The pale creature was curled over one of the officer's bodies as it ripped at its flesh with its mouth. The other's throat was ripped open. Naydeen lay to the side, clutching her bloodied face. She was frozen by fear. Dr. Mardin, the dog handler, and Natasha were missing.

Arjun vomited onto the flashing asphalt of blue and red. He swayed and rested against a vehicle to his side. The maggot-coloured creature ripped at the middle of the body, no livelier than a rubber doll. The creature suddenly stopped and slowly tilted its human-ish scowl to him. It didn't have the eyes of a thing that looked satiated. The deep red stones that were set into its face were deadly smooth and looked starved. Its entire face looked tout and sucked into its cheeks like a corpse. Sprays of its victim's blood dripped off its chin. It propped massive, pale, blood-stained hands onto its meal and postured itself as if to pounce.

"So bland and tasteless," the demon said, as it spit a chunk of the police officer onto the road. "But you…I smell you, and you smell…" The creature sniffed the air, stopped, and returned a frightening display of stained teeth to him. It crawled toward him, leaving smears of the officer's blood with each inch. "Fear makes the meat rich." Arjun pressed himself against the vehicle. He couldn't move away. The demon stood on its hind legs and looked down on him. "Pray to your creator, dark meat." Its saliva hit his face.

An ear-splitting shot rang off the trees. The tall creature arched backward and screamed a cry that was more man than beast. More deafening shots rang out. The beast swung its great white arm, like the limb of a birch tree, and tossed Arjun. The world spun in a flash as he lifted from the force.

He felt his body hit a solid object and the air was pressed out of his lungs. The world didn't stop spinning. He had had her…He had had her. Blue and red closed in around him. A scream pierced the enclosing walls of flashing light. He heard a thumping like a tenderizer. He heard the splatter of drops on the pavement. Heavy footsteps stepped toward him. He shut his eyes. He felt the nothingness of his childhood hideaway box. He could feel its restrictive walls as he tried to stretch out.

The heavy steps sounded like soft slippered feet on creaking floorboards. He felt warmth pool beneath him. He curled tighter inside the lightless chest. He thought he could hear the repetitive slap of a paddle off Khatta ma'am's hands as she marched toward him. The noise stopped. He held his breath. He felt the chest shake as something lifted the lid. Blue and red light blinded him.

"Natasha?" he whispered weakly.

A hideous face swirled above him.

Chapter 12

Yuuta huddled into the nook of a broken cliff. Pine needles from above softened the rock floor. A Summer evening cold bit through his thin shirt. The world said nothing. The trees lower on the rocky slope seemed distracted, like a crowd watching a play. The night sky was vibrant. Each twinkling giant a reminder of his sofu, as they watched the nightly display on camping trips. He remembered the old man's boyish excitement when he got to point out Orion's belt, and his happy ramblings on the Shinto moon god. The memories were strangely fogged. Yuuta reached for them, but they pulled further and further away, until all that was left were the playful winks of an old man.

A popping noise floated from the distant trees. Four more followed quickly after. He poked out of his hiding spot and looked over the treetops, expecting fireworks. The white of the moon brought light to the world. The horizon glowed despite the black sky. Two more echoey pops shook the trees awake. Crows crowded in swirling clouds over the forest as they took flight. The wild birds filled the forest top with their yapping, circling as if searching. He shivered, cold at the sudden realization of his aloneness. He twisted his toes together in his shoes as they began to pinch. The Summer cold felt strangely out of place. He tucked himself back into his nook.

The puk-wudjie's dead weight was heavy in his backpack. The devilish laughter had sung the song of the creature's death, as he carried the lifeless bundle into the heart of darkness. He pulled off his backpack to look at it. It was like a dusted collectable stuffed carefully beside the axe wrapped in the stained towel. The thought of her scent on the towel comforted him. He could feel a tingle that buzzed like a blanket-shock on his fingertips. He knew it was her. He felt her in everything. She was interconnected to the threads of the nature around him. He tried to smell her. The thought of her suddenly nude body frightened him. He struggled to reflect on the whiplashed torso that thumped with the enraged pounding of her heart. The image of her breasts sent a flare of sensation that forced him to shift his eyes in search of his humility, as if he was caught watching his mother undress. She was more woman than beautiful. He zipped his backpack up horridly and swung it back to his back.

The eternal cawing was replaced for a quick moment by another pop. The echo carried ominously off the walls of the cliff. There was a deadly silence as the black birds maneuvered out of ear shot. Three deep claps followed the birds. The shallowness of the bursts unnerved him, and he tucked himself into his knees. He knew they weren't fireworks.

He looked for warmth as he cuddled himself. He

wrapped tightly around his legs. The world's energy became deafening. He fought his mind for sleep. He counted to it, he prayed to it, he tried to trick it, but its reinvigoration abandoned him. He stared into his lidded blackness. It was cold. It was loud. He shivered again. He thought of her…of Natasha. Anger stirred inside him like a graeae's pot. He thought of her whipped and tortured body. He thought of her bloody nudity. He clenched his teeth.

"Why would they do that? Why would they hurt you?" he said angrily to nobody. He gripped tightly on his shins. "Why?" His face vibrated with the clenched word.

"Tears, child?" a young girl's voice spoke. Fear caught him. He looked up. He unwrapped his arms and tried to push himself closer to the wall he already rested against. He stood and looked around quickly. There was nobody. "Child…child, do not fear us. We are of the river." The voice had a familiarity that calmed him. "We wish to share with you, child."

"Share-sh-share what?" He asked, as he continued his search for the source.

"The truth, child…The truth," she said.

"Of what?"

"Of her, child. Of the daughter of Muzzu-Kummik-Quae, the mother whose face smiles with the light of the star that dances in the day."

"I don't understand," he whimpered.

"Come child…Come child. We will teach you."

"Come where? I…I can't even see you," he

blubbered.

"Our voice, child. You must follow our voice. Come," she said, excitedly, like a girl convincing him to come over to her house to play.

"It depends…" he questioned. "What side are you on?"

She laughed. Her laugh was rich and fun and innocent. It reminded him of Kimberly. He listened closer.

"Side, child? Side of what? There is only life," the girlish voice said.

"There is always darkness and light…Death and life. The Devil and God. In every story…Always. It's like people can't think there is no other way to life…It's always light or dark, male or female. So, it must be. If that is all people say there is for all of time, then what else could there possibly be? There's always a side."

"Child, we will teach you. Come to us. Follow the sounds of the veins of the earth. Come," she repeated.

He hesitated. Something held him there, an unknown gravity that gripped him by the shoulders. He suddenly realized that the voice, the voice of the river, and the feminine incantation that had whispered in his head held the same ghostly coolness.

"Jadis…" he whispered under his breath.

"Child, we feel the fear flowing through you. Icy cold like a wintry eve. You must seek the river. Seek the brook. The stream. The world's flowing blood of life. We are but its voice. We can teach you. We must teach you."

"I'm…I'm scared. I think…I-I…I think this has been as much as I can take," he said and stepped back into his nook. "Leave me alone…Please, just leave me alone."

His stomach churned. He clutched it consolingly. He was starved. He could still taste the vomit on the back of his teeth. Each swallow struggled through a swollen throat. He didn't want to make any more choices. He felt wrong. He fell back down and tucked into his legs. He rocked back and forth. He slapped his head repeatedly with both hands. He realized the voice inside was his own. He knew he would never escape it.

"Child, your father is with us," she said.

"My-my dad?" he questioned, as he lifted his tear welled eyes back to the sparkling night. "It's a trick… You don't know anything." There was no response. He propped his head fully up and looked around. There was only the black silence of the world, now a graveyard of life. The phantoms of the forest faded in out of the wall of darkness: ghosts of a spotted light source. He stood and breathed out deeply. He stepped out of the nook, looked around quickly, and walked slowly toward the trees that compelled him. Their sudden life source vibrated as he walked through them. The broken logs, snapped sticks, the dirt, the grass, the needles that were spilled across the earth, all swelled with the vibrations of being. "Can you bring me to her!?"

Only an air choked echo responded. The darkness of the forest unnerved him. He looked quickly behind himself. He continued his spin on the spot and looked around wildly. He saw pale shapes in every branch. A crack in the bushes caught his breath. He wondered if it was even real. He swore he heard something behind him. Each breath was too loud. He tried to hold them in to listen more closely. The treetops shifted.

"H-hello?" he called out. "I'm just a kid… I need some help. Please."

"Do you?" a man asked.

"Please…I just want to go home," Yuuta pleaded. His breathing quickened.

"Where is home?" the man pursued.

"Who are you? Are you…another one?"

"I do not understand," the man confessed.

"It's, umm…Don't worry…Don't worry about it," Yuuta said, ashamed of the valuation of his reasoning.

"Boy, we have little time. Hahnunah has starved for long enough. The daughter, she must be found. Her seed is the potential difference that powers the flow of life. Such is the foul exchange made for the life of the Anishinaabeg. Such is the cyclical destiny of our servitude to Creator, blessed be He," the man expressed mockingly. Yuuta saw a person's tall shape fill a gap in the trees. The man could've been a lightless apparition if not for the warmth he emitted. "You must guide me to her." The closeness of his voice struck Yuuta.

"How do I know I can-can trust you?"

"Trust? I am only truth. I cannot speak to how

it is I differ from the falsity of those you have conjured in your thoughts."

"I don't understand…" Yuuta said.

"Ahh, then we have come full circle, boy," the man exclaimed. "We must not waste such time with this banter. We must find her. We must find the daughter of Muzzu-Kummik-Quae."

"Muzzu-Kummik… Quhy? Is that some kind of… god?"

"God? She is All Mother. The mother of life and of the great turtle's eternal burden…Through me, she created the Anishinaabeg. Thus, I am kin to man."

"Kin?" Yuuta said under his breath. "What is your name?"

"Boy, we must not hesitate here. My brothers are foul beasts that will rape the seed into the daughter: the soul of she that stirs like a threading root through you. They have been much in the world of my wanton propagation…As such, they have grown hedonistic, ravenous, and vile. They have forgotten the teachings of All Mother and Creator."

"I don't know where she is," Yuuta admitted. He felt awkward in his confidence.

"No, but you can feel her, can you not?"

The man stepped forward. He was completely nude. His body was marked with crusted blue streaks like dried paint. From his head sprouted a great set of antlers that were like thick black claws reaching upward. His visible skin was golden-tan, and he had a twisted braid of deep black hair. He was extraordinarily tall, but not as frighteningly so as the pale monster.

"I think I feel her…I don't know," Yuuta said shyly.

"I see her essence through your blackened eyes. Seek her not in yourself, but in the world of life. Feel her connection with the universe of living things. Touch the earth and let its voice guide you to her." The man seethed with energy.

"Who are you? Why can't you do this yourself?"

"Creator, blessed in His wisdom, cursed us to this search. A game, you see. Children playing chase the butterfly. Wild boys set free in the long grass at a cliff's edge. We are predators, untamed and hungry. Meshkwadoon is our bond to this corporeal demise. Our purpose is to plant our seed in the depths of she under the whispering boughs of the Great Willow tree."

"What will happen once your purpose is… done?"

The man hesitated then walked toward Yuuta. His nakedness drew Yuuta's eyes, though much was hidden in shadow. His chest and stomach were muscled. His legs were thick. He had big shoulders.

"Decide, boy. Death or design?"

"I-I don't know."

"You must decide, boy!" The world vibrated with the man's intensity anger.

"I can't! I can't choose…"

"Decrepit worm. You are nothing then. Death is your choice, as it inevitably is for all Anishinaabeg."

The man shook his antlered head and turned

abruptly. He drew away from Yuuta. Each step left a footprint of life before it crumbled like flowers withering in a flash of time. He was gone. The forest returned to contemplation. Yuuta waited. His heart raced. Time blew by on the runaway breeze. The spectres of his fears were complicit in the silence, faceless monsters that taunted him. His stomach stung, as if something ate him desperately from the inside. He needed food. He needed water. He needed to find her. He took deep breaths to calm the pressure building in his chest. He twisted his hands together for warmth and comfort. His ears suddenly began to ring. The persistent tone quickly faded into the quiet. He was left listening to his nasal inhales and exhales. He closed his eyes. The blackness was barely thicker behind his lids than what he witnessed with them open. He breathed in through his nose. The air was crisp and smelt like a forest. His feet felt planted into the dirt. A tree whose roots were shunned by his burrowing neighbours. He breathed out from his nose. His toes tingled. He shivered.

He turned to a tree and unzipped his pants. He looked around to ensure his privacy before he began to urinate against the bark of a thick trunk. His pee dribbled like a rolling stream down the crevices to form a pool. He looked at the dark pee puddle. Three nights of nightmares stared back at him with sunken eyes.

A cracking of branches broke his thoughts, and he looked around as he tucked himself away. There was nothing he could see. A flapping of wings lifted from the treetops. Insects' throaty calls sang out to him. He walked towards the closest source of the natured music, while it played all around him in a festival of sound.

As the calls grew louder and more distinct, he caught himself from slipping into water. He swatted a crowd of mosquitos that buzzed around his head. One bit his neck. He quickly slapped the vampirical bug that feasted below his ear. His presence disturbed the sounds and they all adjusted further away from him.

"Water…" he whispered. He knelt in the damp earth that dipped into the black pool.

He cupped his hands and drank the cool liquid. It tasted earthy and left him crinkling his nose as its aftertaste tingled in the back of his throat. But it refreshed him. He took another sip and splashed some on his face to wash away the buzzing insects.

"Welcome, child," the voice of the girl spoke. "We are so happy you came to us. We can teach you. We can show you."

The water rippled away from his disturbing hands as he quickly pulled them out.

"Are you frightened, child?" the girl asked, her voice arising from the water before him.

"I-I-I'm cold," he shivered.

"Child…" she said, in barely a whisper. "Come to us…Into our embrace. Your father is here."

He felt her smiling. The giggle in her voice was playful. It brought warmth to something inside him, and he felt he could trust her. He considered her age and her happy tone and walked deeper into the pond. Despite its cold bite he felt warmer, as if coddled in a hug while standing outside in the snow. Each step led him deeper and deeper along a gradual slope. He felt undergrowth graze his arms like wet tissue paper. His clothes clung to him. His backpack dragged him down.

"You're almost there!" the girl cheered.

He walked until the pond was up to his shoulders before he slipped into the full embrace of its gnawing cold. The sounds of the nighttime creatures and his body marching through the pool flushed out of his head as the swirling sounds of the deep overcame them. He realized he couldn't swim as he sank toward the bottom of the endless black body of murky ink.

"Child, feel the life inside you." Her voice rang more clearly than when he was above.

He felt his feet hit the pond's murky bottom and he pushed himself up. The water was too thick with stirred mud to see the top. He abruptly broke the surface and sank back down. He began to wag his arms searching for a way to move. He hit the bottom again and shoved upward, but his waving arms slowed his ascent. His heart raced. Water rushed into his mouth as he tried to yell. He heard a vile feminine cackle. He choked on the water, and it flooded him further as he tried to regurgitate the fluids that he was already drowning in. His body convulsed and fought the gripless liquid. He waved his arms erratically. He was drowning. *He was drowning.*

A force suddenly wrenched him upward. He lifted partially out of the water and was dragged along its surface. He vomited as oxygen tried to find a way inside him. His nose burst cool liquid out of his nostrils, and he gagged up everything inside him. He felt himself pulled onto the earth and left to lay on his side, sniffing and spluttering. He whimpered at the realization of his own death. He shivered and curled into a ball. He dry heaved onto himself and gagged painfully.

He felt a sharp claw grip him and turn him on his back. He followed the voiceless direction and found himself staring into glowing blue eyes. He fought for his breath. The rock-skinned puk-wudjie stared curiously down at him. It shook its head mysteriously before it burst into a barking laugh.

He continued to choke. The creature took a few moments to settle and return to its raspy breathing. He gripped its arm and silently pleaded his thanks to its flickering blue fireballs as he found specks of air. It simply stared back at him. It looked strong, as if it was never anything but strong. His memory of it crumbling like an unstable stack of lifeless rocks seemed false in his mind.

"How?" he croaked. "Water?" It made no distinct acknowledgement of his theory. "Was it the water…I think…I think Mr. Ogi mentioned something about rock and water?"

It didn't reply. It stared like a dog analyzing its owner. He turned to the pool and considered the near-death experience. There was no sign of the girlish voice or the murderous cackle that stirred in its depths. It was as if neither were ever there. The water faintly reflected the faint glow of the puk-wudjie's eyes. Insects continued their calls to each other. He felt their songs' sincerity. The world flowed on. His death would have had no impact on any of the life that flourished there. The stars shimmered. He felt empty. He laid his head back to the wet dirt. He was cold and the darkness frightened him. He shivered as water trickled down his face. He adjusted his ripped backpack off and shut his eyes.

Chapter 13

The creature carried Arjun like a jute sack slung over a farmer's shoulder. His ribs ached. His shattered arm raged beneath the loosening wrap. The motions nauseated him. He couldn't spit out the building paste in his mouth. He felt Natasha's absence like an empty room in a hoarder's house. He lifted his eyes from the bloodless wound on the pale spine of the tall beast and saw the ground was no longer hidden in blackness. The forest revealed itself to him like an undressing woman.

"I smell your awakening, meat," the demon spat through deep exhalations.

Arjun caught his breath. The vibration of it speaking reignited his fear. Sweat tingled along his neck as it dripped from his back. He clenched his jaw. He suddenly felt gravity pull his weight into the fiend as it slid unstably down a slope. He could hear his heart thump, as it beat against the creature like a dull butcher blade. The creature swayed and his stomach's contents swirled inside him like a sloshing weight. He closed his eyes as he tried to calm himself. He was too scared to release the pressure that built in his bowels, despite the aches. The trees watched them curiously. He felt their reservations in the presence of the deathly white monster.

He dropped his head back down to face the forest floor. The creature left paths of broken foliage behind it. Dark blue shadows slithered toward them like snakes in slow motion. The world closed in around them. The trees grew dense. They leaned inward. There were few spots of light under the thick canopy. He smelt life like a wafting cook's wok. Something fluttered out of the trees above. He shook with a fluish chill.

The creature began to breathe heavier and faster. It quickened forward as if excited. The roots it maneuvered through were a clayish red. They grew thicker, more invasive, and redder as the beast swatted its way through the hanging extremities of nature. The pulse of the world grew distinct. The trees waved to the sky. He felt bathed in natural wonder, as the sun cracked through the boughs above. A sharp and putrid smell abruptly disturbed his reverie. The horrid stench permeated the air like an unclean porta potty. He gagged and his moment of peace fled him.

"It is gaasiiyaakizowin," the fiend breathed heavily. "Here decays Anishinaabeg flesh and bone of rotted spirit. Eyeless and bloated corpses. Turned meat."

The hunger of the beast seemed to quiet in the silent chirruping that fluttered through the tripping wood. Everything survived seamlessly in the stench: monstrous trees that were thick and dark, wild foliage that twined with reddened roots, and the bubbling of water that rolled like the shoulders of Bindu Bolar. It was grotesque but beautiful, a fitting place for this creature that was both animal and man.

"Where are you taking me?" Arjun braved to ask.

"Silence. I speak only," the beast snarled with a deathly bass that vibrated uncomfortably in his ears. Its vile breath carried to his nostrils.

"Are-are you going to kill me?"

"Kill? No. We do not kill. We harvest. I am a mouth that feeds the beating heart."

"Whose beating heart?"

It snarled in clear frustration but said nothing.

The trees began to thicken around them, until they eventually split into an opening. The clearing was tangled with protruding roots like long fingers from one great bark-skinned hand. He shut his eyes against the stench, no longer interested in watching the wiry veins sprawled under the beast's naked pale feet. Soft whispers tickled inside his ears. The beast clenched its grip, and he could feel its long claws press dangerously against his skin. He tried not to breathe in an attempt to mitigate the stench and the potential for a deadly accident.

The whispers grew stronger, like a breeze picking up. His burden on the fiend seemed to grow heavier, as it struggled to twist through the throbbing red roots. He heard a fragile woman speaking indistinctly on the air, as if guessing for a language he understood. Her voice was melodic, but frail.

"Arjunkaul," she said from somewhere in the

trees to his left.

"Protect her, Arjunkaul," she said from the trees on his right.

"She needs you," she said from somewhere he couldn't trace.

"The daughter must fulfill meshkwadoon, Arjunkaul," she said directly into his ear.

"Arre baap re...I'm done with this!" he spat, as he punched his fist into the side of the monster.

It snarled and shifted him around uncomfortably. He barely held back a vomiting spell before it settled him. The twisted roots were like a whirlpool of blood in his unstable vision. The image of the mauled cops sent a twinge to his lungs. He shut his eyes and breathed deeply, trying to brace his arm. He felt like a palm tree shirted tourist gasping for breath on a tossing cruise. Everything spun violently inside the darkness of his head. He opened his eyes. The roots grew denser and thicker around them.

The fiend suddenly stopped. Its breathing was scratchy and harsh. He felt it clench its claws through his sweater and lift him up. It tossed him onto the root strewn earth. His body ached from the uncomfortable impact on the uneven surface. It grabbed his face and shoved something rubbery between his teeth. He tried to shake its forceful fingers away, but it choked him with whatever it shoved into his mouth. He was forced to swallow it. It crumbled down his throat like a misshapen clump of dirt.

"Watch," it said as it pushed his face back to the

root floor. The stench masked its rancid breaths.

He traced his eyes along the roots to see them return into a great tree. It was a monstrous willow that curled like a disgruntled hag whose ragged clothes hung from her bent shape. He felt the roots below him flex, like pipes carrying pressurized flows. The tree shivered.

"Come closer," the aged female circle of whispers said. "Come closer…Into my embrace…Come to me… Flesh warms me…Come."

"What are you?" Arjun demanded.

"Me?" the whispers rolled. "Life."

"Saala kutta…" he exhaled.

"Come closer, Arjunkaul. Let me feel you"

He slowly adjusted to his feet, but hesitated. He felt a wrongness no different from biting unexpectedly into a rotten fruit. The wind slowly wheezed through the greenery around him. He looked back to see only trees. The beast was gone. He spun on the spot to search for the vile creature, but there were only trees. Trees like a parading battalion of soldiers formed around their Commanding Officer. Trees hiding the rest of humanity from him. They were a wall in a memory he couldn't comprehend getting around. Then there was the great one at the centre: a twisted and bent embodiment of the land. Its roots were a network of cables that split into the earth, carrying the signals of unseeable life.

"Who are you?" he asked.

"The voice of the land," the whispers stated. They seemed to fill the root entwined hollow as if they spoke from each corner. "Do you still seek her, Arjun-kaul?"

"Can you help me find her?"

"That is not the way," the whispers advised.

"What do you mean?"

"She must choose," they said softly.

"Choose what?"

"The way."

"Arre baap re, what are you saying?" He grumbled. He felt his head bob. "I'm sick of this…What is she? What is this? Why can I see and hear things? What are you?" There was no response. He looked up at the tree. The wakening light revealed a slope of roots delving into a pond near the rear of it. He could feel a force of life emanate through its bulging veins, as if they drank from the world's atman. "Why am I here?"

The wind sighed.

"Arjunkaul…it is life. The seed of the daughter of Muzzu-Kummik-Quae must be born unto me. With the birth of the Anishinaabeg and from the creation of the crossing came meshkwadoon. The exchange. The exchange of life for life. The daughter, a child of Anishinaabe, shall bear the fruit of a son of the same mother to sustain the flesh of the Anishinaabeg. She is of us…but she is gifted with the mortal bonds of the Anishinaabeg. I am the vessel from which life must be fed to bring life. I am timeless, Arjunkaul…but I am withering and bent. I starve for life…for it is all I know. Those who feel me, who feel the spirits, pain at my hunger, like a starving elder on her deathbed fawned by her progeny. They grow desperate to fulfill mesh-kwadoon, and desperation may be the end of the Anishinaabeg, for the lust of Aayaash has deprived me and has broken the covenant." The massive willow creaked faintly, twisting for comfort under the weight of time and the burden of its drooping boughs. "I grow tired, Arjunkaul." The whisper's encircling sound grew distant. "You must serve her, Arjunkaul. Guide her to my roots, for where the seed is sown so must it be reaped. Now come, Arjunkaul, let me feel your warmth before you depart. I much crave the sensation of the flesh, for it has been many cold years and I, a decrepit and misshapen extremity of Hahnunah, do so crave the touch of the flame of mortality."

He didn't move. He stood and watched the willow. It showed no signs of thought or pain or hunger, but in his eternal self, he saw its vacancy and its weakness. It was a hollow shell. Although he didn't trust its words, he struggled to pull away from its coercive grasp on his heart. It softly groaned. He waited. The whispers didn't speak again. His body tried to pull away, but he couldn't. He put his face in his hands.

"Holy Deva," he maoned to himself. He pinched between his eyes and sighed.

He had to find her. She was the only thing he knew he had to seek. His mind had no sense of duty to his job, the kids, his father...his mother. He had a flicker of an image in his mind of his ex-wife, but he forced it back into the gutter where she would rot with her new family. She was a vampire that sucked him dry. He had to carry the weight of her mental abuse like a bruise on his face.

He turned to the forest behind him. It watched the willow's hollow reverently. He limped away from the aged tree and back into the dense woods. He stopped to look at the phone he was surprised to find was still there. It was dead. He felt for his wallet and keys. They were gone. He sighed and looked around in contemplation of his options. The forest was a village of sound. The shuffling trees, the bird songs, the animals in the brush, the chirps of strange insects, and a splash in a hidden pool were the bustling life of this world. He still felt her, like an anxiety that kept his heart racing despite any serenity. He slid his phone back into his pocket and limped to a tree to sit at its base. He felt his age through his knee and the pinch in his lower back as he slipped to the earth. A crack of branches caused him to flinch, and he looked around nervously. He saw nothing.

"What am I doing?" he said to himself. He scratched his head. "What the Deva am I doing?"

He shifted himself back to his feet. His pains accompanied his hunger, but he knew he had to find her. To feel her. He had to see the circling universe that swirled in her hazelnut eyes. He pulled out his phone again. It was dead. He realized he just checked it and looked around with an unusual sense of shame. He threw it into the darkness. He scratched his chin. His fingers scraped with a tearing noise across the recent beard growth that had snuck onto his face. He closed his eyes and listened. He hoped the world would direct him to her, but he heard nothing. The morning matured as he anxiously sought direction. He found nothing. He looked at the trees. They had no answers. It was as if he suddenly awoke from the dream that led him here. Desperation began to develop inside him. He felt his heart quicken.

"You have pain, man?" a strange voice asked.

He spun on the spot and saw nothing through the uneven lines of trees.

"Arre baap re! Hasn't there been enough of this?!" he called out.

"You trick me, man?" the voice said. It was like a squeaky old crone.

He examined the trees with squinted eyes. He spotted a soft movement of orange and caught a fox watching him from behind a trunk. It looked consideringly at him, then blinked.

"Is it… you?" he asked.

"I am I," replied the fox. Arjun sighed but didn't take his unblinking gaze off the small snouted animal. The fox took a step from behind the tree and sniffed the air. "You are not of this skulk, man. From what glade do you come?" It looked down to its paws, as if thinking.

"I'm not from around here…I think that's the- That's what you mean…I think," he stammered. "How can I hear? Is it because of her?"

The fox didn't respond. It tilted its head and analyzed him.

"You are a clouded man," it eventually said. "You do not see."

"Help me see."

"A man must teach a man to see, for what does a fox know of the colours behind man's eyes?" It lifted its head proudly. A rustle in the treetops suddenly spooked it and it returned quickly behind the tree trunk. "Man must find a den, for crows' eyes hunt from above."

The fox turned and ran away.

"Hey! Come back here! Hey! F-fox? Blessed Vishnu, burn these monsters," he spat with a curse.

He kicked a loose stone that shot off with a quick clatter. His head felt heavy. He stumbled forward. He gripped a nearby tree for stability. His feet spun below him in a slow vortex. The light seemed to refract off the branches above him. He closed his eyes and tried to shake away the disorientation, but when he opened them all he saw were black spots floating everywhere he looked. The ground undulated like a mirage. He dropped to his knees and vomited up the chalky chunks of something unknown. He tried to spit out the acidic remnants left in the back of his throat. The horror of the creature shoving something into his mouth flashed across his mind. He puked before he could reconsider the substance it had forced into him.

"Shoot…" he whispered as he struggled to his feet. His arm was numb. His thick saliva dripped to the earth. He wiped its stream away and attempted to walk forward. Before he realized, he was on his hands and knees crawling through the thick brush. His hands pressed against the hard earth and unsmooth rocks as he dragged himself through the overgrowth. His arm felt like a weight he slogged around without feeling.

"Help!" he called. There was no answer. "Help!"

He stopped for a breath and then tried to quicken his crawl. He felt like a helpless creature mucking through the mud as it shifted around him. The ground inclined forward, and he pulled himself down with a root that broke through the dirt like a boney arm. He reached the rock bottom and a small creek dribbled in front of him. He dragged himself with one hand to its edge. He rested on his elbows and bathed his hands weakily in the cool water. He tossed it onto his face and washed his mouth with it. His face was a Van Gogh on the surface of the pool. He watched the ripples calm. He judged himself before he looked to the opposite bank where branches and long plants slouched toward the water. It was serene if not for the haunting images of the night's demons fighting for space in his mind. The branches suddenly seemed to reach towards him like the pale beast's monstrous hand. He pulled himself to the slope and away from the creek. The water from his face dripped onto his sweater. He was too weak to wipe it away. He tried to pull himself to his feet again.

"Saala kutta," he cursed again as he collapsed back to his knees.

The world spun slowly around him, as if its rotation was sped up just enough to be distinct. He did every breathing technique he could think of to avoid puking again. He crawled back to the creek's side. He stared into it again. Soft-edged pebbles littered its base. He looked against the current and saw a boot slowly thumping against jutting stones and a fallen log. It was barely carried by the weak waters. He continued to watch it until it rolled into reach. He grabbed it before it could float past. The low-ankled black boot was smeared with crusted mud along its laces. He threw it in shock as he realized it still had a desecrated portion of a limb inside. He barely held back his upsetting stomach.

"Hello?" a young woman called. "Is anybody there?"

"Hello?" he called back anxiously, as he wiped his mouth. "Here. I'm here!"

He sat back on his heels and looked around. He wrestled with heavy breaths as he tried to listen for the voice's source.

"Are you there, Dell?" the voice called from the top of the slope on the other side of the stream. "Dell… I'm scared."

"Shit," Arjun whispered.

"Dell…Dell, I can't go back!" the girl cried.

"I'm coming, hold on!" Arjun assured her as he forced himself to stand.

He rushed on to a rock that wasn't quite consumed by the water. He stumbled for the next one but caught his balance. He made a final jump to the soft sloping growth on the other side and pulled himself to the top.

"Where are you?" he called. "I'm here. I-I can help."

"Dell? Dell…they're coming for me. They're

going to find me again. Please help me get out of here?" The girl began to sob. She sounded frightened.

"I'm not Dell, but I'm a—a teacher. I can help you." He stumbled into a tree and slouched forward. Vertigo tortured him. He struggled to hold himself up.

"Nimaamaa? Nimaamaa?!" another girl's voice called. "We're waiting for you nimaamaa."

"Keep talking girls! I can hear you. I'm-I'm coming," he panicked.

He stepped forward then stumbled. He punched the ground in frustration. He heard the patter of feet running toward him. He looked up, expecting to see the girls, but there was only the morning enriched forest.

"I-I'm here girls. I'm here to help you…J-Just…" he trailed off into deep breaths.

"Dell!" the young woman screamed.

"Maamaa!" the other girl followed.

He felt trapped by the barrage. The pattering surrounded him like a class of children flocking to a stray puppy. He heard whimpering and sniffing, crying and laughter, whispers and worries.

"They hide from maji-manidoog," a woman said. "For those are indeed frightening creatures."

He looked forward and saw her. Her legs were a deer's legs, and her stomach and torso were that of a tan-skinned woman. He mentally restrained himself from watching her breasts.

"What are you?" he asked. Her face was indistinguishable as it warped with the rotating world around him.

"What are *you*?" she snapped back. "Is it not better to ask *who* are you?" Her voice was clear and low. "Now, how does an inini find himself in this place… unsolicited?"

"I–I'm not sure." He took a deep breath. "I'm lost, honestly."

"Bagwanawizi…" she said.

Bushes rustled and girls and women in a motley of tousled clothing exited the shadows of the forest. Many had dark hair, some had bold noses, but most had dark eyes.

"Bring him to the glade," the deer-legged woman said. She turned and pranced off seductively, as if unaware that her lower half was not human. He felt compelled to watch her.

Two thick armed women pulled him to his feet from his spot in the dirt. Their skin was ice cold, but he didn't resist their guidance. They pulled him away from the creek and into the trees. They were silent. A little girl in ripped blue jeans and an oversized black sweater skipped ahead of them. The other girls and women followed them silently.

It wasn't long before they dragged him into a meadow. A hare lifted its head with a start from the grass it grazed and watched them enter. It bolted away as they crowded the clearing. The deer-legged woman waited for them ceremoniously. His women crutches released him, and he fell into the grass. He stared into it with struggling breaths. He cradled his burning arm against his chest like a dying child.

"How have you come here?" the deer-legged woman asked sternly.

"I told you; I don't know. Why…why are all of these girls here?" He wiped his bearded chin as he looked around. The crowd of females seemed to slowly close in around him.

"They are the silent spirits," she lamented. "The ones taken unjustly by the tortures of an unrelenting world of flesh. The lost ones. The innocent ones. Now, they seek healing and peace."

"They're not… alive?" he wondered.

"Alive? Your words are senseless, inini," she scolded passionately. "They were ones who lived among you. Children, girls, women. They are here before you now. Does that not constitute their life?"

"I'm not sure," he admitted.

"You are strange, inini…Why have you come to this place, our place of solitude? You dare disturb the beaten spirits of the lost ones? Speak!" The girls and women drew closer.

"I think I'm the lost one," he said.

"You mock us?" She kicked her left hoof along the ground. "These forsaken children are already the mockery of your corporeal world. You dare to come to this place of harmony and disturb it?"

"No, I-Of course not!"

"Then why have you come!?" she demanded. An unspoken malice sparked in her eyes.

"I seek a woman!" he blurted out, frustration overcoming him.

"Ahh, so, the truth is hidden in the mud," she smirked.

The air in the glade grew cooler. The crowd of females closed in around him. The deer-legged woman was barely visible over their heads.

"She's not dead. She's not dead…She's important. I must find her and-and guide her." He had no confidence in the words coming out of his mouth, as if he was coaxed into speaking.

"What do you seek of this woman, inini?" She eyed him suspiciously. The others had their eyes on the ground as if ashamed.

"Am I so frightening? Arre baap re, I'm a schoolteacher. What I seek is…her safety. And from what I've seen, she needs me." The meadow was silent. "Help me help her."

"Look at their faces. Look! Abandoned, manipulated, forgotten, murdered, raped. Look at their eyes!" The deer-legged woman wailed as the other girls and women lifted their eyes to his. "What do you know of what a woman needs? A teacher? A fool. You are not welcome here, inini."

A woman grabbed his shoulder, and he could feel her cold grasp through his torn sweater. He tried to pull away, but hands pulled him in every direction. Some dug their nails into his skin. He stumbled into a cold body as he tried to step away from the clutching fingers and fell to his knees. The bodies and stretching arms blocked out his view of the deer-woman. His arms were forced to his sides. He winced. They drew in closer and closer.

He fought for air. Something struck his head, and he grew disoriented.

"Natasha!" he desperately called. The cold bodies fell in upon him, shutting out the new day's light.

Chapter 14

Yuuta shivered awake. His sobo's words were in the back of his head, as he laid there in his damp dirtiness. A dwindling dawn accompanied his wakeful blinks. The flaming warmth of the naked sun opposed his cold bones. He shivered again. His sopping clothes were a soaked blanket draped over him. His hair was a dripping mop on his head. He hugged himself to stop the chills. A musty smell clung to him. Hunger moaned in his stomach. The thought of Mr. Kaul's starving eyes replaced the thoughts of his sobo. He felt like a stupid kid chained to the hate inside him as he imagined the sickly man. He was desperate for direction in what he knew he had to do. He was desperate for approval.

The puk-wudjie realized he was awake and stood from its cross-legged position. It came over to him. It had a beaten little apple in its hand. He sat up and took the offered apple. The bitter fruit's insides spilled out of his mouth as he devoured it. He wondered if he should thank the creature. He chose silence instead, as it passed another small apple to him. The creature sat patiently beside him. It watched him.

"Do you have a mom or a dad?" he asked through a swallow and a shiver. It tilted its head slightly. He thought of his own parents as his chewing filled his head. "The water…She…she said my dad was there? How would she know anything about him? Do you know anything about him? He-he went missing, after he put my mom in the hospital…and then I lost her too. She just…died. She couldn't move. She breathed with a mask…And then she was gone. As if…As if someone forgot to turn her back on. She was so cold…I'm so cold."

He laid his head back onto the grass and curled his legs into his arms. He thought of the slowly pumping ventilator. He thought of her eyes easing closed. He jolted as the puk-wudjie's sudden movement startled him. It growled and stood to its feet.

"Boy," a raspy voice choked. "Do you mind?"

The ragged man limped between the trees. He stumbled into a kneel at the edge of the water. He held his side. Yuuta could hear his raspy breaths like a kid with asthma. Yuuta pushed himself into a sitting position and rubbed himself for warmth.

"It doesn't get easier…" the man said slowly through hoarse breaths. "The cold…Hunger…Fear… It'll always be there. You must find balance…You must find balance."

The man suddenly winced and curled his body inward. Yuuta saw the deep red and looked away.

"I-Are you-are you okay?" He felt afraid to shame the man by acknowledging his wound.

"A windigo is a monstrous beast," the man coughed. The ragged man ripped the sleeve of his patched suit jacket and pushed it against his dripping belly. His slow, ragged breaths matched his clothing as he cupped his other hand in the water and used it to clean his face. "Memegwesi…" the man said as he splashed more water onto his face, "did she try it?"

"I don't know what you mean," Yuuta said honestly.

"Did she call you?" the man clarified, as he leaned over the pool.

He let the droplets drip from his shaggy beard and into the water. Yuuta could hear pain in each stuttering breath.

"What can I do? I-I can help you," Yuuta felt invigoration grow inside him at the man's suffering.

"Boy, there is not a thing you can do for me… Natasha…You must focus your thoughts on her." The man coughed and spat into the water. "Tell the dog to heel."

Yuuta looked at the creature standing like a threatening bear cub. Its blue eyes sparked wildly.

"Why should I?" Yuuta said. "He's the only one who has helped me. Guided me. He's the only one who listens. It's so funny, all of you people, and monsters, and things, you all just see a kid. You think you know what I am. You don't know anything…You don't know anything!"

The man coughed gutturally, and fluid shot into the water.

"Boy…listen. I'm dying. I've been alone for a long time…So damned long. I was alone at the beginning…

when I was cursed to this. I watched for a thousand years as my body crusted with dirt, dust, and waste. A decaying statue standing over the grave of rape and death. I wasn't much older than you are now...I was strong, and I was becoming a promising man. I had a name then...Thorgils...Yes...Thorgils, son of Leif. A name now forgotten by all things." His voice tightened as he struggled into a coughing fit. Thorgils dropped onto his butt and groaned. Yuuta saw a dark puddle that deepened beneath the man. The creature continued to growl. "Damned fiend...Don't trust any of it. Not of him, not of the spirits, or anything of this world..." He paused and winced. "You cannot trust even the Anishinaabeg skraelingjar, who'll think you're nought but swallow's shit to their type. Trust only yourself. Seek only Natasha. She is the only truth worth its weight in salt."

Thorgils coughed and laid completely onto his back. Blood soaked through his clothes and covered his hands. Yuuta walked slowly over to him. The sun shone mockingly down upon them. Yuuta knelt and looked at the man's face. Blood crusted his beard. It was smeared like dried syrup across his cheek. Bubbles at his lips spluttered as he rasped out a shallow breath.

"Boy...I have so much to tell you...So damned much still to say...I failed you and I failed her...I have no memory of using this word...In all my time, I've held it in. No man deserves it. No man or woman or child deserves the prostrating resignation, but...I'm sorry. I'm sorry for the path that has been laid before you...A path…A path bridged by death. I'm sorry…kid…But I…to…to…to Val-"

Thorgils let out a choked gurgle. He convulsed for a moment and then was empty. Yuuta saw the same fogged eye look of his mom and his sofu: a mysterious peace, the peace of a long-sought sleep.

He continued to kneel in the blood. He looked at the open-eyed face of the man. He hoped Thorgils would blink to reveal his ruse. He didn't blink. He didn't breathe. He was dead.

Yuuta stood from the puddle of blood and stepped backward. The creature no longer held its aggressive stance.

"Who was he?" Yuuta asked weakly.

The creature stepped over to the corpse. It waved at Yuuta to join it. He motioned forward, but the sight of the blood dizzied him. He tried to look at Thorgils's face, but the sudden spinning of the world forced him off balance and he slipped into the puddle of the man's fluids. It splashed everywhere. He tried to stand but fell again. His heart pounded. He began to hyperventilate. Everything spun in a whiplash of weeping red. He shut his eyes in hopes to block out the death. He heard slithering vines in his head. They were joined by the squishing sound of violent chewing. His sofu's face smiled out of the darkness. Yuuta screamed. He kept screaming. He couldn't tell if what came out of him was in his head or out of his mouth. He didn't care. He just screamed. He opened his eyes and the world was no different. He was soaked through from the blood and water.

He caught a dark shape in the corner of his eye. On the ground, curled into a ball, was a faceless woman's body. He knew she was dead. Her face was mauled. He saw only a shape. He focused on her. She looked alive, but he knew she was dead. He stood to his feet. He walked slowly toward the dead woman. It shifted. He suddenly was aware that she was alive. He rushed over to her. Her head shot up and stared into him with soulless deep black eyes. Her face was spread open and indistinguishable. Maggots spilled out of the gaping hole where her mouth should have been. He tripped backward and vomited toward Thorgils's corpse. He shut his eyes again and cried.

He cried until he realized the shadows had shifted. He looked up to the cloudless sky. A splash in the water frightened him, but he saw the result of a duck's landing as he shifted his gaze. He pushed himself to all fours and crawled to the pond. Once he reached the bank, just at Thorgils's feet, he looked down to his reflection. His face was painted with a circus mask of blood and dirt. Streaks were left as lightened paths on his cheeks from the tears. The girlish voice lingered inside him. He shivered at the realization of the water's intent. He heard a shuffle and caught the puk-wudjie rummaging the corpse. He looked quickly to the spot of the curled woman, but he only saw a small dark boulder. He quickly double-took the rummaging creature.

"Stop that!" he yelled. "Let him be…Stop it." He rushed over to shoo the puk-wudjie, but it dodged him and returned to sifting through the corpse's neckline. It dug around slowly until it ripped off a string necklace. It held the necklace in its stone-claws. The string was frayed and old but dangling from its center was a shimmerless black ring. He reached out his hand and the creature dropped it onto his palm. It was cold and heavy, but it was too big for his fingers. "Why?" The creature ignored him and walked to the edge of the water. He looked at the ring more closely. "Should I...keep it?" The puk-wudjie said nothing. The ring felt no different than any of his sobo's jewelry. He didn't know if it was supposed to mean something or if he was supposed to feel something. The need for meaning nagged at him. It stirred something ugly in his stomach. He felt the bubbling cauldron at the brim of overflowing and his stomach rage in a fury that twisted and tightened. "What does it mean?!" he screamed at the body of the man. "Why...Why...What does it mean? Please... Why is everyone dying?"

He whipped the ring. He turned away without trying to spy its demise. A hunger inside him spread through his limbs and filled him like a slow numbing toxin. It was like the sucking tentacles of a demon making its nest. The trees shivered when they saw his face. A path seemed to open before him as his vision absorbed the vibrations of life. He felt the invisible sensation through his soles. The energy was like life's web touching all things. He felt the world shift below him. He felt pulled into the trees. Pulled from humanity. It coaxed him. It called to him wordlessly. He looked back at the creature. It watched the water thoughtfully. He looked at the man's corpse. He hesitated. A white butterfly hovered around a patch of light and disappeared into the trees. He followed it.

He knew where he was going this time. He could see the flow of life running toward her. He followed it without thought or fear. He saw the glow of her being like a signal in the distance, through and beyond the forest. He began to run. A Christmas morning excitement swelled in his chest. He felt himself smile. His face cracked with the dry dirt and blood. He knew Thorgils was right, he had to go to her. The opening of the path matched his pace. He felt relief in the exhaustion of his run, as despair was replaced by the tightness of his lungs.

His path led him to a trail. He sped onto it from the trees and continued his run along its shoulder. The light of day glowed with an unwavering consistency that made him hesitate. He suddenly realized that he didn't feel or appear any closer to the raging beacon of life. He gradually slowed to a walk as the realization continued to dawn on him. The trickery of the world seemed to circle around him in a dancing mockery. He stopped and focused on his breathing. He listened curiously to the whispers of the nature. The sound of a vehicle cruising past became a vulgar interruption. He scolded the now apparent roadway just ahead of him.

Dust settled in a cloud. He adjusted the damaged backpack he realized he was still wearing. The image of the rusted axe was clear in his head. He flipped the backpack off his back and opened it. He unwrapped the axe and examined it. He placed it on the ground and brought the towel wrap to his nose. He wanted to smell her. Something in his groin begged him to smell the towel, but an unknown restraint held him. He looked around to see if anyone was watching. He strained his ears but heard nothing. He hesitated for a moment then sniffed the towel deeply. He felt his own oddity as he smelt only the residual metallic scent left in stains by the axe. He threw the towel to the ground. He quickly picked up the axe and examined it again. It was spotted with orange and brown; its edge had a dull sharpness. He gripped it and swung it twice. He sighed and return-ed it into the backpack.

"Your choice is wise, boy," a man said. Yuuta whipped his gaze to the trees and saw the nude antlered man kneeling with his eyes closed. His dark braid was slung over his shoulder. It was strung together with threads and beads. "A willow whispers under the eyes of the crows. She who comes, the seed of the earth and the mould of Nanabozho. A guardian spirit to witness the offering…And for he to guide the seed's blossom. To the willow she must return. To the dirt he must go."

The man opened his eyes slowly but remained kneeling. Yuuta held his gaze on the crusted blue stripes across the man's chest.

"Help me find her," Yuuta begged.

"You will suffer," the man said. A soft breeze shifted small strands that weren't caught in the man's thick braid. "You will know a pain that slices deeper than a healer's tools. She needs a man, a warrior."

"I can be those things!" Yuuta shouted. The man said nothing. He raised himself to his feet. "I can be what she needs. I have to be what she needs."

"Did the corpse of Thorgils, son of Leif teach you nothing?" The man stepped forward and lifted Yuuta's eyes toward his own. "So, *you* have been chosen. There is much that is hidden inside you. Dark secrets. Great determination. Fear and hate. Childishness. Boy," the naked man walked to the towel that Yuuta left in the dirt, "follow the signs."

The man picked the towel up and smelled it. He held his eyes closed.

"You must show me how," Yuuta pleaded.

"To be a man is to live with the weight of your choices," the man proclaimed. "The true man, he is driven by a power of will to carry the greatest choices. Make your choice, or you are nothing, boy."

"Why are they monsters, and you are not?"

"Monsters?" the man considered. "Are bears monsters? Are wolves monsters? Are men monsters? They are what they've been made to be."

The man held Yuuta's gaze. He didn't feel frightened; he felt…calm. He felt comforted by the man's strength and power. Life swirled past them in unseen sparks and crackles.

"Who am I?" Yuuta asked.

The man hesitated, squinted his eyes, and shifted his head.

"You are you, boy," the man said.

"That sounds…underwhelming."

The man held his squint and then returned to a statuesque posture.

"Now is the time. Find her," the man reasserted.

Yuuta licked his lips. His breathing was heavy despite the tightness of his lungs being gone.

"Teach me. Please, I don't even know where to start. I can't drive. How do you get around?"

The man laughed. Yuuta wondered at its dustiness, like opening an old book in an attic. The man shook his head then turned away and walked barebacked into the forest. Yuuta watched the man's shape vanish into the trees. He watched for a long moment, then threw the axe and towel into the backpack and swung it securely onto his shoulders. He slowly turned and followed the trail in the direction he had been running. He felt alone. He looked around. The puk-wudjie was gone. Fear nested inside him with the tentacled demon.

"Puk-wudjie?!" he yelled.

He fought the surge of helplessness. He tried to return his focus to his breathing. His semblance of will crumbled hopelessly between his fingers. The insecurity of his loneliness curled over him like a monster of Tartarus.

"What am I doing? I'm just a kid. I'm just a friggin kid," he reminded himself. "What am I doing?"

The sounds of a vehicle approaching reawakened his spirit and he gripped his backpack straps. He burst through the brush and thin trees to the road. He judged the distance of the hidden vehicle and waited by the treeline's edge. He saw its dim lights wrap a bend just in front of him. He waved out his hands. The vehicle gradually slowed as the driver leaned forward to clarify what she saw. His backpacked burden dug into his shoulders as he considered the exposure of the axe.

"You alright, eh?" the driver said, as she poked her head out of the rolled window of her black truck. Her brow was heavily clenched. "You're a real mess, you know that?"

"I, uh, I'm looking for Ogi, Ogi and Chloe Blackleaf," Yuuta said.

"Why would you be doing that, eh? Out here like this…Are you sure you're alright? You're an absolute mess," she repeated. "Here, let me lay down a towel and you can get in." He watched the woman reach under her seat and shuffle around until she pulled a towel out and covered the passenger side. "I guess it'll be the most I can do for now…Ogi you said? Ogichidaa Blackleaf? Now what is he doing to be involved with a kid like you?"

"It's nothing, mam. I…I, uh, I'm looking for someone, and he can help me," he said as he pulled himself into the truck seat. He felt as if each word was a lie that was written all over his face. He wondered if all the woman really saw was a crusted blood and dirt creature. "I had to…fend for myself out there."

"Your unspoken words are my plausible deni-ability, eh?" she smiled.

He squinted his eyes to understand, but the woman was watching the road as she pulled away from the shoulder. She ignored his silence and turned on the radio.

Chapter 15

The sun sank slowly from its peak. She couldn't imagine it rising again. Everything she knew, her education, her childhood, who she was, leaked slowly out of her perception. The swirling flashes of painted and frightening faces drained from her head and down to her toes. She stank with the smell of campfire. It was in her hair and stained to her skin. She revolted herself. She was a de-armed dumpster mannequin. She was a mockery version of the girl that ends up on the news like a fragile housewife caught jogging by a perverted stalker. The girl scarred so badly that the eyes of watchers and strangers see it like a mark on her face. The girl that knowing women send blessings to God isn't them. The girl locked in a hospital wing, a story from others' mouths.

The day's summer heat added sweat to her body already dampened by blood. She would have been calmed by the comfort of her judgementless nudity, if not for the wounds that bubbled and crusted in the sun's rays. The breezes seemed reserved for the forest prison she was hauled from.

A woman squatted in a bush just beside her. The woman wheezed with each breath as she peed.

"Dr. Mardin?" Natasha questioned, as she recognized the woman's lined face.

"Eleanor, Natasha," the Doctor said. Sweat dripped from Eleanor's forehead. Her curled posture made her look older than she seemed at the hospital. Her hair was a mess tied poorly into a bun. "I have so many questions." The woman looked up from her feet to Natasha. Natasha was discomforted by the woman's humanity.

"I don't have any answers…" Natasha said.

"Do you always expect to have the answers?" Eleanor followed.

"I…I don't know."

"Natasha," Eleanor stood and pulled up her padded underwear and pants in a quick motion, "what is all of this? Has this always been your life?"

Natasha looked around. The world was filled with a buzzing haze. She saw no answers in the long grass of the rolling field. She forgot the question as she focused on a hydro pole in the distance.

"I'm sorry, Eleanor. What did you say?" she wondered without shame.

"What is the truth of this?" Eleanor asked as she sat beside Natasha.

"The truth? The truth is that I'm also searching for what all this is. The truth is I don't even know if there is a truth. Everything I think I know, it all seems locked in a cage in the back of my head. I see it all, like… like a sign just out of eyeshot. I know the words are right there, but-but I can't read them. I can't connect to them. I can't feel them, or taste them, or touch them. They're just black squiggles... like untranslated hiero-glyphs. The truth is, Eleanor, I'm scared. I'm scared that at any moment whatever is out there or in my head will find me. It'll see me for what I am. It'll know. It'll realize I'm nothing. The hunt will end and I–I-" Natasha silenced herself as her eyes twinged. Her pain intensified as she sought comfort where she sat. Her chaffed and rashed skin screamed through her nerves as if it was remembering the horrors of the previous night. She cloaked her upper body in the blanket Eleanor had wrapped her in. "How did you find me? Why did you look for me?"

Eleanor stared into her. The old woman had aged years in the days between their hospital meeting. Her wrinkled eyes seemed even smaller under the developing bags that darkened her expression lines. Her tight graying hair was frayed and spindly beneath her bun.

"It is strange how things somehow seem to fall in exact order. There always seems to be an odd fictitiousness to reality." Eleanor looked down at the ground between her legs and picked a piece of grass. "I apologize. Please ignore my old woman ramblings." She threw the blade of grass back down to the ground. "We pursued a boy. A boy connected to you in, what is still, an unknown manner it seems. The OPP put an amber alert out for him. Although we did not find him, we found you and a man in the forest the boy was last known to have been. The man was known to us...My recommendation is that you be cautious of him. He has…lost himself. The rest is honestly a blur. I am not sure what to say to it."

"Say more: the boy and this man? I saw them. Who are they?"

"Strangers, I expect. Happenstance victims. I am loath to admit it, but I unfortunately do not quite understand it myself," Eleanor admitted.

Natasha winced from a sudden painful reminder of her injuries. The ground seemed to harden beneath her. "What do they want with me?" She shifted uncomfortably.

"I am not positive. Based on my confrontations with the man, Arjun Kaul, I believe his name is, it appears he seeks to aid you in some capacity," Eleanor reflected. "The boy…well, I have not personally seen or met him, but he has left a trail of violence from what I hear."

"How? Why?"

"I was hoping you had the answers, Natasha," Eleanor sighed. "I am afraid I do not know. There is more than a little violence that is connected also to you."

Natasha lowered her face to hide the sobs that revealed themselves with her breathing. Hopelessness burrowed like a predatory insect inside of her. She focused on the hair she realized she twirled between her fingers.

"My mother…they said she was crazy my whole life. We were close once, I think, but that feels like a lifetime ago. I have so few memories of her now. I always thought she was strong. She was always taking care of something. Somehow, I know…I know that this all connects back to her. The things she saw and the things she did. The things she was in secret. This all seems to link back to her, but it all seems so sudden. She could have reached out. She could have explained. I would have understood. I-I would have gone to her," Natasha stuttered. She pressed her hands into her eyes and angrily twisted them to block the tears. "She…she's dead. I know it in my heart. She's dead."

"Well, she was a mother. I know it is an old trope, but everything she did up until the end had you at the centre of it, whether she wanted you there or not. Do you remember how she passed?"

"No, I'm not sure. Umm, I don't specifically remember anything about it. She…I was – She was in my arms…I see her. She was limp, like a…a doll," Natasha found herself recalling.

"Where were you?" Eleanor probed. "Did she say anything?"

"Why is my body so hot, but I feel so cold…" Natasha hugged the blanket gently closer to warm her shivering limbs. She hoped her visible suffrage hid the shallow truth of her inability to recollect the image of her mother's face.

"Just hold on, Natasha. Let me have another look at the lacerations." Eleanor squatted beside her. "We need to wash these…"

Natasha sensed a strange reservation with Eleanor's examination of her. She tried to shift closer to the woman, but Eleanor pulled her hand quickly away.

"Am I...contagious? Does it affect everybody? What-what is it?"

"I have theories, but it appears to impact people differently. The only variance between the four notable cases, which appear to be distinct in purpose, is gender. Of course, this is rather all speculation, as I can only ascertain based on the evidence I have collected in piecemeal," Eleanor considered. "Anyway, we should be moving. Who knows what is behind us? Your injuries will have to wait."

Eleanor took a pair of folded latex gloves out of her pocket and stretched them on. The gloves' wrists and fingers were rolled and stretched from previous use. The woman looked down at her own clothes before she tucked her hands under Natasha's armpits and assisted her to her feet. Natasha leaned unsteadily into Eleanor, using her as a crutch. They stumbled awkwardly together.

"How do you know whatever this is isn't airborne? What if a strand of my hair has brushed you?"

"I suppose I would have already been one of your victims," Eleanor said thoughtfully.

"What if you are? What if gender has nothing to do with it? What if it has to do with the strength of a person's spirit or the strength of heart or something stupid like that?" Eleanor said nothing. Natasha focused her remaining energy on her legs as they worked to keep her standing. Her breathing struggled as she fought herself from crying out. Eleanor's gloved hands in her armpits were like gripping claws that dug into her skin. She breathed and choked back another whimper. "Stop…We need to stop," she spilled out. "I can't… Oh my god, I can't. I can't. Please. Eleanor…I can't."

"Alright, Natasha," Eleanor succumbed through sharp breaths. "I-I think you are right, but we can only rest for a moment. We have to leave this place as soon as we can."

"Maybe whatever I have is making you do this?"

"No," Eleanor replied sternly. "I would absolutely know when I have lost the capacity of my mind."

"Maybe you're right…I don't know. I just know I can't go another step…Maybe that hydro pole will lead us to people. You should just leave me here and go get help."

Eleanor sighed. She hesitated for a long moment.

"I think you are right, Natasha. That is the most logical thing to do," she said with another sigh.

Eleanor shifted and Natasha found herself following the woman's physical guidance to the ground. Natasha laid her head into the grass as her body was settled. She pulled the blanket over herself. Her teeth chattered from a coldness that reached inside her. She curled like a cocktail shrimp. Eleanor stood for a moment, breathing slowly, then walked off.

The heat of the sun wavered as its edge reached for the horizon. Natasha stared into the grass beside her. It vibrated curiously. An unfelt breeze seemed to sway the thin stocks as they jostled nonuniformly in her direction.

"Do you…hear me?" she whispered into the grass, hesitating under the fear of her revelation.

The grass stopped, as if its wind was suddenly carried off. It was eerily silent. She waited for some form of communication of understanding. Nothing happened. She held back a whimper as Eleanor crushed the grass underfoot when she suddenly returned. The green stocks were left crinkled beneath the woman's stained sneakers.

"There is a road by the base of the pole. I think we should set up there for the night, at least. If a vehicle approaches, we will see the lights or hear it from there. That is our best chance," Eleanor described. Her breathing was lightened, but she held her stomach as if she was hurt.

"Are you alright, Eleanor?"

"I am fine. Please, please do not worry about me. It is a personal burden." Natasha nodded in understandding. "Are *you* alright, Natasha? You look horrible."

"I feel absolutely dreadful." Natasha suddenly realized she had no memory of her last laugh. "Well, I suppose we should just do this now."

She tried to push herself up, but her arms refused her in defying vibrations. Eleanor swooped in quickly and assisted her.

"Come on," the woman said sternly.

They both grunted as Eleanor pulled Natasha into a standing position. Natasha leaned on the taller woman as they slogged the final metres to the road's edge.

The blanket dragged infuriatingly across Natasha's skin with each step. She looked at her toes and saw her own blood dripping down her shins. She felt Eleanor's shame and was relieved the blood was from her wounds. She was annoyed that she was relieved.

Eleanor suddenly stumbled. Natasha felt the woman's grip loosen and slide down her arm.

"Eleanor?" Natasha moaned as she tried to bear the woman's collapse. Eleanor pulled Natasha to the ground.

Natasha moaned into the dirt as her body shook from the pain. Her vision was spotted, and the world spun. She attempted to drag herself up, but everything seemed to move in slow motion. She dug her fingers into the earth, but they only dragged through the soft dirt as she tried to pull herself forward. She ached to be on her feet. She tried everything to move, but her body was as stubborn as a resolute cat. She turned her head to see Eleanor on her own back. The woman breathed heavily with her open eyes to the sky. "What do we do?"

"We wait, I suppose," Eleanor breathed out hoarsely, keeping her eyes on the sea above them.

"What if no one comes?"

"Then no one comes, I suppose," Eleanor said easily.

"I…I don't think I'm going to make it, Eleanor. I really-I really can't go any further." Natasha's mouth quivered. She fought with everything left not to cry. She shivered again. The cold bit at her through the heat like a hellish torture. She attempted to spit out some of the dirt that she breathed into her mouth but choked Each cough felt like her last as her lungs fought for air. Her throat was dry from the gritty dust and the dehydration. She choked and gagged and coughed. Her prayers were coming true in a final abuse as she heaved for air. Her chest struggled under an invisible weight that pressed down on her. "Thank you…"

Eleanor stirred beside her and began to shout. Natasha saw the shape of the woman leaning over her, but her vision was spotted. She struggled for air. Her throat tightened. She tried to call, but nothing came out. It was the end. She felt it. It was finally the end. A hideous, ugly, and tortured end, but she found it. Her body resisted her thoughts as it fought for each breath. Her mind opened. Everything was a kaleidoscope of colour. She was no longer aware of her breathing. The shapes of the universe spun in her mind. She felt her body lift from the earth and into the blue sky, through the clouds, into a darkness speckled with patches of light, past flickering metallic shapes and orbiting bits of debris, and into blackness. She lifted toward nothing. Everything was utterly dark and cold, until her universe shook, and she suddenly felt air rush into her. The energy and glow of life burst like an explosion into view as she was turned to her side.

"Damnit, Natasha…God damnit," Eleanor heaved. Frustration waded in the woman's brown eyes. Natasha felt Eleanor's warm hands against her skin.

The woman's face was sickly pale. Natasha said nothing. She struggled to swallow. Eleanor suddenly turned her head. "Hey! Hey! Can you help us?" The woman struggled to her feet.

"You alright?" a man called out. "She alright?"

"She is alive, yes. Do you have any water? Can you help us?" Eleanor dropped back to her knees.

Natasha didn't see the man, but there was a long hesitation.

"Listen, the closest hospital is in Sudbury and we're a bit of a ways from my truck. I don't think – Shit, umm, shit. Just hold on," the man said. She could hear his shuffling movements. Footsteps approached and a shadow hid her from the remaining light of the sun as the man's dark shape blocked its weakening molestation. She rolled back to her back. "Jesus…" He stepped backward. "Listen, this ain't right for me. I'll have to call someone."

"For god's sake, give me that water then," Eleanor demanded.

"Here, I just opened it," the man said. He sounded nervous.

"Is it me?" Natasha said through tears, into the sky. "Such a hideous thing not even my bare breasts can redeem? Am I so fucking beaten and bloody that people no longer see a person?"

"Natasha, take a drink. Come on," Eleanor demanded. The woman kneeled by her head.

"Who are you? I can't trust you…I can't trust any of this," Natasha spat. Droplets from her eyes became domes in the dirt as they made hesitating dives off her cheeks. "Please, Eleanor…Eleanor, just let me die…"

The man's shadow turned everything into a dark blur. She felt her head lift from behind. She suddenly gagged on water as her mouth was propped open. Her handlers cowed her. All sound was distorted as if replaced by the crackle of a fizzing TV screen.

"This world is no good for you," the red-gloved thing said to her. It stood at her feet like a twilight phantom. Its ghastly face, scarred by her nails, broadened at her recognition of its hollowed-out tone. "Look what you've done to yourself. My my, such a shame… Such a shame."

It smelled the air with a deep inhale. She watched its round unpainted nostrils flare and flutter obscenely. She felt suspended in time. Eleanor and the man were gone.

"You're not real… You're not real…" she said to herself. "You're not real!"

She blinked and it was gone. Eleanor was kneeling at her feet. She watched the man as he spoke on the phone. She tried to direct her focus to Eleanor's eyes, but they were indistinct through the veil over her vision.

"Stay with me," Eleanor said as she re-snugged the blanket around Natasha.

"Your eyes…Your eyes are brown," Natasha whispered.

"Yes, they are brown. Now just lay your head

back down. Come on…Good…Good. Now, Natasha… where are you from?"

Natasha closed her eyes and laid her head into the dirt. Her body was a tingled numbness. Whispers were like fluttering insects in her ear.

"I'm from Marmora… Marmora, Ontario," she said with a breath of annoyance.

"And…what do you do? Are you in school?" Eleanor pressed.

"School…I'm-I'm not in school…but I don't know. I don't know…This isn't the time for this… Please… Please. Let me at least just sleep," Natasha moaned.

"Come on, Natasha. You are a smart woman. You know what I am doing here. Stay with me. Listen, I am exhausted too: absolutely beat to hell. I feel like I just did a Dwayne Johnson four AM workout blitz, but you have to work with me. You want to die? You think death is a better option? Well, I cannot provide you with any wisdom to say death is not the better option, but you will not be dying while a damn doctor is here. You will not. I did not go through years of turmoil and suffrage. I did not read and write papers and my dissertation. I did not just drag you through miles of forest for this to be acceptable. You will listen and you will understand right now, Natasha. You are going to force yourself out of this or so help me god," Eleanor demanded. "Now tell me, what do you do for work?"

Natasha's nose tickled with fluid. Eleanor was a Niobean bust looking down on her.

"I'm a…a Historical Analyst…I-I just need to close my eyes for a second… Maybe if I sleep this off, I'll be okay," Natasha felt herself murmur.

"Natasha, you will not. What is your mother's name?" Eleanor asked desperately.

"Eleanor… Please," Natasha begged. The world seemed to bristle with light above her. The sky was cloudless and empty. "My mother…She…We are the same. The world speaks to us…"

"What do you mean?"

"Can't you hear it?!" Natasha yelled. "The trees. The water. The earth. They call out in throbbing whispers, like a web of living things. They are searching for something…And I…I'm at the heart of it as it closes in around me. My death…my true death, will be at the whims of these otherworldly demons. I see it now. They will turn everything against me…Their utter design is my demise…I smell the hunger on their breath, like belligerent drunks at a bar. They have that look: the nurses, the man, the boy, the-the things…They all have it. A look that is so ill intentioned that it stains their eyes…But you…You have brown eyes. They're average and…and they're small…They're beautiful. Oh my God, they're beautiful."

Natasha was driven by an urge to caress Eleanor's face. Despite her numbness, she felt her arm lift slowly.

"Natasha, I cannot take your hand," Eleanor said as she kneeled back down.

"Am I so disgusting that I can't even be touched…" Natasha winced from a sudden stabbing from her maimed stomach. She rushed her gaze back to Eleanor's eyes. They were still brown. Her soul reached out to the woman's maternal instincts, but they were greeted by a barrier strained by a hidden sadness. "Why are you here? Tell me, Eleanor…Why have you stayed?"

"I had a daughter once…A husband too, if you could believe it. It seems so long ago now. We were so close, the three of us. They were amazing…And then there was me. I am no mother. No mother like a mother is expected to be. He was more mother than I ever was. Well, nevertheless, they died in a car accident. As all such things are, it was horrible and painful. I dug into the confines of my studies and my work. It became my opiate. Soon enough their death became my badge and my mask; I hid from the world. Now I am old without being old, and I have nothing but my badge, my mask, and my work. Then, as all these stories seem to go, there was you. Though, it was not my daughter that I saw in your hazelnut eyes…but myself."

The man coughed conspicuously as he stepped away. The silence was a strange comfort. Eleanor's personal suffering was a strange comfort. Natasha breathed deeply and smelt the particles of life trickling around her. She felt the living energy of the pollen she inhaled. Whispers were carried by the floating dandelion umbrella hairs. The world awakened with her self-awareness, as the sun set.

"Eleanor, I'm sorry, but I can't be here...I-I have to go…I need to get out," Natasha said weakly.

"Well, you can try if you like, Natasha, but I do not think you are going to make it far," Eleanor said.

"Further than if you let me get taken from this place…My story's done. You don't need to pretend anymore…You think I'll be an acceptable woman once I get out of here? Do people so easily overcome this kind of trauma? What will I become? Who will I become?" Natasha wept.

"You are not getting taken, Natasha. Now listen, a story is not over until there is no one left to breathe life into it. Yes, you have seen the underbelly of abhorrent violence. Maybe you have experienced worse. I do not know a thing about you, but hate, violence, rape, death, they are all as much a part of a story as love and hope. Maybe the words of another paint you as an eternal victim, but you must live the image of yourself that you want to see, otherwise, your unauthentic self will become unsustainable. You will crumble under the unrelenting feet of society. You must accept your sufferings, as you accept all other things. Through acceptance you will find hope. Hope for yourself. Hope for your children. Hope for a world that whips its inhabitants around like debris in a storm…Now please, let me help you."

"Everybody is trying to help…or lead me…or guide me. I don't want any help - I didn't ask for any. I'm not your daughter. I'm not you," Natasha spat. Eleanor sighed. Natasha's stomach curdled as she watched the woman's tired expression. "I'm sorry, Eleanor. I'm so sorry."

"Stop being ridiculous. I am not here to argue with you. I am not here to mother you. We are going to get out of here and get some serious help." Eleanor hesitated. She seemed dazed. "I think that this is bigger than you. There is something out there…a monster. It-it slaughtered them."

"You have to leave me. You have to go on," Natasha begged. "It'll come for me."

"I'm sorry to interrupt, but my wife is on the way with her truck," the man said. "She won't be long now. We're just down the road there."

"Thank you," Eleanor said.

"What colour are his eyes?" Natasha whispered up to Eleanor.

"They are dark…like a brown, maybe," Eleanor clarified after a moment. "Why?"

"The sign, it's in the eyes…I told you…The man, the nurses…the boy, they all had it." Natasha clenched her teeth as a spasm of pain erupted from her chest. "We can't wait here."

"I saw it in Arjun: the black eyes," Eleanor whispered.

The cawing of circling black birds penetrated the power of the world's whispers. They flew overhead in large patches of black.

"Hey, there's someone coming. Are you both alright?" the man put in. "It looks like some kind of nurse or something? Is she with you guys?"

Natasha turned her focus to the man dressed in vivid orange and camouflage. He looked down a long gun he had pressed into his shoulder.

"Who is it?" Eleanor inquired, as she spun. "Is that...Cheryl? Natasha, the nurses that took you, what happened to them?"

"The Filipino girl, she...she was murdered. The other, the bigger one, I-I don't remember...The ambulance...she drove it right off the road. I thought she died in the crash...but I saw her again. I don't know what happened to her."

"She looks like hell. Can you grab some more water?" Eleanor hissed at the man.

"Sure," he said, bringing his rifle down. "This woman is with you?"

"In a sense..." Eleanor said.

"Here." The man reached into a pouch at his waist. "Can't say I'm upset that I actually get to use this thing."

The memory of the black eyes of the nurse in azure made Natasha's rattling nerves even colder. She expected to see her own breath despite her sweat soaked body.

"I am going to help her," Eleanor said as she began to step away from Natasha.

"No. Wait...Don't leave me again," Natasha moaned as she grabbed Eleanor's shin. "She's one of them...She had the blackened eyes." Eleanor looked down at her. The woman hesitated before jostling her leg free from Natasha's grip. "Don't! She'll kill you."

"Cheryl, are you alright? What happened?" Natasha heard Eleanor call out.

Indistinct chatter followed. The man cradled his gun and kept his gaze in the direction Eleanor had walked off.

"Don't worry. My wife is a healer. She'll be able to help you until we get to a hospital. I'd've called an ambulance, but that ain't much help around these parts. These women…Are you alright? Are they alright?" The man squatted down. "I'm sorry I don't know a thing I could do to help."

"No, it's not you. Just stay away, okay? Just don't come near me," Natasha urged.

"Alright. No issue. Not any of my business. I was just checking. Not usual with a thing like this."

The women returned. The nurse in azure was broken and bent. A stream of blood had dried from a crusted spot on her head. Her dark clothes were covered in dust and mud and speckles of black red. Her eyes hovered momentarily on Natasha as she followed Eleanor.

"I-I-I don't know what h-h-happened," the nurse stuttered. "I was g-guiding Gail on a f-follow-up and then suddenly I-I was here. I-in this p-p-place. I saw a man and a-a-a boy. I don't-I don't know. I-I-I'm sorry."

"My God, Cheryl, just have a seat. Yes, right there." Eleanor assisted the bent woman to the ground. She looked away from the disheveled nurse as she stood back up. "That must be your wife there now."

Natasha held her gaze on the nurse. The big woman deliberately avoided a reciprocation of her glare.

"Who the hell do you think you are?" Natasha

spat. She shifted uncomfortably. Hate added pricks to her torn body. "If you're still one of them, just do it. Just kill me."

The nurse stared at the ground and remained silent. A vehicle pulled up and quick footsteps followed a closing door.

"Oh jeez, Francis. What happened?" a woman worried.

Before anyone could stop her, the woman bent down and touched Natasha's forehead. Natasha slapped the woman's hand away instinctively.

"Hey, stop th-"

"No!" Eleanor yelled.

"Don't touch me," Natasha panicked. "Shit… Use hand sanitizer or a disinfectant wipe or something. You can't touch me."

"Listen lady-" the woman began.

"Okay, okay, relax. What has ignorantly been done is done. We will have to work through it. Damnit, I was not thinking." Eleanor rubbed brown eyes that were sagged by exhaustion.

"Francis, what is going on? What are they talking about?" the woman huffed.

"The taint…" the nurse whispered. She lifted her head from her stain patched knees. Her black eyes turned on Natasha. "This stubborn g-girl. She reeks of a poison so foul that she en-en-ensnares any who t-touch her. Her victims are left to serve the whims of f-f-faceless masters…"

The nurse stood up sharply and jabbed something at the unsuspecting man. The gun fell to the ground as he shot his hands and eyes to his stomach in shock. The nurse pulled back and blood immediately pooled through his jacket.

"Francis!" the woman cried. "Shit! Francis?"

The nurse slapped Francis's wife and she fell to the ground. Eleanor tried to grab for the gun, but the nurse easily shoved her away. Eleanor hit the ground with a thud and stopped moving.

"Y-y-you stupid b-bitch," the nurse said. She gripped a roughly pointed stick that was now dripping with the man's blood. She stepped over the woman and slammed the stick into the wife's throat. She pulled it out with a horrid squish and jabbed it down again.

"No!" Natasha screamed.

The nurse stepped over to Natasha. She gripped Natasha by the hair. Natasha felt the tug as her face was forced to meet the nurse's. "He n-n-needs you. H-he hungers for you. It must be d-d-done."

Natasha tried to grab at the woman's hand pulling her hair, but she was too weak. The nurse pulled her hair tighter and coiled it around her fist. Natasha choked out a squeal. The nurse tugged and then tugged again. Natasha felt the strands pull against her scalp as the nurse began to drag her. The pain trickled through her numbed limbs. The world watched her pensively as she was pulled like a street whore to her defilement. Her dying body stopped calling for relief. Her sandpaper lungs begged for the deep burn of a final cigarette.

Chapter 16

The blood from Arjun's nose congealed like mucus in his mouth. He tried to find satisfaction in its liquid quality, but the tightness of his throat denied him the feeling. The women and girls sat in a circle around him. They talked as if he wasn't leashed to a pole in the centre. He heard giggles and laughs. They had smiling and listening faces. A skinny woman, with short dark hair, passed a pipe to a girl who could've been a student of his.

He spat a build up of the blood and looked around for the deer-legged woman. He lost sight of her after the beatings had stopped. He strained his muscles against the restraints. His efforts left him limp. His bitten arm was feelingless. Blood mixed with sweat. He brought his focus back to the women as he realized only the whispers of the trees stirred in the background. The eyes of the female circle were all on him.

"Inini, you will speak truth here. You will remove your mask of flesh while you look into the eyes of the broken daughters, sisters, and mothers of the Anishinaabeg," the deer-legged woman whispered into his ear from behind. A sharp object pressed against his lower-back and he felt the humility of mortality in his stomach. "Do we scare you, inini?"

"I'm not here to hurt anyone…" he urged as he tried to turn to her. "I'll tell you anything. I-I have nothing to hide."

"Good." She traced the pointed object from his back to his lower abdomen. "Very good."

He twisted uncomfortably to see her. He could see only her face. Her eyes looked his body up and down. He crossed his legs impulsively to hide his unshaven shame.

"The fables all say do it, inini. Cut it off…All the stories say it. Dismember the vile monster. It is such a fine gesture. Look at these women and girls. You will see their devotion to that need. To that justice. They whisper it to me. They speak through the wind, inini. Have you not heard their cries?" She grabbed him and he clenched his eyes shut. Her hand was warm and feminine. Her touch wasn't aggressive. She laughed. The eyes of the girls and women encircling them didn't blink. "A stirring? Do I arouse you?"

"No. Stop this," he begged.

"A creature that can't control its urges. What do they call that? Ahh, yes, a beast." He felt a sharp pain at his side. He shuddered. "Don't be afraid, beast. It's better this way, trust me. The hate, shame, and fear never leave a survivor. It is always there like a revealing shimmer in a woman's eye. She would rather spill her insides than reveal the bottomless hole that sits in her stomach like an ever-hungry parasite devouring everything she is connected to."

"I wouldn't. I wouldn't do that. Natasha - Her name is Natasha. She's connected to you somehow… Arre baap re, I'm just trying to get to her. Everything in me is pulling me there, voices in my head thundering like a stampede. Everything pulling me toward her is pushing me away. This feeling, this world. I-I don't know what the Deva is going on. I'm just trying to get to her. Something inside me is linked to her. The trees… The flowers. Nature, all the nature, it will speak to this. It knows. I can feel its connection to her like some kind of energy or-or chakra or something. The world shakes with it…and when she's near, the world is an eruption of sensation and life that I-I can't describe. Please, I know I am nothing to these girls, as many men must seem…but really, I am just another person. I'm not driven by a need to harm or hurt anyone or anything. Deva, I teach children!"

She looked down at him. Her dilated eyes were tilted ovals filled with brown. He felt the sharp object's point hesitate against his skin. He struggled to hide his discomfort.

"You hear the voices of the All Mother?" she asked. Her innuendoed tone was missing.

"I don't know what I hear or feel, but there is something, something out there pulling at me."

A phantom pain was left at his side as the pointed object was slowly pulled away.

"Ganawenjige…" she whispered. "Do you know your fate, inini?"

"I only know I need to get to her - to Natasha."

"Yes, the trials of meshkwadoon," she sighed. She released the hold she had on him. The missing pressure against his groin left an instinctive feeling of vacancy. She turned her back to him and stepped toward the encircling girls. "Take comfort, for he is not of those we seek. Go, return to peace," she concluded to the girls.

They immediately broke the circle and left at individual paces into the trees. They faded out of sight like soundless ghosts. A bird called out. A response followed. The glade's normality resurrected like a busy street following an accident. He made a struggle of his bonds to remind the deer-legged woman that he was still there. She turned back to face him.

"The spirit behind your eyes says you speak truth, inini. Be wary, however, for your honesty is corrupted by a need. A need that will drive you to your death." She tilted her head to the sky. She sniffed the air. "The willow stirs."

She stepped toward him and cut the bonds at his feet. She threw the sharp object, and it landed unseen with a thud. He closed his eyes and basked in the sensation of freedom.

"Thank y-" he began, as he lifted his eyes to her, but she was gone. "Arre baap re…This place. Saala kutta, I'm *sick* of this."

He went to hit the ground, but realized his wrists were still bound together.

"Son of a-" he spat angrily as he twisted aggressively against the rope bond. He clenched his teeth and hit the dirt at his knees. His injured arm tingled with a concerning pang. "Come back here!"

His echo was the only response. He struggled to his feet and leaned weakly against the stake he was released from. He thought of his rope handcuffs and looked for the thrown sharp object to cut them with.

He limped over to the dull stone blade that protruded from the earth. He awkwardly wiggled it loose. He sat down and struggled to find a position where he could restrain it. He finally was comfortable with the bone handle between his bare feet. He spent many frustrating minutes sliding the rope against the loftily held edge. His biceps burned. The dog bite pulsed. When the final rope strand snapped, he spent a moment searching for peace.

When he found a feeling of pained balance, he brought his thoughts to his clothes. The glade was empty except for spots of grass. He covered himself with one hand, held his other arm weakly to his matted chest, and slowly followed the ubiquitous whispers into the trees.

The sun was high, and his hairy body glistened from each colliding ray. He walked slowly, with a searching gaze. He felt watched. The whispers and vibrations carried with them an awareness. Their awareness frightened him into humility, as if the gods watched him shamelessly from above. The sun's revealing rays were like spotlights in the trees that he avoided. The shaded ground he stuck to stabbed with unseen pebbles at his feet. He couldn't gauge his direction. Natasha's reverberations were unclear. She was an idea that drove him, but she no longer was a passenger in the back of his mind. He had to find her. The uneven earth began to slope upward, and his limping malcontent grew deeper.

"This damn forest," he angrily whispered to himself, as he struggled up the slope. "Arre baap re." The climb slowly became treacherous as it grew more vertical. He pulled himself to a flat portion and stopped. He tried to focus on his options. He looked up to a cliff wall and looked back down where the slope returned into dim light. He wondered if he should climb down and go around, but he resisted the idea. He sat on the smoothest rock he could find and shook his head. "Holy Deva…"

He looked out across the trees. The sun was already dipping to the edge of the earth. He saw a lake, swarming murders encircling the treetops, a river, and a forest that expanded out of site. He shook his head, stood up, and turned to pee against the rock wall. Pushing the pee out caused him to clench as something inside his stomach burned. He looked down at his bruised abdomen and groaned.

Once he finished, he sat back down on his rock and scratched his unwashed hair. He put his head in his hand and listened to the world he blinded himself from. He listened to its layers, picking between strands of the harmonized network. A vibration ran through his toes. It trickled up his back. His head moved with its sensation. He lifted away from his hand to see only the blinding light of day. He tried to focus on his deep breathing, but the soft sound of shuffling movements distracted him. He looked quickly around to catch the shape of hideous creatures sitting cross-legged on the edge of the flat landing. The bark-like figurines watched him with protruding beady white eyes.

"What the Deva are you?" he remarked, catching his breath. They were silent. They watched him like curious monkeys. He shifted his eyes along them, squinting to confirm his vision. "Are you like that other…with the blue eyes?"

One of the creatures twitched its head to the side, its own chalky eyes focused on him. Dust swirled at his feet. The hair on his arms and chest lifted. The cold breeze heightened his insecurity. Trees moaned. The sound of his own heart thumped in his head. The earth vibrated. He felt it in his soles. He tried to lift his feet out of fear, but they were magnetised to the ground.

"Mino giizhigad," a demonic voice spoke. It carried a hideous reminder of the taste of soil. He turned from the creatures to the deranged red vested figure. Its face was angular and painted chalky white. Its penetrating grey eyes were edged like a sword. "Aabawaa."

"What do you want with me?" His resolve dwindled at the site of the monster.

It laughed with a vulgar shriek. "The petals of our ivory flower have begun to open. I can smell her blossoming." It inhaled deeply with its eyes closed. "She runs. Yesss, she flees like a runt of Nanabozho's frightened litter. And you, you are but a starved hound on a scent. Fulfill your design, mutt."

"I can't. I can't feel her," he stressed. "You must tell me how."

The being cracked a hideous grin. It stepped forward and lifted his hand by the wrist. Its touch was like burning ice. It was uncomfortably close. He could feel its cold breath. It let his hand fall limply back to his side.

"Embrace your instinctual needs."

"What if my instinctual needs tell me to kill you?"

The figure's shrill laugh rang down the slope. The trees shriveled in its strength. The repeating thumps of his heart grew in intensity. His feet gripped the earth. A crow landed on a rock nearby and cawed. He jumped from the sudden interruption. It flew off with an annoyed bark.

"It senses death," the deranged figure claimed.

"Whose?" Arjun asked, struggling to focus with the pounding in his head.

"Omens do not speak. They are only messengers of fear."

"Why do you keep me alive? What is your name?"

"Jiibayaabooz." The forgotten beady eyed creatures shook as if energized by the strange word.

"Why do you follow me?" He felt the dirt under his butt dampen from his body's pooling sweat. "Tell me what you want!"

"What I want? Noooo, no. You're not listening. You're not listening! This isn't petty chatter for the sake of entertainment, you mutt." It slapped him. "Did you not feel the boy? You expect to be given power for nothing? Power is will, fool. Flesh and bone are nothing. You must seek beyond the bounds of your rotting shell."

Arjun was too stunned to react, the sensation of the being's large frost-bite hand hitting him rang in his head like a bell's clapper. He gurgled up the blood that he tasted in his throat and spat a red pile of bile on to the dirt at the figure's long-nailed feet. He traced his eyes from the ground and up its loose and frayed animal-hide pants. He stopped as he realized the breasts partially hidden underneath the red vest.

"Just tell me what you want with me," he implored through his teeth.

Its cold grip wrapped around his neck and lifted him off the rock. The excess fluids in his throat clogged with the pressure. His body shook as it fought for air. His voice was caught in a silent gag. Panic flooded him as the world called out like a warrior's drum. Everything blurred. The monster's grey eyes were grotesquely large.

"Find her," it snarled.

It tossed him to the ground and released a haunting shrill. He spluttered and coughed into the dirt. The vulnerability of his nudity anchored him. His anxieties fought with his terror.

He looked up and saw across the trees. The sun

kissed the horizon. The monster and the beady eyed creatures were gone.

"Saala fucking kutta…" he cursed, as he pushed himself up into a sitting position.

He curled his arms into his chest. He looked around with the capacity of a pitiful child. The world was ugly and dim. He got to his feet. His body ached from the violence of the Lost Girls. Their eyes were imprinted in his head as he searched for a spot to relieve his nerve loosened bowels. He felt their lifeless stares through the dimness watching him squat at his most vulnerable. He clenched his eyes to hide from the fear and the shame, but he was comforted in his release.

The unblinking leers carried him blindly onward, naked and unwashed, until the whispers of the world returned. The trees were curious strangers that watched him. It grew colder and louder as the forest darkened. Mosquitoes buzzed around his head and began to peck at his body. The welts left behind swelled and itched. He swatted at the biting insects as their swarms thickened. He attempted to escape the assault by outpacing them but was limited by the forming blisters between his toes and his lungs' reminder of his lapse in self-care.

He tried to focus on Natasha as he altered his pace, but the compiled irritations left him limping weakly. He tried to breath methodically. He repeated in his head a prayer to the universe for rescue.

He was forced to stop under the weight of his dumbbell breaths. He leaned against a barely visible tree trunk. Everything was eerily dark. He bathed in his own frigid droplets of sweat. He couldn't comprehend how the light of day had slipped away. The bark of the tree was moist with life. He closed his eyes. He could feel something inside the tree like a flow of life. He followed the feeling down the trunk and to the dirt where it faded. He wanted to slam his fist into the ground, but he couldn't summon the energy. He struggled to his feet again.

He stumbled and tripped through the thick bush until his torn feet met gravel. He hesitated and stepped backward. He could see a road like a dark river of stone running between two walls of trees. A shape moved through the dimness along the opposite shoulder. It was close enough to stand out, but far enough where he couldn't determine what it was. It slowly moved forward then stopped. He felt it consider him. He heard its heavy breathing. He somehow knew it was a dog. Its breathing quietened and it began to growl. He turned to flee but his movement triggered it to run. It came at him in clicking steps. He tripped and felt its body crash over him with a thump and a squeal. He looked up and saw it savagely rise. Drool dripped from its curled mouth. He could smell its nasty breath and unwashed fur. It dove at him, and he wildly reached out his hands. He felt its head and body flail as he gripped his fingers into its fur. He squeezed with an unrelenting fury that blinded him.

He awoke from a sudden stupor. There was no light, but he could feel the warm blood dripping down his arms. He realized the dog was still gripped in his clenched hands. His thumbs were hooked horrifically into its eye sockets. Its jaw and tongue dangled lifelessly. He pulled his hands away and puked. His hands shook as he wiped puke residue off his face. He began to sob. He looked at his bloodied fingers. He tried to wipe them in the grass, but nothing came off. He looked at them. They shook. His eyes were filled with their red stain. He heard something in the trees, but all he saw was red. He sobbed into his shaking bloody palms.

Chapter 17

"How long you been out here?" the woman asked Yuuta, as she turned her head to him.

The truck rattled with each bump. Its shakes unsettled his stomach. A song on the radio filled the gap of his hesitation.

"I can't remember. A couple days?" He couldn't look away from the road. The feeling in his stomach worsened with the punishing thoughts of what he'd unknowingly reveal. "What day is it?"

"It's Monday, June twenty-third or twenty-fourth, I think. I'd have to check my phone," she said as she kept driving.

Time suddenly hit him as he watched the truck lights break the darkness with their white beams.

"Oh, well, how far away does Ogi live from here? And I'm sorry to ask this…but do you have any food… or some water, please?"

"Umm, I-" She hesitated as she looked around quickly. "I've got nothing for you, sorry. Ogi though… I know he's got some land on Whitefish, but I can't remember for the life of me exactly where it is. I'm going to take you to the local APS to get you figured out, though. They should have som-"

"No!" he shouted. His ears warmed with the realization of the outburst. He looked at the woman. Her collared shirt was untucked over a pair of loose jeans. Her chin length hair was a black dusted grey. Her cheeks had pits like miniature craters. He watched her peek over at him with wrinkled eyebrows. She had an aunt-like face. "I just think - I really think I should see him." He felt the axe in his backpack like a beating heart against his back.

"Listen, eh... I've had my share of sights and such. This chick is done with that stuff. I'm on my two feet with the goals of peace and comfort now. It's them or the highway, my friend," she went on with a sigh. "By the way, my name's Dell. What's yours?"

"You don't understand. I-I-I'll give you money! I have some money on me." He struggled the backpack off his back. "I have some money. Please."

"I don't want your money." Dell took her eyes from the road and looked at him. Suddenly she shot them back and swerved slightly. "Jesus! Did you see that sucker?" He looked quickly back to the road. She pulled the vehicle to the rocky shoulder. It shook sketchily. "You alright, eh?"

He nodded. He looked at his door's mirror and saw nothing.

"What was it?" He wondered. Dell twisted to unbuckle herself. "I-I think we should keep going. We should go right to Ogi."

"Keep going? Not down here. Take this," she said with a grunt as she reached under her seat and pulled out a long object. She pulled off a decorated leather cover to reveal a long blade with a leather wrapped handle. He grabbed the blade's hilt gingerly. He felt uncomfortable with it in his hands. "It's just a knife, eh. It'll only do what you tell it to."

Dell adjusted her blue jeans and struggled through her door. He felt the truck shift and looked in the rear-view mirror. He watched her wrap around to the truck's back, open it, pull out a long black case, open it, and remove a long gun. He followed her with his eyes as she walked to his window and tapped it lightly with her knuckle. She motioned with her head for him to follow.

"Wh-what are we doing?" He asked skeptically, as he stepped out. The long black gun made his stomach churn, despite the long knife he held. "Do you know what it was?"

"Hard to say out here. Could've been a black bear, but I don't think so…and hopefully I'm right, 'cause this rifle ain't shit against a bear."

He followed her slowly down the gravel shouldder. Flickering orange from the truck signals made it hard to focus beyond the lit spots. The wind sighed through the trees. He stopped and focused on the sensation of movement nearby, but it lifted with a shuffle and flew into the branches above. Dell stepped off the gravel and onto the grass. The sound of her footsteps vanished, but a strange moan grew distinct in the darkness.

"Eh?" Dell grunted.

"Help…" a voice replied.

Yuuta grabbed the back of Dell's shirt. His palm's sweat built like slime on the knife's handle. Dell stopped and fumbled through her baggy back pockets. She immediately clicked on the flashlight she pulled out. She moved its light slowly along the gravel before she shifted it to the opposite side of the road. There was nothing but the run of the pavement and trees in the resonant glow. She swiveled the flashlight to a spot on their side of the road. There was nothing strange.

Another moan to their left drew the flashlight and their eyes from the gravel shoulder to where the trees were thin. Yuuta's stomach brimmed in his throat. He felt his body pull back to the truck. Dell's persistence pulled him like an unwilling prisoner.

"Who are you?" Dell called into the darkness. He felt some assurance in the woman's confidence. "Are you alright?"

"Holy Deva! Praise them all. Praise them…I'm here. I'm here," a man cried desperately.

Dell motioned the ray of light to the shape of a naked hairy man crawling toward them on all fours. His eyes reflected the beam like black crystals. Yuuta gasped. "Mr…Mr. Kaul?"

The man said nothing as he struggled toward them.

"Jesus fuck!" Dell swore. She swung her rifle over her shoulder and ran over to the bruised and naked man. Yuuta watched her squat down. "Can I help you? We got to get you out of here… Shit, eh. What happened? Buddy, do you know this man? Are you alright?"

Yuuta stared into his teacher's inhuman eyes. He didn't see the man this thing used to be. He saw only a wounded beast edging away from death. The naked man's eyes swallowed Yuuta's in their hunger for life.

"Yuuta? Wha-what's going on? I–I-I can't feel her. Everything is quiet but for the poison in my own head. Blackness…A dark curtain pulled in front of my eyes. I-I can't see…Oh Deva…What have I done? What have I done? What have I done?" Mr. Kaul whimpered. His eyes glistened. Yuuta pulled back in embarrassment. His body resisted any sensation of pity as he focused on his hate for the begging creature. "Help me find her, Yuuta." The man edged forward weakly.

"Whoa, whoa. I can't let you do that. Come on," Dell huffed as she struggled to pull Mr. Kaul to his feet.

The black eyes of the naked creature's drooping head held to Yuuta. Its hairy body reiterated its animal-like state. Yuuta felt no shame in seeing it bared without reservation. He found momentary relief from fear as the wounded shell of the man was guided back to the truck like a psych-patient.

"He's my…teacher," Yuuta confessed, as he cautiously followed behind the pair.

"Jesus. This is exactly why I don't do this shit, eh," Dell ranted, as she shook her head. "What the hell happened to you? You're a right mess too. You and this kid…What happened out there? Is this a school trip or something? Jesus." She assisted the sad man-creature through the truck's passenger door.

"Yuuta…" Mr. Kaul breathed. He turned his head slowly toward Yuuta. "We-we need to find her."

"Hey, you're not finding anyone like this-"

"Listen!" Mr. Kaul interrupted. Yuuta and Dell froze instinctively. Mr. Kaul had his eyes closed and his nose lifted to the sky. "They're watching us…"

"Jesus man," Dell marvelled. "Let's just get you some help, eh? I'll have cursed myself Christian if I don't stop hearing the two of you."

Mr. Kaul didn't acknowledge Dell, but he followed her final guidance into the seat. She shut the door. Yuuta and Dell wrapped around to the driver side. Yuuta looked into the cab to see the brown, hairy creature slumped weakly against the passenger window. His bruises and bloodied arms were distinct in the vehicle's interior light.

"I can't go in," Yuuta claimed, feeling the presence of the man like phlegm caught in his throat.

"Eh? Things are complicated now, buddy. I'm not sure what happened out there, but you…you do what you need. I know that feeling. Jesus, I wish you didn't remind me of it," Dell said with a shaking head. "The yelling inside your heart like some asshole shouting demands that you had no plans for. Don't listen to it. It's just noise. That's all it is. Go if you have to, but don't be ascared to ask for some help, okay? Now, I best be taking him out of here. Don't need some man dying in my truck."

"You're going to let me do what I want?"

"Yeah, why not? It ain't my responsibility to be

taking those who're unwilling. Don't care how old you are," she admitted.

She removed the gun from over her shoulder and adjusted it into a slot behind her seat. She pulled herself inside.

"Take that for now, eh. It doesn't take being something special to sense the anger out there." She turned the key in the ignition and shut the door. She rolled down the window and stuck out the flashlight. "This'll do you some good too."

He watched from the grass beneath the trees as the truck pulled away in a cloud of dust. He swapped the knife and flashlight between his hands as he wiped away the sweat from his palms. He put the flashlight in his pocket. He used the bottom of his damp shirt to wipe the knife's leather handle. He gripped it and swung it. A tingle trickled down his neck. Something in the sheen of the clean blade felt murderous. His breathing quickened. He gripped the handle with both hands and looked to a spot before him, imagining a figure kneeling. It was like the shape of a man from a dream, faceless, yet disting-uishable through the sensations of his heart. He looked into the thinning dark curls of the man's hair. His heart beat against his ribs. He felt excitement. His arms tightened with expectation. He lifted the blade above his head. He felt the crevices of his dry lips with his tongue. The trees watched him at the peak of pleasure. He imagined Natasha spying on him. His body cowered as his groin swelled. Then suddenly his grip loosened in uncontrolled shame. He looked around. Everything was hidden but for the blade he still held in front of him. He breathed out in gasps as the ecstasy abandoned him. The feeling in his groin softened, although he still felt its control.

"Natasha…" he whispered to himself.

He kneeled down, placed the long knife in the grass, and removed his backpack. He shakily put the knife inside and swung the bag back to his back. He removed the flashlight that bulged against his thigh. He flicked it on and followed the whispers of a sleepless world into its wooded domain.

Chapter 18

Arjun's breath fogged the window the top of his head leaned against. He shook with a biting chill, despite the warm air from the vents. He opened his eyes only to remind himself he wasn't dead. Each time he chose to flee the dark and twisted expanse of his mind, he noted the tree lined road never seemed to change. The absence of change soothed his battering thoughts. He closed his eyes. He listened to the old truck's questionable rattles and the groan of the engine. He had no concern for his driver, who carried him like a charioteer in a dream. He hated what he had become. The eyes of the girl he couldn't save glared with the same soulless glaze of the Lost Ones'. The water was like a tar that pulled her in. He reached for her desperately. His fingertips touched hers, but his arms were like stretched spaghetti. His muscles were at their limits. Her fingers pulled away as the water consumed her. Her face was one of a child's horror, with a human understanding of her end. The black tar flooded over her wide eyes and into her mouth. Any sound she made became bubbles as she gurgled to her death.

"No! No!" he screamed.

The water swirled in the darkness, until it

stopped. Everything stopped. Everything was silent.

"Natasha…" a whisper echoed in his head.

A thumping filled the void that consumed the world above the black lake. It grew louder and louder. It beat to the whispers of the trees, and the wind, and a world he saw like a pencil sketch. Whispers continued to speak her name, but the beating drum drowned them like Emily in the lake. He looked into the water. He saw nothing. He leaned closer. He saw only a shadow of the endless depths. He leaned until his face touched its surface. It was like the surface of ice. He took a deep breath, closed his eyes, and plunged into it. He saw only a swirling blackness. He blinked. He saw a road lit by the lights of the truck. He left a head-shaped imprint against the window as he straightened awake.

"Where am I?" he asked.

"Jesus. You scared me." The woman driver tensed.

He turned his head and examined her. She was butch, with dark hair that hung just above her shoulders. Her tight collared shirt accentuated her round figure.

"Who…who are you?" he continued.

She sighed and shook her head.

"Someone who's really deserving of a drink," she clucked. "I'm Dell. I found a kid earlier, we found you, kid left. That's pretty much the long and short bof it. Now we're off to the APS. They'll get you to the hospital. You alright, eh?"

"APS? A kid? A boy? A young Asian boy?" His

heart knew she meant Yuuta.

"Yes."

"Yuuta…Arre baap re, we have to turn back," he panicked. "We have to get him. Why did you let him go? Shit!"

"Listen, I'm nobody's keeper. I'm taking you to the police and that's the end of it. You can explain to them your shit. I ain't having nothing to do with it." Her gaze was locked determinedly on the road. He looked down at himself and remembered his nakedness.

"Arre baap re, I'm sorry. Do you…do you have a blanket or clothes I could use?"

"I've got nothing for you, unfortunately. I would've covered you if I did. I don't mind me a hairy man, but you think I'm some kind of pervert?"

"No, I-if you can't go back for Yuuta, is it possible you know Chloe Blackleaf?"

"Jesus. What'd those Blackleafs drag here? Been messing around with peyote again, I'm thinking, eh? Fuckers think they're Navajo," she sniffed as she shook her head. "A bit of a drive still left. What's your name?"

"Arjun." He looked down at his hands. They tremored unconsolably. "What's the APS?" The truck's rumbling vibrations pacified him.

"Anishinabek Police Services. You both are on tribe land and, personally, I'm done with dealing with shit like this and getting in trouble. I let the kid go because he wasn't beaten half to the spirit, but you… I'd be shamed by my own self-berations if I didn't do the right thing with you."

He watched her. He suspected that she could sense his gaze on her, as she straightened her back. Her throat shifted from a swallow.

"There are things out there…" he warned.

"Any of us living around here could've told you that, eh."

"No. No, listen, uh, Dell, listen to me. I'm not talking about bears or wolves or whatever. There are things. Things like walking nightmares with eyes that pierce like a god's damning wrath. I've seen their faces, their monsters…their violence. There is death behind me. I-I'm not sure what any police can do."

His hands were clammy from the sweat. He shifted uncomfortably against the towel that covered the seat beneath him. He tried to pull its edges over his thighs. She said nothing.

Flashing lights drew his eyes back to the road. He felt her decelerate. As the truck slowly wrapped a bend, police cars and ambulances filled his vision. He felt his stomach turn. He felt hot. He rolled down the window wildly. They were all going to die.

A uniformed figure stepped from the roadblock and signalled for Dell to stop and roll down her window as he walked to the driver side.

"Evening, Dell. What're you doing out here?" the officer inquired with rural town mannerisms.

Lightning flashed across the sky. A rolling thunder followed seconds after.

"Jesus, Jack. What happened, eh? You guys finally doing your job?" Dell chided with a shake of her head.

"Come on, Dell. We'll find her," Jack insisted, looking up as droplets clicked off his cap. He suddenly shot a look into the truck. "What the hell? Who is that? Is he alright? What're you up to bringing a guy like that down this way?"

"I found him at the side of the road, Jack. Now let me through so I can take him to the station…Give him to someone who will actually be able to help him."

"Come on, Dell. You always end up in this shit. You're going to have to step out of the truck," Jack imposed. He looked back to another officer who waited with analyzing eyes just in the dimness between the different sources of light.

"Wait," Arjun disclosed. "There's a boy. We were attacked. A woman too…She's in danger. I have to go. I, uh, I mean, we need to go back for them."

He flicked his eyes to the barricade as he noticed other officers begin to approach.

"Fuck, Dell, really? What is this?" Jack pursued, as he shook his head. "Okay, both of you out. Sir, are you alright to get out by yourself?"

Arjun examined the police officer, whose posture changed with his approaching co-workers. He felt his heart thump against his chest as their faces seemed to melt with the rolling drops of rain that ran down their faces.

"I have to go. I have to go," Arjun whispered to himself.

Lightning lit the roadway as thunder roared in

an explosive clap. He pulled the door's handle aggressively, but it didn't move. He swore under his breath as he tried it again.

"Whoa, whoa. You calm down now. It's locked," Dell insisted.

"I have to go. She's out there alone. Unlock it. Unlock it!" He panicked.

They both stared at him with eyes that brewed with fear and disgust. He found the lock and pulled it up. He opened the door and his body folded onto the wet pavement. He saw black boots. He heard indistinct voices. Thunder growled like a threatened beast. A shape curled in above him. He slapped away a black gloved hand and rolled. He stumbled to his feet. The gravel stabbed at his blisters, but he felt her in a sudden burst. He felt her.

Whispers from the trees encouraged him. He heard shouts like a mob chasing him. His feet squished through the mud and wet plants of the forest. The urgency of his need drove him like a starving Dalit. He felt the pain of his hunger like a knife in his stomach. The smell of the sopping forest clouded his senses.

Her sensation quickly faded as his pace slowed. He stopped and looked around. He saw nothing. Cawing crows mixed with the engulfing shower of rain. The sensation of her throbbing spirit seemed to wash into the earth with each drop that fell from the umbrella of boughs. A flicker of light hovered through the trees before him. He hesitated. He could see a crowd of black shapes flitting around it. A great drum boomed in a single deep echo that shook the earth, eclipsing the sky's growls. He ran from the light.

"Arjunkaul…," a voice called, penetrating all things, "she is here, Arjunkaul."

Drops fell like cold beads on his head as he looked back to spy the illuminated clearing. There was nothing. He couldn't see. He strained furiously. He sensed watching eyes to his right and he spun to catch them. There was nothing but droplets slapping the leaves in a melodic lullaby.

"Where are you!?" he yelled. "Where is she?!" Shrieking laughter broke the whispers. The music of the world shattered with the horrific wail. He felt hate in him open like a flower bud. "Where is she!?"

"Now, now. Do not let anger be your demise. You must breathe, mutt." The deep voice vibrated through a clearing that suddenly burst into light around him.

Crows swirled in frantic crowds among barely composed corpses that ringed the circle of trees on piles of red bulbs. The air was immediately heavy with the blinding scent of spice. Crudely carved pillars of wood faces stared at him from an inner ring. The centre was lit by a stack of burning logs. Sitting by the fire were frightening figures with haunting glares. His eyes were pulled from the scene by the painted stare of what could only be an apsara. The light of the flames died on the matte white paint that hid her face in a worldly mask. Her slender, barely dressed figure was a toxin that flushed him in his impurity. He fell to his knees. The drumbeat became melodic and slow. Her eyes pulled his in an unflinching wrench. He caught his breath as he felt something violate the sanctity of his spirit. Each breath was an exhaustion of life. She smiled, blinked, and the enchantment broke. He looked around at the laughing world. He recoiled. He tried to crawl backwards, but something blocked him. He turned to confront the barrier. The painted face and grey eyes of the red-gloved figure stood over him.

"Do you smell it?" The tone of its voice shook in his head like the wind top bellow of a mountain. "Death and life." It pulled him to his feet with ease. "Before you sits the mother of all things. Bring your shame before her, mutt."

It pushed him back to the ground. The dry grass chafed his palms. The whirlwind of crows cawed fiendishly. They were strangely uninterested in the corpses.

"Do you fear us, ozaawi-ma'iingan?" the woman spoke from her stump like throne. The crows silenced immediately with the resonation of her voice. He forced his eyes onto the beaded necklaces around her neck. Below them, the golden-brown skin of her cleavage flowed like a river to her stomach. "The eyes of the flesh cannot comprehend the world of the spirit. What you see before you is simply a conjuration of your own mind." He craved to hear more. "Come."

He walked weakly toward her. His feelingless arm was crusted black in the yellow light. He had no memory of when the wrap unraveled off. The faces of strange creatures, animals, and unknown things looked curiously from various sitting positions on the ground. He limped in a wounded spectacle before them as he entered their circle. The heat of the burning fire threatened his skin with its lashing flames. The beating drums grew with each step as if the circle of creatures were beating them themselves.

"Good," she said. She returned her gaze to the fire. "Bring us Nanabozho's pipe." The circle cheered. Some stood and danced in a spin of stomping, as they made noises to the sky. "I understand your fear now. You are like an infant who witnesses their first Pow Wow." She stood to her feet. A vibrant skirt of swaying layers of feathers, beads, and fabrics hid her legs. "This…this is the coming together of all things. The spirits of oeh-da, of the wind, of the water. The spirits of life, of death. Death. What could be more frightening to the flesh? I do not see that same fear in you. You are here to serve a purpose greater than your understanding. A fulfillment of life for life. Maybe you do understand?" She reached down to a strange creature like a moss-covered toddler with beady white eyes like the creatures of the red-gloved figure. It passed her a long-stemmed wooden pipe. She examined the roughly carved curvature of the object, then held it out to him. "Breathe in the cleansing spirit of fire and death," she whispered. He realized the leering watchers were silent.

"Why?" Arjun asked. His maintained resolve was a surprise even to him.

"To understand life, one must know death. That is such with all things. A tale told by a thousand tongues, and yet, forgotten by all flesh," she proclaimed. He looked up to see her casting her gaze upon him. He felt small and shriveled in his nakedness.

"Will it-will it be my death?"

"What does your spirit tell you?"

He hesitated. He sought for a voice inside his mind, but all he heard was the echo of his own search.

"I just want to see her again," he admitted.

"Then your spirit has spoken." She stepped forward and re-offered him the pipe.

He stared at it, then stepped toward her and took it. He saw the flicker of her smile as the shadow of her lips shifted with the tossing light. He brought the stem to his open mouth. He looked around without moving his head. He could see the red lit substance in the pipe's bowl. He struggled to smell its fumes over the wafting smell of spice. He closed his eyes and inhaled without reservation. The heat of the substance flooded into him. He choked and coughed. An indescribable taste of herbs and smoke were left in his mouth. He coughed in a fit as the laughter of the circle swallowed him.

He was back on his knees and before him was the painted face of the red-gloved monster. He caught his breathing and spat some of the foulness from his mouth. He dropped his gaze to its feet. Fractals of glistening light framed its veiny, long-nailed toes. He blinked and the feet were gone. The crackling flame was gone. He smelt earth like the fiend's foul fingers in his nose. Crystals filled and fell from the trees, glistening in the vivid light of the sparking sky. The trees sneered at him.

The twisted roots and nature of the ground stabbed into him in defiance of his obstruction to their desire for each drop of stilled rain.

He closed his eyes and life's network splayed out to him in a map with a throbbing pulse at its center. He reached out to it, but it was as untouchable as the stars. He stood up and opened his eyes. It was gone. He closed his eyes. The world appeared as a residual outline in the blackness. He clawed his hands against his face and screamed. Laughter danced around him in moving circles.

He walked into the darkness. He felt his way blindly through the trees and falling shimmers of light. He smelt a familiar foul stench. He thought of his ex-wife. He missed sex. He missed companionship. He didn't understand his loneliness until he recognized the gap that had formed inside of him. He thought of his mother. He never called her back. He considered school and the kids. He thought of Yuuta and his beetle-black eyes. The image of a girl drowning in inky waters suddenly flashed at him in a violent gushing of memory. He stopped and leaned against a tree. The forest was silent. His heart raced despite the tranquility.

A sudden splash rippled across the air. Snapping foliage approached him through the trees. He froze. Cool drops plopped onto his head. He could hear slobbering breaths. He watched the world with bouncing eyes, too afraid to move his head. He could feel slow approaching vibrations off the ground. He caught a black shape slumping through the trees. He could feel it watching him.

"Strange smell," he heard a gruff voice whisper.

"What are you?" Arjun called out. It didn't reply. He squinted and quirked his ears forward as its heavy breathing ceased. "Please…d-don't be frightened."

"Man do not speak," it grumbled.

"It's—it's just a dream…so my guess is all things can speak here," Arjun advised. "What are you?"

"I am hungry," it said. Its voice was rough, but gentle.

"Arre baap re," he said with a bob of his head.

"Man is strange," it said. "I do not speak to man."

"Why? Have we done you…harm?"

"Harm?" it questioned. "I never speak to man."

"I see…You have never spoken to a man? Do you speak with other things?"

"Only as much as things speak to me."

"Riddles from men and beasts…" Droplets continued to dive in fractals of moonlight. "I can't get a straight damned answer from anything around here."

"Maybe you ask wrong questions."

The shuffle of heavy steps accompanied its panting breaths as it moved confidently forward. He saw a black shape between the shadows of trees. He caught his breath as a large bear grazed between a set of twin trunks.

"Holy Deva," Arjun exclaimed. "Y-you're a bear."

"As you are man." It stopped just in front of him. It sniffed him. "Your flesh rots."

"I was attacked by a, uh, dog," he said as he tried to lift his feelingless arm to the bear.

The bear sniffed his wound, then licked it several times with its long, slimy tongue. It coughed throatily and held its mouth open as if in hopes the air would remove a foul taste from it.

"That I do often for my own. Stinking wounds lead to stinking death." It moved away from him and sat with its back against the nearest tree. "What are your questions?"

"Honestly, I don't know…Uh, how–how many can I ask?"

"How many do you have?"

He sighed. He ached to sit, but his anxiety of the hulking beast kept him on his feet.

"Why can I speak to you?" he pursued first.

It looked at him for a moment then shifted its gaze around as if done with the conversation. It stretched its mouth in a large yawn and licked between its teeth. It sniffed then hesitated.

"The wind speaks of ganawenjige," the bear revealed. It scratched its back in distinct scrapes across the tree it bent with its leaning weight.

"What is that?"

"Ganawenjige is what it is." The bear scratched its front with its clawed paw. "Ganawenjige protects seed."

"What seed?"

"Seed of life. Seed of man. I care not for seed," the bear retorted.

"Then why speak with me?"

"I care for speaking. Man has deep roots."

"Is there more than one ganawenjige?"

"The wind has spoken of two. I know not what can be."

"I-I think I understand…"

"Do not have fear, man. If no speaking, I no eat, but I care for speaking. Let us speak," the bear confided.

"Uh, who is the-the red-gloved thing with the painted face?" Arjun asked, releasing the first image that came into his head. The bear said nothing. "Then what-what is meshkwadoon?"

"That is big question." It sat forward slightly. "Meshkwadoon is life for life. Exchange of seed for man. No meshkwadoon, no man."

"Why? For what purpose?" He bobbed his head in an attempt to shake the riddles into clarity.

"For man," the bear said simply.

"What must the ganawhenjeegay do?" he continued slowly.

"Ganawenjige. Ganawenjige protects seed."

He clenched his fists in unconscious restraint. "What seed? Is Natasha the seed? How do I find the seed?"

"I care not for seed. Daughter of daughter, she is of man. If man can not smell man, how does man know of man?"

"Well, we see each other. We hear each other…" he lectured in frustration.

"Man is strange. Man must know to follow wind.

Daughter of Muzzu-Kummik-Quae speaks on wind. Daughter of daughter is seed."

"I – That…that is actually the clearest answer I have gotten. What about the men-like things. They're not like man. One is a snake-man, the red-gloved one… it-it or he or she is hideous. They hunt for her."

"Cubs of Muzzu-Kummik-Quae. They are of meshkwadoon. They carry seed for daughter. They are not food. They are not hunters." The bear laid down and rested its head on its front paws in his direction.

"They carry the seed for the daughter of the Muzzu-what? What does that mean?"

"Seed of life planted in belly of Oziisigobiminzh."

"Planted? Do you mean they're going to plant their seed in… what? The-the daughter, their sister?" Arjun's heart began to race as the idea of her seemed to fill like the droplets in the leaves. "Is she that thing you said?"

"Meshkwadoon."

"I just-I don't understand gana-wen-jige? If it is meshkwadoon for her to die for all this stuff, then why do these brothers push me to her…and then threaten me and humiliate me and-and k-kill those around me?"

"Fear different when no others around. Life fear. Death fear. You only see fear," the bear sagaciously advised.

"Okay…Saala kutta…" Arjun leaned against a tree. Every inch of him groaned. "I'm really trying to understand."

"Man angers. There no understand. Words no

truth. Wind truth. Comfort truth." The bear scratched its back on the tree more aggressively. "Ganawenjige protect. Bears eat. Man hunt." He stared at the large creature. It looked oddly domesticated in its ease. It sniffed and looked around more intently. "I go. Man must go," it said as it lifted itself onto its four large paws. "I have no answers."

The bear sat up then walked slowly back into the darkness of the trees. Arjun straightened, but a fear of the reality of the beast forced him to hesitate. Wind shook more shards of crystal from the treetops. The cool droplets that slithered into his body hair forced him to shiver.

The shiver stayed as the breeze shifted. The cold's bite stung his wounded arm. He limped forward. He felt no urge to follow the bear. He stopped. He looked at his hands. The dog's blood stained them. His years of self-deceit stained them. He remembered Emily's smiling face before she fell out of the canoe. He remembered her cold, pale skin when she was pulled from the water. Her dead eyes had ripped a hole in his self-assurance. A fear of living had soaked his insides in black tar. The eyes of others were like the poisonous stares of Kaliya. Eyes that questioned his karma. He tried to focus on his breathing as the anxieties seemed to wash over him in a flooding release. His mouth was pasty despite the remaining droplets of rain. His tongue ached for the taste of a morning's glass of water. The trees whispered faintly. Colours swirled in a mystery of madness around him.

The world suddenly vibrated. He felt her. He stumbled forward as he limped toward her sensation. He began to run. He knew he had to save her. His path opened before him. Ecstasy brewed inside him. He had to find her. Her call was more than the whispers of the wind. The lightness of his being carried him effortlessly onward. He felt the freedom of his righteousness, empowered with the sensation of purpose.

He felt the shedding weight of his humanity as he suddenly understood the essence of the immortal breath of his atman. He felt liberation. Liberation from mortal irrelevance, from fear, from hate, from memory. He found the empowerment of each breath in its endowing blessing of earthly sustenance. He found the empowerment of each breath in the invigoration of his eternal being.

He flew with the rush of life, a bird seeing a world of green from above. He was free.

Chapter 19

Yuuta's flashlight torch was the only light in the roofless cavern until a flash made everything clear in a moment of mythical brilliance. A roar from the deep reminded him of the necessity of his journey. He grew sick of the sight and smell of trees. He tried to imagine the shapes as towers of an ancient city.

The land was perilous and haunted. His only fear was his failure. In the tower tops, pattering like tiny footsteps began. Drops of some hidden creature's venomous saliva dripped down in splashes around him. Neither his sword nor axe served any purpose against the hidden fiends. Their whispers penetrated his mental wards. He knew a single drop swallowed would be his doom.

He ran with his torch and gaze pointed to the ground in front of him. The venom droplets fell in showers. The towers of the abandoned civilization served no cover. He ran. He couldn't stop running. He hurdled the fingers of the ground that reached for him. The whispers grew and grew. The towers had eyes he knew watched him. His clothes and hair were soaked in the foul saliva. Shadows of beasts and demons peered out from the spots between nature's rubble where his torchlight hit. His hand called for his sword, and he found himself pulling it from his back as he ran.

A flash of light split the darkness and the beast of the deep's growl swallowed the whispers that floated like fireflies between the spikes of the world that never was. He ran desperately toward it. The sloppy drippings of the demon army above him flooded the earth. His footsteps splashed in their salivations. He looked back to catch the night creatures that swarmed in behind him like a pack of starving wolves stalking their prey. He caught yellow snake eyes that fell away in a swirl of rushing noise as he tripped forward.

He pulled his head out of a small puddle in the root twisted mud. His chin quivered uncontrollably. He gripped furiously into his palms. He screamed. The rain washed over him, and he let it dribble into his mouth. He choked tears into his hands. He forgot the rain and the cold. He forgot the nightmares and the blood. He forgot the faces and the feeling of a smile. He saw only black canvases with blurred images of thoughts that meant nothing.

He fixated on finding his flashlight. He tried to stand, but he stumbled. He forced himself to crawl toward a spot of glowing white on the ground. His chest heaved through his sobs as he crawled through the clinging moist earth. His hand slipped and he clenched his teeth in a broiling anger as he tried to find stability in the slime. The whispers never stopped. The arching trees laughed at him in his childishness. He felt the burden of his youth like a knife at his throat. He felt the burden of time. He felt his stupidity. A child crippled by an imagination of nothingness. Defeated by a tale he thought belonged to him. A victim of his own inability to believe that he was nothing. A child.

He stopped and leaned against a large rock that stuck out from the base of a slumped tree. The light he pursued seemed to pull away. His bones vibrated beneath his wrinkled skin. His story was at its end. He felt strange relief at the realization. Storytellers always seemed to forget that the only real end to things was through death. It was a recoiling reality that revealed that the stories of others were simply made on the idea that a moment in a life is simply a moment, like a flash of his sofu's camera capturing an image of something that is staged and designed for viewing. He was a child, and his tale was to be told in a foreshadow of his demise like the hanging ornaments of Aokigahara. He hated the world.

"Gmiwaan nangwaa," a familiar voice spoke, breaking his mental spiral. Yuuta wiped his tears in a panic. He couldn't stop his chin from quivering. The lightning flashed white above the trees and the monster's boom followed. He saw the outline of the antlered man like a goat-headed demon. He swallowed deeply and breathed slowly with the prayer that the rain hid the shame of his crying. "Silence is wise."

"Is this the end? I-I don't even get to see her again?"

"Ishkwe-aya'ii? What does a boy know of ends?" Yuuta clenched his fists and tucked closer to the rock.

He felt the violence of nausea and shut his eyes. He heard the man step forward. Yuuta opened his eyes. The man basked without motion in the rain. His arms were stretched toward Yuuta. His palms cupped pools that splattered with the falling drops. "Drink, boy. Drink of life. Feel the rolling drums inside you like the beat of your heart. Move, boy. Dance with the spirit of a world tainted by flesh. See her tears. Embrace her. Feel her. Take her. See her. Take her. See her. Feel her," the man chanted. His voice was like a thumping drum that drew Yuuta to his feet.

"I can't feel her…" Yuuta whispered. He felt the tickle of drops on his lips but was too stilled to move another inch. "I can't feel her." The man suddenly threw the pools in his hands to the ground. Yuuta felt his face pull upwards as the man yanked him to his feet. The man coaxed him to look into his eyes. The darkness and the rain disfigured everything but a nose that was thick with curled nostrils. Yuuta forced himself to pull away. The man's grip was surprisingly loose and unrestraining. Yuuta could still feel the thumping of the chant inside his body. The whispers of the trees joined it in a swaying of sound. Lightning split the sky and the man before him glowed like an antlered god. "I can still find her. I have to."

"If your will says it is, then it will be so," the man stated.

"If you won't help me, then let me go. Let me find my own way." Yuuta felt the desire to twist his hands, but his clenched fists stopped him.

The man turned and held his hand out in the opposite direction. "I seek only the fulfillment of your will. Go. Find her. Face the fear that festers inside like hemlock. Become the man you feel you seek to be, boy."

Yuuta hesitated. He was afraid to move. His fear in the choice frightened him. The reality that he had never chosen a path faced him like a monster standing over his bed. He prayed to Natasha for guidance. The rain continued its toxic drippings. The blood of Thorgils was washed from his conscience, but it still clung to his clothes like dried patches of paint. He threw off his backpack. He took off his shirt. He let the rain caress his white chest. He hesitated. He had never shown a soul but his mother his naked body. He felt weird. He rubbed his arms.

"What is flesh but the seedling of the spirit. Look to the world of life and reveal to it what it reveals to you," the man said as he stepped forward. Thunder spoke in a low grumble in the distance. Yuuta looked down at his legs. His shoes squished with the flooding of water beneath his soaked socks. His breathing quickened. He tried to control it, but he couldn't keep up. It began to outrun him in heaves. He hyperventilated. He yelled and removed the rest of his clothes in an encompassing mania. He tossed them like dirty rags to the side. "Embrace her. Feel her. Take her. See her. Take her. See her. Feel her." Yuuta's heart felt the mud between his toes. He imagined her naked feet in the soil, warmed by it. He looked to the treetops and screamed again. The antlered man laughed. "Take me to her," the man said sternly, as his laughter subsided.

Yuuta looked down at himself. His fear was a tyrant controlling his thoughts. It carried him to his backpack. He stretched the rip and removed the axe. He looked at its rusted spots. He gripped it how he imagined a warrior would. He felt a cover of security. He took out the long knife and threw it to the side where his clothes lay. He threw the lightened backpack and stood up straight. The antlered man was gone. Yuuta didn't care. He felt her like a throbbing in the trees. Each fickle touch of the living universe around him was an exciting shock through his body. He walked toward it. He ran. The throbbing grew and grew until its beating filled his head like the hollow echoes of a strige's hoots. He gripped the axe. His feet splashed through the puddles and his footing was strangely sound as the path began to slope and thicken.

"Yuuta…" a feminine whisper joined the echoes in his head. "Yuuta, I'm here."

"We're here, chiisana kuma."

"Yuuta…Yuuta, come to me."

The whispers grew wild and afraid. The world around him had a shaken energy. Roots curled like pythons along the ground. He gagged as a wave of smell like the rotting sweetness that tainted his sofu's corpse penetrated the air. He no longer felt the rain. A dim blue lightened the world, and he could see the roots leading through the trees.

"Welcome, child," whispers spoke faintly from all sides.

He kept running until under him the roots became large enough to bridge a rolling stream. A fish splashed in the water then swam away. The water's lulling glide through the running crack in the earth called to him in a familiar voice. He fought it and crossed the root bridge. The trees broke open on the other side and a path ran upward through a rocky grove. He twisted through the maze of boulders, fallen trees, and cliff sides, and broke into a clearing twisted with roots as red as blood. The roots ran like intestines into the largest tree he had ever seen. The tree was ancient. The leaves of its drooping arms sagged like unwashed twists of dried hair. It seemed to lift slightly as he stopped in its root twisted clearing.

"Do not fear me, child. Come. Come," the whispers lulled, filling the area with their sound.

He walked towards the tree, knowing it was the source. He gripped the axe again to remind himself he still held it. The tree motioned in a breeze that he didn't feel and drops of water fell like tears to the ground from its hanging leaves.

"Is that why they call you the Weeping Willow?" Yuuta asked, moving closer to it. Despite the water being what was left from the rain, he somehow felt the tree's sadness.

"Child, I am called many things." He felt the strength of its being with each step closer to the great tree.

"What do you think your name is?"

The air lifted as if the tree smelled deeply of the

world around its trunk.

"A masterpiece..." the whispers humoured, echoing until they faded into the trees beyond.

"What is?" He felt less certain about the axe in his hand with each step toward it.

"Anishinaabeg," the whispers mused softly.

"I-I...What do you mean?" he asked, barely holding his frustration.

"There is too much to understand, child. It is the blessing of mortality, to be free to know nothing. To wither and die. To have horror, malice, and error cleansed with the final closing of your eyes." The tree seemed to sigh as it groaned. "It is the true beauty of all living things."

"Are you a living thing?"

"I am life," the whispers confided.

"Why am I here?"

"You have like thoughts," the whispers said.

He didn't realize he had stopped. The tree hung over him like an ancient dome.

"Who?" he demanded.

"Gikinoo'amaagewikwe," the whispers offered sternly.

"What are you speaking? I don't understand any of the things said by your kind."

"You hear nothing but the wind, child, for a tree cannot speak."

"I - Please...I want to understand," he begged. "Who is she?"

"A daughter of Muzzu-Kummik-Quae. Her spirit is bound to meshkwadoon, as her mother's before her." The whispers grew more focused but remained like embodied voices from various sources.

The great willow groaned and leaves and droplets fell again on his naked skin.

"How did she do this to me?" He looked down at his hands as if to see his skin becoming green.

"It is a tale few yet remember. Such is the way of things that are spoken, like a passage of wind that never dies but is never the same. Just as life in its glory must end, so must all tales. Few are blessed in their knowledge of this understanding. Few still know that the wind only speaks what it still carries. The truth is carried across the streams of many winds. Few know that what has been spoken is now of the rivers and of the trees and of the earth."

"Do you remember?"

A wind sighed through the tree's drooping strands of leaves.

"It is Muzzu-Kummik-Quae's tale to tell," the whispers said slowly.

"That's-that's it? After all of this and what I've seen and what I know, that is your response?" He released the anger that shook his arms in a yell. "Why am I always tucked away in the darkness like some fragile doll. It's-it's not right! What kind of monsters are you to run a kid through such things and expect him to be…to be…satisfied with that! I thought this was different. I thought this was life. That there was a necessary balance. A light to the darkness. You were the voice of reason…of wisdom. What-what is this? What are you?"

"Child, do things that grow in the light not also grow in the dark? Your thoughts are of fear. Do not let it consume your spirit, for it is the spirit that connects the Anishinaabeg to life," the whispers spoke in an unaltered tone.

"Wh-what can I do?" He squatted down and placed his head into his hands. The axe clanged at his feet.

"Do only what your spirit speaks inside you," the whispers recommended.

He grunted angrily. He sought the throbbing that brought him here and felt it in numbing vibrations all around him. But he didn't feel *her*. She was taken from him. Extracted like a bone from his body. He begged to everything in his head for a sensation or a tingle, but he felt nothing but cold nakedness.

While he stood in his childish hesitation, he felt the wind continue to swirl in circles around him. He felt the eyes of all things shift to the barricade of trees that walled the clearing. A figure pulled something with a struggle into a gap in the roots lit by the moon. The figure was bulky with a ripped and stained white top and dark blue pants. He recognized the stuttering nurse, before she collapsed to her knees.

"It is time, child…" the whispers said.

Chapter 20

Twilight draped the sky like black paint with purple on an easel. Stars speckled white like the peeking specks missed in the dark mix. The trees' curses were no longer an abuse, but an expectation. The same memories repeated like flickering photos of moments in Natasha's head. Nothing made sense to her. She forgot almost every image of who she was before she awoke at the edge of the forest. The idea of her behind her desk with stacks of paper became a blur of a life lived by another. A story she knew she was a part of but couldn't remember. The only blessing was the nothingness she felt. She glided like a passenger in a ship, watching the sky from its deck. If there was trouble below, she wasn't wise enough to notice it. Dark clouds flooded the sky, and what was once dim patches with sprinkles of light became a black backdrop.

The trees quietened. Their stillness made them appear like haunting statues. A cool wind rustled in a wild dance between the carved wonders of the forest. Drops began to fall in a soft patter against the ground. They obscured the choking breaths of the nurse who dragged her inhumanly through the forest. Light split the sky. She counted to two before the rumble of thunder followed it in an engulfing boom. The time between the flashes became uncountable as the world of nothingness blinded her.

She faded in and out of its waking nightmare. She struggled to understand what was real. A flickering image of a woman she knew was her mother convinced her it was safer inside her head.

She opened her eyes and the rain had softened, almost invisible in the darkness. Her senses began to resurrect as a putrid smell trickled into her nose. She blinked.

She lay on the ground looking into a cloudless black. The nurse kneeled beside her. The bulky woman's chin slumped on her own chest. Her azure top was gone, revealing a blood-stained white t-shirt, soaked through to her bra. She looked dead. A man stepped behind the nurse. He placed his hands on the woman's shoulders.

"Bear witness, mashkikiiwikwe, to the true healing of oeh-da. Stand!" He pulled the woman up by the back of her throat with one hand. She crumbled as he let go. Her body was lifeless. The handsome man stepped away casually. Natasha recognized the yellow swirl of his eyes as he walked past her.

She turned herself to face a root engulfed clearing. A monstrous willow tree stood like a Hellenistic wonder in the clearing's centre. The boy, Yuuta, stepped out from under its great hanging branches. She was struck by his nudity, despite her own. He gripped an axe and looked upon her with wide eyes. His face was pale and sunken, like a starved child. He looked sickly and deprived.

"Abinoojiinh, come," the handsome man said as he stopped between them.

The boy looked back to the tree. He watched it, then turned to face her again. He stepped shakily forward. His eyes sought hers. She tried to look away from his nakedness, but he continued to walk slowly toward her. His face suddenly wrinkled, and he recoiled in fear. She wondered at his sanity until she realized the footsteps behind her. She twisted her head to see the dark-skinned man step out of the trees. He was nude and covered in bruises. He held his blood-spattered arm to his chest. His eyes were unforgivably black.

"You're-you're here," he said. "Holy Deva…"

"Don't!" the boy yelled frantically. "Don't go near her!"

"Yuuta…Yuuta we have to help her. We can get her out of here. You-" the dark-skinned man stopped and directed his attention to the handsome man. "He-he will kill us all. We must go. We must take her from here." The handsome man laughed, and his yellow eyes twisted mysteriously. He looked strangely reptilian despite his muscled body, sleek black hair, and human features. The boy stopped. The glow of the moon brought much of the clearing into view. She turned her head to watch the dark-skinned man step closer. "Yuuta…Don't listen to this shit. They offer nothing but death. We can save her.

"Chiisana kuma…" a soft woman's voice spoke from the darkness between the roots. An elderly Asian woman stepped into clarity. Yuuta went red and turned awkwardly away from her. "Do you not recognise me, Yui-chan? Have you forgotten the love and care your sofu and I put into you?" Her voice was lovingly stern.

"Yuuta…" the dark-skinned man urged. Natasha stressed at his forgotten name.

"Sobo? Is this…real?" Yuuta asked with wide eyes.

"Yui, they are not monsters," the elderly woman advised.

"But they…they killed sofu. And you, w-why're you here? It doesn't make any sense." The boy stepped backward.

Crows casually started to fill the treetops. They watched like spectators at an arena. Natasha pulled herself over to the nurse, who had not moved since her collapse. She shook the woman's shoulder. The woman moved with the motion but showed no signs of living.

"Who are all of you?" Natasha demanded weakly. She felt the dark-skinned man step beside her. Cawing began to ring in bursts as the birds began to jape and cheer for blood. "Where am I?"

"Let me help you up," the dark-skinned man said as he kneeled down and grabbed her arm. She pulled it away aggressively.

"Don't touch her!" Yuuta squealed harshly.

"Wait, abinoojiinh," the handsome man demanded as he stepped into the boy's path. "There are others who must witness the sowing."

"You will not touch her!" Yuuta shrieked.

The handsome man lifted his hand and slapped the boy. "You will heel, animosh." Wind lifted the man's hair. It blew behind him in a wave of liquid black. His slit eyes turned back to face her. Everyone looked down upon her expectantly. Nothing happened. No one moved. The old woman was gone.

"Brother!" a man's voice bellowed from the trees. "We will have peace in the glade of Oziisigobiminzh!"

"Oh…" the handsome man rolled with charm. He glared into the hidden forest with a visual anger that made his smile twitch.

The shape of a large figure hugged the darkness of the trees. Glistening dots hovered behind him like blue fireflies.

"Meshkwadoon is not a sacrifice," the unseen man stated with a voice that commanded all things. "You will allow the daughter to choose."

"What power do you have, manijoosh?" the handsome man called out. "You are but a cripple! From trickster to decrepit. You shame us all."

The crows cawed wildly. The feeling of Natasha's tortures began to trickle through her numbness. She crinkled into herself with a struggle as she tried to suppress the pain. She felt burning like Band-Aids of flesh being ripped from fresh wounds. She shook and the pain intensified.

"Natasha, I'm taking you from this place," the dark-skinned man whispered, as he squatted down.

She felt his arms scoop under her. He struggled awkwardly to lift her.

"Stop!" Yuuta yelled. The boy ran down the sloping roots athletically. The axe he held in his hand became distinct through the darkness. "Don't touch her!"

The dark-skinned man pulled his hands away and stepped back.

"Yuuta, we can go over this another time. We need to get away from these things…Arre baap re, what are you thinking?" The dark-skinned man looked unsure of himself.

"I will not have you treat me like a kid…I will not let you treat her like some kind of object of your perversions!" the boy cried.

"Come on, Yuuta, I-I don't know what to say," the dark-skinned man pleaded.

"Admit it. Admit your thoughts, you psychopath. I see it in your eyes. I see your hunger. I know the stories. I-I respected you. I thought…I thought it was all rumour, but you did it didn't you? Emily's death was your fault, wasn't it? And now, look at you. In this place…You're the real monster." The boy whimpered. The ground seemed to shake with the energy of his passion.

"Yuuta, I-I won't hide from this. You're right. There's something wrong with me…Deva, even I know it. I fucking know it…I've lost everything. I've lost the respect of my colleagues and the parents. My wife. My life. I have…nothing left. Emily's eyes watch me from the dark like riverboat lanterns carrying me to the depths of Naraka. No-no, Yuuta. Fuck…This is not the place. You're a fucking kid, and you're going to follow behind us, or-or I'll have to let you go…"

"Arjun," Natasha said slowly, as the name finally came to her. "Leave me here."

She caught his black eyes. They watched each other for a moment longer than she knew why. A timeless magnetism locked their gazes into place. His shoulders lifted as his chin quivered before he broke the unseen bond. He dipped down hastily and went to scoop her up. He struggled to get his arms under her. She could hear his distinct breathing as he bent down over her. She felt the heat, hair, and sweat of his battered body.

"No!" she heard Yuuta yell.

Arjun wrapped her into his arms like a father cradling his fallen child. She looked up and into his eyes. He smiled.

"I know he has it in him…Please find it," Arjun whispered.

She heard a blunt thud. A spray blinded her. The weight of the man collapsed onto her as she fell back to the ground. She used her last bit of strength to wipe her eyes, as his weight pressed onto her. She looked at the back of her hand in realization of the source. Fresh blood was smeared in a streak of red across her fingers. She tasted it in her mouth. An axe was cleaved into Arjun's skull.

"Oh…oh god," she whimpered.

The tears came to her as if she had never cried before. Her chest begged for air as she quivered. The red-gloved figure's shrill laughter collided with the sounds fighting for space in her head. The weight of the now dead man she never knew laid like a ragdoll against her naked skin. She felt the hand of the boy on her back. His touch was strangely warm.

"It's okay, Natasha…isn't it?" he asked with a sad quiver.

"Yess, yess. From three to one. From three to one," a voice groaned through the air. She recognized its hollow depths. "Nanabozho, welcome. Welcome." The hidden fiend sniffed distinctly. "You smell like hoed earth, brother. Your relationship with the Anishinaabeg has become you. Disappointing."

Beating drums broke into a chorus in the trees. Their rolling song called to the world with echoing booms.

"Boy," the figure of the shadowed man called out as he stepped into view. He was carved like a bronze Promethean sculpture, with the realism of the flesh. He had a braid of deep black hair slung over his shoulder. He had antlers like an ancient buck. "You have tainted your spirit in this act upon the flesh. There is only reprieve through cleansing."

Yuuta dropped to the ground. He tried to drag the weight of Arjun off her then stopped. He clutched the body in soundless sobs that shook his shoulders. He gagged and vomited on it and himself. The world vibrated with the thumping of the drums.

"Animoshag!" the handsome man yelled out from behind the shaking boy. Moonlight blessed the clearing and the handsome man appeared godly amongst the roots of the willow. "By domain or by tradition, I have posed the right to implantation." The handsome man's face clenched, and his skin seemed to peel in a slow drag down his body. His reptilian eyes grew with him as he slithered into a horrid iteration of a gorgon. He flexed his masculine torso. The space seemed to fill with an umbrella of darkness. "Great spirit, I thank you. For the spirit, I am thankful. I thank the All Mother. I thank the seamstresses of tradition: Giiwedinong, Waabanong, Zhaawanong, Ningaabii'-anong. I thank them."

The swirling eyes of yellow were a torturous reminder of her sufferings. She froze as they held her in a trance.

She heard the dragging movements of the man-snake's tail as it slithered toward her. A resounding thud silenced the reverberations of the beating drums. The man-snake stopped with a grunt. It broke its gripless hold on her and she dropped her head as she realized the struggle of holding it up. Her eyelids started to droop from the waking burden of her body's exhaustion. She forced them open.

The man-snake was looking at its clawed hands. Blood dripped like onyx stones from off its fingers. It tilted its head down to a gaping whole in its chest. Crows cawed violently, flapping up from their spots in the trees in bouts of excitement. She could sense their eyes on the crumpled naked Arjun bleeding in Yuuta's arms. The lifeless body seemed to come to life with the boy's sobs. Shrieking laughter filled the air like a harpy's screeching.

"Nana, dear Nana. Never has the blood of a son of Muzzu-Kummik-Quae been spilt in the shade of Oziisigobiminzh. Your odium to the tradition of mesh-kwadoon is…oh, it's enriching in its irony. Look upon her flesh. Agadenim your perversions." The haunting voice spoke like a deep echo in a tomb. "Let us feast!"

The roots shivered under the shaking of the drums. Little shapes dragged sticks and branches to a hollow between a twisted pair of roots. A flame burst to life as the drums deepened and slowed. A thing like a moss-covered child carried a bowl of smoke around the edge of the clearing at the bottom of the trees. Different faces and creatures followed in the smoke's trail. The drumming filled the root torn base of the willow. The man-snake slumped into its coiled tail, as if hiding from the light. A puddle of shimmering black formed around it.

"Jiibayaabooz!" Nanabozho called out. "The daughter must choose."

"She will speak the words, Nana…Yes, she will." The red-gloved fiend pranced out of the trees in a theatrical mockery. The moss covered being stopped beside it and offered the bowl of smoke. It bathed itself in the bowl's twisting fumes. "I smell your flowered petals." It sniffed the air and laughed. It cracked a hideous smirk and moved among the roots toward her. "Nanabozho, do you smell it?"

The drums roared with excitement. The encircling world of the spirits began to chant and dance. They passed around the long-stemmed pipe. Its burning herb reminded her of her undying need for a cigarette. She twisted her head to Nanabozho who watched the scene with sullen eyes. He held a bow at his side.

"Yuuta," she whispered, desperate for the sound of sanity. "Yuuta, talk to me."

The boy sobbed like an inconsolable child. She pitied him.

"Girl," Nanabozho called out, "it is the destiny of the daughter of Muzzu-Kummik-Quae to sustain the world of being. The great turtle bears the world on its back in an eternal servitude to this life. You must birth the seed in the embrace of Oziisigobiminzh in servitude to the spirit, but you must choose. Misiginebig has been pacified in defiance of the will of Creator in fulfillment of your choice. Speak it, girl, speak it now."

The violent smell of burning wood and leaves filled the clearing, as the drums rolled in her head. She blinked away specks of sourceless white from her vision. She tried to focus on Yuuta, but she struggled to see past Arjun's discolouring corpse.

"Yuuta…please. At least let me remember the feeling of life…Please," she cried. Her vision was blurred. She dropped her head to the ground and rolled her forehead in frustration. "Please!"

"Ahh…a pity. To see the daughter like a sapped sow. Yes, yes, a pity. I expected more of a child of Muzzu-Kummik-Quae. I see only the weakness of the Anishinaabeg," Jiibayaabooz said, as it stooped over

Yuuta to examine Arjun's body. It laughed. "Tsk tsk tsk. Now that was a foul deed indeed. I do not envy the gana-wenjige, but it must be so…blissful, to know nothing."

"What do you want?" Natasha demanded.

It lifted its cloud grey eyes on to her. Its face was twisted in a horrid smirk. It sniffed the air. The drums rolled slow. The boisterous watchers hushed.

"Great spirit. I thank you for the flesh I am to taste," it said. Madness was in its eyes. "Daughter, speak now the words. Do you choose the spirit or the flesh?"

"Fuck you," she snapped. She would've spit if she had spare saliva in her mouth.

Its laugh punctured the eternal rolling of the drums.

"Ahh well, only fools live by the demands of tradition," it mocked. She could feel its bitter breathing as it looked down on her. It smiled. Its teeth were stained and vile. It leaned deeper. Its smile widened. The four-line scar across its painted face was vivid. "I know the flesh of your kin. Its taste has lingered on my tongue for many cycles. My fingers will know its warmth again."

She felt her hair pull back, the nerves on her scalp reignited under the tug. She couldn't stop herself from crying out.

"Let go of her…" Yuuta said weakly. "Let go of her."

Its laugh shook the treetops, as crows lifted and then came back down. It pulled her by her hair with ease. She kicked her feet wildly. A slap broke her resolve. She stared at the trees drawing away from her. She felt the roughness of the roots dragging against her skin. Her vision fluttered. She saw the bark-like shapes of beady-eyed creatures pop out of the roots like moles. They stumbled in a pack toward Yuuta, who contorted underneath the weight of Arjun. She saw the utter desperation in the blackness of his eyes. The flames whipped shadows in a maelstrom around the engorged roots.

Whispers, screeches, and squeals filled the air. Howls and hoots called from the forest. Nanabozho was silhouetted in flaring blue balls of light.

The hideous fiend tugged her head and pulled her in beside it. It stood over top of her. She could see a set of breasts under its red leather vest. Scars maimed its stomach and torso. Its great mane of black hair heightened its wildness. It squatted over her. She could feel its frosted exhalations against her wounds as it examined her.

"Do not fear life, daughter. You must taste life, as I do. You must bathe in it," it teased, pulling her face toward its own. "You would dare let life grow cold and die like a forsaken elder in her final throes? Tsk tsk… And they name me monster." It stretched her mouth with fingers of frosted iron and stuck the fingers of its other hand inside. She gagged as it forced her to consume a foul-tasting substance. Its laugh filled her head. She had no strength to resist. It lifted her by her armpits and held her in a standing position. She felt its body press against her. Its cold breath brushed her neck before it licked her. It sighed. "Will it be the flesh or the spirit, ivory flower?"

"J-just kill me," she pleaded through her teeth. She had to tilt her head up as it stood to its full height. "Just do it!"

"It shall be done," it smiled. The feeling of the air seemed to change. She looked up and realized she was inside a hollow of the tree. Its walls throbbed as if its great beating heart was on the other side. Her vision blurred. The smell of the earth nauseated her.

"Breathe, child. Breathe," a woman's ancient whisper seeped from the walls.

The air rushed from her lungs as she was suddenly forced to the ground. A blur of two figures shifted aggressively around her. One of them stepped on her arm and she heard the snap before she felt the stabbing pain. Grunts and unknown curses were hurled in inhuman tones that shook the tree's hollow.

"The daughter has chosen. She has spoken the words," the fiend laughed.

The laughter broke as the two figures collided into a wall of the hollow. The beating heart of the tree resonated with the wild drums banging among its roots. She rubbed her eyes and blinked the figures into focus. She saw the red-gloved fiend impaled through its chest. It wriggled for freedom, but Nanabozho held it in place by its shoulders.

"Maji-manidoo, seek peace in the embrace of Oziisigobiminzh," Nanabozho thundered.

Nanabozho closed his eyes and roots wriggled

around the wrists and ankles of the impaled Jiibayaa-booz. It laughed. Nanabozho walked over to her under the burden of the laughter. He lifted her to her feet. She swayed.

"The choice must be made," he conceded, as he looked down upon her.

He placed a warm hand on her lower stomach. She tried to focus on the world as its colours spun into a pool like mixed paint. She vomited on herself. Her skin began to burn, and she screamed. He pulled her tightly against him.

"Return to the flesh, child of Muzzu-Kummik-Quae," he whispered into her ear.

She felt his naked body against her. It was smooth and warm like marbled stone in the sun. The shrill laughter rippled off the walls of the hollow. She fought her drooping eyelids, but her body encouraged the soothing darkness. She heard nothing. She felt nothing.

A world of light blossomed into life. The sky's blue face stared back at Yuuta. He turned away. His breath caught as he found beside him a woman. Her eyes fluttered behind their lids. He focused on the mole on the edge of her nose. His breathing was shallow and quick. He tried to focus on her, but haunting black eyes stared back at him from his mind. He shuttered. He looked to his other side. Mr. Kaul lay facing the sky. His dark skin was purple and pale, like a plum with splotches of white. Yuuta stared at the man's discolored form.

"Where are we?" the woman asked quietly, as if waking from sleep. He quickly looked at her. She held an arm with an engorged wrist against a bare chest lined with large slashes. "A forest? Ahh-Shit…W-what the hell happened?"

"I-I don't know. I, uh, I - Are you okay?" he asked.

"Oh god…" She shot open her mouth. He saw that she could see Mr. Kaul on his other side.

"I'm sorry. I'm sorry. I-I don't know what's going on. I'm…" he panicked. Her hazelnut eyes forced him to look away. He suddenly realized Mr. Kaul was dead. Yuuta sat up and looked around. There were only trees. Some birds called, but they seemed distant and uninterested. He felt as if he was just unplugged from a world he had been connected to his whole life. His feeling of nakedness had nothing to do with his nudity. He looked at the woman and quickly looked away from her unblinking gaze. "Why are we here? What happened? Can you…help him?"

"Oh god…Who is he?" The woman motioned to move, but she stopped and winced.

"He was my teacher. He, uh, taught me in school…I don't know….Are we still at Algonquin Park? I need to get home…My sobo and sofu must be losing it. I-I need to get home," he choked. He looked at the body. Its skull had a large gash wedged grotesquely into it. "Who are you?"

She was silent. Her silence frightened him. Her eyes never left Mr. Kaul's body. Yuuta was too tired to move.

"My mother…She–she's dead. Oh god, she's dead, and I, uh, I don't know…Everything's black. Her face in my hands…But she-she's dead. Oh god, how did we get here? What day is it? I need to get home. My brother, he needs to know. Oh god…"

The woman twisted a strand of her hair savagely and then stopped with a wince. She put her hand to her head and brought it back down as if to investigate it.

"What should I do?" Yuuta rubbed his eyes with his palms. "What do we do?"

He peeked at her nakedness and shied as she turned to face him.

"I don't have any answers…" she said with a look that suggested she wasn't lying.

A crow cawed. He looked in its general direction. He spotted it watching them. Its hungry black eyes made him shiver. He huddled into himself. He looked at Mr. Kaul. He saw the lifeless face of someone he seemed not to know, as if staring at a poor wax figure of a friend. He put his hand to the gash in the body's head. It was cold.

He looked up as he heard the faint sounds of strange birds. Their calls were like Discovery channel monkeys. The sound grew closer and closer. A beating of noise matched the calls. The woman beside him shook his shoulder, but he was too tired to move. He couldn't hold his eyes open. They drooped as they watched the pale blue. An orange speck dotted it. The winds seemed to change. He heard nothing. He saw nothing. He felt nothing. He blinked.

The End of Book 1 of the tale of Meshkwadoon.